Rob laid the things aside and shook his head, watching her sleep there.

What kind of woman would run away when given the news of an impending marriage? Especially a marriage that would hold benefits for both families involved.

She shifted on the furs and mumbled some words in her sleep. Though he could blame some of her restlessness on her illness and fever, she never seemed to be at peace when she slept. She called out names, mostly the one, throughout the time when sleep claimed her.

Something was wrong here. Very wrong.

If she did not know him or the Mackintoshes, then they could not be the reason for her refusal to accept the marriage. Yet, she did the unthinkable and left the safety and protection of her father's keep to avoid it. Was it just maidenly fear or something more? Though clearly fear was not something that seemed to rule her life if she was brave enough to do what she'd done.

D1409979

Author Note

I knew halfway through writing *Stolen by the Highlander* that Rob Mackintosh would have his story told next. He was quite vocal and rather loud and...ahem...insistent about it, really. So it did not surprise me when I wrote the epilogue in *Stolen* and he told me how to set up his book!

Rob has become used to people wanting to use his influence with his friend and chieftain Brodie since their clan triumphed over treachery. So the fact that someone doesn't want him is a shock to him.

Eva has her own problems that have come from youthful follies and falling in love with the wrong man. And she is certain that Rob is not the right man and now is not the right time. So she runs away, for many reasons.

Two proud people who fall in love in spite of themselves.

Sigh... I hope you enjoy reading it as much as I enjoyed writing it!

Next? Well, since the feuding between the clans Mackintosh and Cameron lasted more than three hundred years, I've got lots of ideas and stories planned.

Happy reading!

PS: I've wanted to use the name Eva for a heroine ever since seeing the movie *WALL-E*. There's a Gaelic form, but it would have you tripping over it every time you saw it on the page. So I compromised and used Eva—but FYI the original form is Aoife, pronounced "Ee-fa" or "Ee-va"... So it worked for me!

Terri Brisbin

The Highlander's Runaway Bride

HARLEQUIN® HISTORICAL

Recycling programs
for this product may
not exist in your area.

ISBN-13: 978-0-373-29874-7

The Highlander's Runaway Bride

Copyright © 2016 by Theresa S. Brisbin

Printed in U.S.A.

Terri Brisbin is wife to one, mother to three and dental hygienist to hundreds when not living the life of a glamorous romance author. She was born, raised and is still living in the southern New Jersey suburbs. Terri's love of history led her to write time-travel romances and historical romances set in Scotland and England.

Books by Terri Brisbin

Harlequin Historical
and Harlequin Historical *Undone!* ebooks

A Highland Feuding

Stolen by the Highlander
The Highlander's Runaway Bride

The MacLerie Clan

Taming the Highlander
Surrender to the Highlander
Possessed by the Highlander
The Highlander's Stolen Touch
At the Highlander's Mercy
The Highlander's Dangerous Temptation
Yield to the Highlander
Taming the Highland Rogue (Undone!)

The Knights of Brittany

The Conqueror's Lady
The Mercenary's Bride
His Enemy's Daughter
A Night for Her Pleasure (Undone!)

Visit the Author Profile page at Harlequin.com for more titles.

This story is dedicated to friends
and writing brainstormers extraordinaire—
Jen Wagner Schmidt and Lyn Wagner.

I began this story knowing only that the bride
would be kidnapped on her wedding day and little
else. With their pointed and relentless questions,
I ended up with an entire story plotted out.
And I will always be grateful for their help!

Prologue

Scourie, north-west Scotland

Eva MacKay was utterly in love.

The exhaustion and pain and fear of the last days faded as she stroked her finger down the soft cheek of the baby lying on her chest. The perfect rosebud mouth pursed and the tip of a tiny pink tongue could be seen. And when the wee bairn's eyes opened and seemed to meet her own gaze, Eva was lost.

She leaned down and kissed the babe's forehead, whispering soft words against the damp skin. Through the hours of labouring to give birth, Eva could only think of the man who should be at her side. He would never see his daughter. Never see *their* daughter. Tears filled her eyes and spilled over as she whispered his name to their child. The babe squirmed a bit and closed her eyes then, drifting to sleep. Eva then whispered the name they'd chosen if a daughter was born to them.

Mairead.

Eva moved her closer, tucking the blanket tighter around the little body and holding her close. The only way out of this would be to throw herself on her father's questionable mercy and beg to be allowed to keep the bairn. Yet, from her mother's cold response so far, she knew she would have no allies for her argument.

Her body needed rest now before she could make her plans. She ached deep inside, both from the birth's trauma and her broken heart. The babe sighed and Eva closed her eyes, enjoying the feel of the little one's warmth. Drifting off to sleep, Eva woke when someone lifted the bairn away.

'What are you doing?' she asked the unfamiliar woman.

The woman said nothing. She simply wrapped the blanket around Eva's babe and began to leave.

'Who are you and where are you taking her?' she asked louder.

Struggling against the pain and the bleeding, Eva pushed the bed linens back and tried to get out of bed. No one would take her bairn. Not now. Not ever.

'Here now, my lady,' Suisan, the woman sent along by Eva's father, said as she entered the chamber. 'I need to see to you, and the bairn will be well cared for while I do it.'

Suisan was efficient in her actions and within a short time, Eva found herself bathed and wearing a clean shift. The bed linens had been changed and all evidence that she'd given birth was removed from the chamber. Sipping a hot concoction that Suisan gave her, Eva felt the pain and anxiousness ease.

'You can bring her back now, Suisan,' Eva said, handing the cup back to the woman. 'I should try to feed her.'

'All of that is being seen to, my lady. Nothing for

you to worry over now,' Suisan whispered as she moved around the bed, smoothing and tucking the bedcovers in tighter.

'Seen to?' Eva asked, trying to push herself up to sit and finding that her body would not obey her commands. 'I said to bring her to me, Suisan.' The chamber grew dim and the room seemed to melt away.

'She is no longer your concern, my lady. You must rest and regain your strength now,' the woman urged.

'She is mine,' Eva argued, but her words came out slurred and confused.

Eva knew she'd been given something to make her sleep, but that was not the alarming part. This woman's words struck fear deep into Eva's heart. But her attempts to sit up and to go to find her babe were for naught, as her body surrendered to whatever herb was in that cup.

'No longer, my lady.' Suisan drew the sheet and blanket higher and tucked it around Eva's shoulders. 'She is gone now. Nothing to worry over now.'

All thoughts fled as she sank into oblivion.

Days passed as she rose and sank into its depths. Days and nights melded into one blur until the day, three weeks later she thought, when her father arrived to take her home.

It took another week to reach their home in Tongue, far to the north and to the east of Durness, but Eva knew nothing but desolation and misery. Her father, Ramsey MacKay, chieftain of the Clan MacKay, never mentioned the child. He treated Eva as though nothing had happened, and Eva understood that this was his way of erasing the 'unfortunate incident' from existence.

Only when the herb-induced haze wore off did the true panic set in—she did not know if her daughter lived or had died. That fear gave her the resolve she needed at her weakest moments, and Eva knew she would find out the truth somehow. If her father would not tell her, she would seek it out herself. That plan gave her a reason to heal and to gain her strength back.

Pretending to be the dutiful daughter, she struggled through the terrible emptiness of loss, while deciding how she should proceed. With no kith or kin to support her, she knew she must do it alone. And she would.

Three more weeks passed when the news came. Not word of her daughter as she'd hoped and prayed, but instead news about her own fate.

She was to be married off to the kin of a powerful chieftain in the south to bind their families together. Her father's edict gave her no choice in the matter of marriage. His declaration that it would happen spurred her into action. Refusal was not an option for her in this—her father could be ruthless in getting his own way. If the Mackintosh's man arrived and Eva was here, she would be wed to him.

So, Eva did the only thing she could do...

She ran away.

Chapter One

Drumlui Keep

Rob Mackintosh, cousin and close friend of chieftain of the powerful Mackintosh clan, glared at that friend and was met by an expression he could only describe as glee. Brodie did not even attempt to hide his enjoyment of Rob's discomfort.

'Damn it to hell, Arabella!' Rob cursed. Brodie's wife had neatly undermined his argument against this proposed marriage with a few words. 'How am I supposed to refuse it now?' He turned and strode out, still cursing under his breath as he left.

The last six months since Brodie had taken his place as chieftain of the clan and the head of the Chattan Confederation had been busy ones for Rob. After struggling to help his friend defeat his treacherous cousin Caelan and undo the damages wrought during Caelan's rule, Rob had taken a position on the council that advised and guided Brodie. But, everyone knew that Brodie trusted Rob as he did no other, and Rob soon became the one to seek if someone needed or wanted something from Brodie.

Rob nodded to several in passing as he made his way down the corridor away from the chamber Brodie used as his workroom. From the way their mouths twitched, he knew they'd heard either the cursing or the door slam.

A marriage contract.

For him.

To some unknown, unmet woman from the north. To bind her clan and his and expand Brodie's sphere of influence.

All of that was the normal pattern of events for marriages and contracts, but somehow Rob had wanted something…more. Something or someone different. Always in Brodie's shadow but not close enough in blood, he'd hoped that would protect him from clan machinations and plans. Clearly, it had not.

Turning the corner, he strode down the corridor and out the doorway that led to the yard. He needed some fresh air to clear his head and think on this matter. Rob did not doubt that Brodie would have his back in this and, if Rob refused outright, Brodie would accept it. But, meeting the gaze of Arabella and saying no would be another thing.

Rob had watched as she, once their enemy, had first given Brodie back his soul and then helped to save their clan. In spite of the long history of hatred and mistrust between the Mackintoshes and the Camerons, Arabella had accomplished what many had thought impossible and, more than that, she'd saved Rob's closest friend.

If truth be told, Rob knew he would have to come up with a strong objection to allow himself to refuse this arrangement. He let out a breath and looked around.

Somehow his feet had taken him into the village, and he stood before his sister's cottage.

Brodie had said that Margaret approved the match. Rob suspected that she would be in support of any arrangement that ended with him married. She'd long decried his bachelorhood and had tried her own hand at matchmaking, but he'd resisted. She was probably chortling with glee over his situation now.

'Margaret?' he said, knocking on the door frame. 'Are you within?' She called out to him.

Leaning down to enter, he watched as Margaret put a pile of clothing aside and stood to greet him. She was always busy, her hands never idle or empty. And though her husband was gone, she worked more now than when he was alive, taking in the strays and the lost and the injured, seeing to their care until they could move on. Just as she had in their mountain camp during their months and months of exile and outlawry.

'Ah, Robbie…' She clutched his shoulders and drew him down for a kiss. 'You have been a busy man.'

'Is that your way of saying I do not see you often enough?' Rob asked as he stepped back. She smiled and nodded.

'Well, now that you are such an important man, seeing to the chieftain's business and travelling so much, I understand.' Rob narrowed his gaze and watched for signs that she was teasing him.

'Aye, Margaret,' he said as he finally recognised the tiny lines at the edge of her eyes as humour. 'I am so important.'

'Truly, Rob, are you well?' she asked, concern filling her tone. Before he could answer, a knock came on the door and it was pulled open.

'Margaret? Are you here, lass?'

A man who called his widowed sister *lass*? Rob turned to see who this man was and was shocked when Magnus, one of the warriors, ducked low and entered. From the man's startled expression, he did not expect Rob to be here. The glances that passed between Magnus and his sister told Rob the answer to the question he'd not yet voiced.

'Aye, Magnus,' Margaret said, walking to the door and the man. The blush in her cheeks both surprised and pleased him in some way. Though he would never have thought of this, clearly there was something more than simple kinship between the two. 'Rob just arrived.'

'Rob,' Magnus said, holding out his hand in greeting. 'How goes it?'

'Well, Magnus,' he answered, accepting the man's hand. 'What brings you here?' he asked, even knowing 'twas neither his right nor his place to ask such a thing.

'I help your sister from time to time with the heavier tasks at hand,' Magnus explained. His voice grew gruff and Margaret's face grew redder. Heavier tasks, his arse! 'With you being off, seeing to Brodie's business, I stop by when I can.' Margaret looked near to choking or exploding, Rob could not decide which, so he took pity on her.

'I am glad you are here to aid her, Magnus. Especially when I cannot be,' Rob said.

He meant it. Though from their actions, the shy glances shared between them and their nervousness, Rob understood the relationship that was growing. Margaret's healing skills had saved Magnus's life during their exile, and the two had spent much time together.

If it pleased his sister to have this man close at her side, then it pleased him. She did not need his approval to marry again or to take a man to her bed. If she found some joy after the bitter loss of her husband, Rob would not deny or question her. The air around them grew tense, and he felt the odd one here and knew he should go. But first…

'Speaking of my travels, Magnus, Brodie has offered my hand in marriage.'

''Tis about time for that, Rob,' Margaret said, laughing and pulling him back into a hug. Magnus stepped aside to let her close. 'I had given up any hope of my efforts working to see you matched.' She let him go but kept her hand on his arm. 'So who is the lass?'

The snort he let out was unexpected, as were her words. Margaret had given no approval. Hell, she had not even known of the offer. Brodie would pay for this.

'A MacKay from the north. Brodie wishes our clans joined, and I seem to be the eligible kinsman to be offered to the slaughter.'

He did not need to see her wince to hear the bitterness in his own voice. If this match did happen, he should not want his resistance whispered around. Margaret leaned in close then.

'Mayhap this is for the best, Rob? Brodie would not ask someone he did not trust to do something as important as this.'

Rob nodded. 'Aye, you have it right, Margaret. I had just hoped…'

He paused, not knowing how to explain his feelings to her. Men and women looked at this from different perspectives and, since her marriage—one that resulted in a deep love—had been an arranged one, she would likely not do anything but support it. Some noise outside caught his attention and gave him the excuse he needed to leave.

'I must see to packing for the journey,' he said. Kissing his sister, he nodded at Magnus and then could not stop himself from a wee tease. 'Have a care with those heavy tasks, Magnus. A man could find himself confined to a bed easily if they are not done well.'

Rob walked out quickly then, but not without hearing Margaret's sputtered curse and Magnus's deep and hearty laughter. It did his heart good to know that Margaret had found joy again and that Magnus would be there for her.

The rest of the day passed quickly, too quickly for his taste, as he saw to his duties that involved training the warriors. Fighting at Brodie's side over the past years had honed his skills with weapons and strategies, and he enjoyed this part of his duties the most.

Then, he gave Brodie, and Arabella, his answer at dinner.

Brodie's reaction was exactly what he expected it to be—a knowing nod of his head and a satisfied expression in his gaze. Arabella, well, Arabella jumped up and ran to him, throwing her arms around him and clutching him close, regardless of her ever-expanding girth.

'I am glad, Rob,' she said, wiping at her eyes as she released him. 'I want you to be happy in this. I pray you will find the MacKay girl to your liking and you will be happy.'

Any desire to argue or correct her dissipated at Brodie's approach. The look in his eyes now promised retribution and pain if Rob dared ruin Brodie's wife's happiness in this matter. Having been at the wrong end of Brodie's anger more than once, Rob decided to allow her to believe the optimism in her words and he just nodded.

'When will you leave?' Brodie asked, as he guided Arabella back to her chair.

'In a day or two. I have some things to see to before I leave.'

'How many will you take?'

Rob inhaled and let it out before answering his laird. He'd thought on this all day while finishing up some tasks. If this failed, he wanted no one to witness it. Whether Brodie would agree was another matter.

'I go alone.'

Silence greeted his words for several long seconds. He met Brodie's stare, waiting as his friend thought on his answer.

'I would rather you take at least a small number of men with you,' he said. 'But you will be travelling through lands held by allies or kin and can defend yourself,' Brodie agreed. 'How long will you take?'

'If the weather holds, no more than a fortnight to get there and another to get back. I will stay there as long as it takes,' he said.

'Rob...' Brodie began. Rob held up his hand to forestall his friend.

'I am at peace with this, Brodie. If I cannot tolerate the woman or have some strong objection, I will speak my mind to you.' Brodie smiled and nodded. 'I am at peace,' he repeated, 'but not happy at all.'

Accepting more wine in his cup from a passing servant, Rob drank it down in one swallow. He'd been truthful with Brodie—if there was something wrong with the lass, he would refuse. If there was some impediment or other reason, he would refuse. And if there was none, he would have to accept her.

As he mounted his horse and gathered the reins of the packhorse in his hand two days later, Rob rode out of Drumlui Keep, knowing that he would be a different man when he returned.

A married man, for better or worse.

He could only pray that it would be for the better.

But the situation that greeted him on his arrival made him realise, it was only going to get worse.

Chapter Two

Three weeks later—Caisteal Bharraich—Castle Varrich—village of Tongue, Scotland

He should have gone by ship. He should have taken men with him. He should have done many things differently than he had. Rob knew that and more now as he neared the MacKay's keep outside the small village of Tongue.

Following the winding path up and around the hill on which the castle sat, Rob heard the guards call out as he cleared the last copse of trees and approached. He called out his name and the gates opened. One man motioned for him to follow and he did, aware of those watching his every move. Once he'd ridden close to the entrance to the keep itself, he threw a leg over his horse and dismounted. A gap-toothed boy ran up and Rob tossed the reins of both horses to him. He whistled to the boy before the young one got more than a couple of paces away and tossed him a coin.

'Mackintosh?' a man called out from the open doorway. 'The MacKay awaits you.'

Rob nodded and climbed the steps, leaning down to avoid hitting his head as he entered the keep. It was smaller than the one at Drumlui, but well kept and brightened by windows high up on the walls in the main hall. Glass from the looks of them. With the winds that blew in from the sea to the north and across the Kyle of Tongue, it was clear to him why those windows were small and thick.

Walking towards the large table at the other end of the rectangular chamber, Rob took note of a woman rushing there, as well. Not young enough to be his intended, she arrived there just as he did. He paused and bowed to the large, bearded man before him.

'My lord,' he said, as he lifted his head. 'I bring greetings from the Mackintosh to you and your family.'

He'd brought several gifts that yet remained on the packhorse that he would present formally later. And, something more personal to give the young woman when, *if*, he accepted the marriage contract. Rob glanced around the chamber and, though he saw several servants and others in the hall, no woman young enough to be the MacKay's heiress was present. Reaching inside his tunic, he took out a packet from Brodie and handed it to the MacKay.

'Ye were expected nigh to a week ago,' the MacKay said, nodding to a servant. 'We heard of storms to the west. Did ye get caught in them?'

'Aye,' Rob said. He accepted a cup of ale from the servant and followed the laird's lead over to a table. 'What roads I found quickly became muck and mire.'

'Not surprising at this time of year,' the older man explained. 'And this year the storms seem stronger coming from the north.'

The talk about the weather continued on and Rob knew it was forced. The rains came and went. The winds howled or caressed. The sun shone or hid. And none of that was of enough consequence for a man like this chieftain and a man like himself to dwell upon. It was, however, a perfect way to avoid the subject they should be discussing.

And why would the MacKay be avoiding that?

'I have been amiss, Mackintosh,' he now said. 'I do not believe ye have met Lady MacKay, Morag Munro.' Rob stood once more as the woman approached them now.

'My lady,' he said with a bow of his head. 'A pleasure to meet you.'

'Was your journey pleasant?' she asked, sitting on a chair across from her husband.

The journey again. Would the weather be next?

'Longer than I expected, my lady.' He kept his tone polite and tried not to let his suspicion enter it.

'These storms have been unusual.'

Rob nodded, smiled and drank from his cup, unable to speak in that moment. Something was amiss here.

Granted, he spent the first week of his journey being angry and cursing his fate. Well, cursing his best friend's high-handed method of seeing to his life and future. And cursing his own inability to simply refuse. Mayhap the storms had been the Almighty's way of slowing him down so that his eventual acceptance of this arrangement would happen before his arrival in Tongue?

And he had accepted the inevitable of this situation. Until now.

He had not lived this long without a healthy amount

of suspicion in his blood, without knowing when to look for more or without knowing to respect the feeling in his gut when it told him of danger. Or betrayal. He'd survived and protected Brodie's life by understanding the signs.

Something was wrong here.

Rob searched for any sign of treachery and found none. The usual tasks and chores he would expect in a keep this size went on around him. Other than several guards posted at the doorway and one closer to the laird, he saw no increase in defence around the hall. Yet...

'Your belongings have been taken to your chamber, sir,' the lady said now. 'If you have need of anything before our evening meal, simply ask one of the servants.'

Rob stood as the lady did, understanding he'd been dismissed from their company, even if the laird remained in his chair watching them silently.

'Lady,' he said, with a bow. 'I appreciate your hospitality and look forward to speaking more at the evening meal.'

With another bow to the MacKay, he followed the servant off as he was clearly meant to do. Rob paused as they turned the corner down a corridor and glanced back at the laird and his lady. He found them watching him.

Oh, aye, something was amiss here. Now all he had to do was discover what it was. Suddenly, his reluctance over this match seemed the sensible approach after all.

The next hours passed slowly as he waited for darkness to fall and dinner to commence. He unpacked his clothing and found the two gifts he'd brought for the MacKay daughter: a book of prayers—from Arabella's own collection—and a silken scarf—suggested by his sister. Lady Eva MacKay was well educated, according to Arabella, so the book should be appreciated. But, as Margaret had pointed out, a lass was still a lass and a lass liked something pretty, too. Hence the pale blue scarf.

A servant knocked on his door and invited him below, so Rob followed, observing the others who preceded and followed him as much as he could. Other than a few furtive glances, ones not unusual when seeing a stranger in their midst, he noticed nothing else. His presence would have been known by now and his position as the emissary of the Mackintosh would assure polite if not deferential treatment.

The hall filled with kith and kin and Rob was led to the front table and a seat waiting next to the MacKay. Strangely, there was no other open place, and his intended was not yet present.

'Lady Eva?' he asked after bowing and taking his place.

'I must beg your pardon, sir—' Lady MacKay began.

With a curt wave of her husband's hand, her words and nearly her breath were cut off.

'When you did not arrive as expected, my daughter asked permission to visit her cousin until you did. I have sent word, and she should arrive back here by midday on the morrow,' the laird explained.

It was not the news or even the fact that the woman they all meant for him to marry was not present for his arrival. It was not even the nervousness of Lady

MacKay or the furtive glances she threw in her husband's direction. Many noble husbands and wives led barely civil lives together and others lived in open warfare.

No, it was the way everyone present there who could hear this conversation paused and seemed to hold their breath that gave Rob concern. As though this delay and absence was not a simple and usual thing, but was instead something big and important. Which made his hackles rise. He cleared his throat, breaking the tense silence, and nodded.

'I look forward to having the pleasure of meeting her on the morrow, then.'

It was as if everyone let out their breath at once and returned to the conversations that they'd paused moments ago. Servants carried platters of roasted meats and fowl to the table, holding them so the laird and lady could select the choicest bits first. They brought the food to him next, as the honoured guest, and then to the rest at the high table.

The meal progressed and no one else mentioned the missing daughter at all. They discussed the MacKays. They discussed the Mackintoshes and the Chattan Confederation. They discussed the storms another time. All in all, it was the usual conversations and the usual fare for a diplomatic meal. Rob knew he would learn nothing here from them.

And yet, something flowed under it all. Mayhap he was right in his resistance to being forced into this marriage that would bring the Mackintoshes into an alliance with this clan? An opportunity to discover more came when one of the MacKay warriors approached and greeted him. They shared a mutual cousin, but Rob had forgotten that Iain lived here now.

'Will ye join us for a wee game, Rob? When ye are finished with yer meal?' Iain asked after greeting the laird and lady. 'Just a few friends, ye ken.' Iain, Rob now remembered, liked to throw dice.

'With your permission?' Rob turned to his host and awaited his word. There was a slight hesitation before a quick nod of consent. 'Aye, Iain. I will seek you out when we finish.'

The table was cleared a short time later, and the lady was granted leave to retire. Once she'd left, the laird spoke to a few of his men, giving orders for the morn and then stood to leave. 'Break your fast with us in the morn, Mackintosh. We can ride out to the coast, if the weather clears.'

'Aye, my lord. Until morn, then,' he said with a bow.

Rob let out a breath he had not realised he'd been holding and turned to see where Iain and his friends were gathered. Now, now he could find out what was going on here. A few hours later and some coin lighter, Rob had discovered some interesting bits about the goings-on in the Clan MacKay.

Rob woke early the next morning and saw to his horses in the stables. Built under the keep, they had their own entrance that faced north and the Kyle of Tongue. A few men nodded in greeting as he made his way back and into the hall where the morning meal would be served.

He held his words all through the meal, never giving any sign that he knew what was actually happening here. A short time later, the laird called for their horses, and he followed Ramsey from the keep, through the main gate and along the water's edge south. A few of the laird's men rode with them, and the first part of the ride was pleasant enough.

The MacKay was clearly quite proud of his new keep and the growing village that it protected a short distance to the east. He led them around in a circle that kept the keep in sight at all times. High on its hill, it was visible from the surrounding lands and made an impressive sight.

When they returned to the keep, climbing the hill and reaching a point that gave them a fantastic view of the surrounding kyle and lands, Rob pulled the reins and halted his horse. Ramsey waved his men on and stared at him. Rob could almost feel the man's growing discomfort as each second passed them by.

'So, my lord...' Rob began, watching the laird's face closely as he spoke. 'In which direction do you think your daughter headed when she ran way?'

Chapter Three

It had seemed a sound plan at first—run away from her home to give herself time to find her bairn. Run away and avoid this impending marriage. The Mackintosh's man would have his choice in accepting this arranged marriage or forgoing it, and Eva had planned that the latter should be his choice.

Surely, a man, no man, wanted to marry a reluctant or resistant woman? And if her disappearance shamed or humiliated him, would he not simply ride back to wherever he came from and seek out a willing woman to wife? Eva sighed again.

Shifting on the cold stone floor beneath her, she tried to ease her way back to sitting up. Her ankle and knee protested, sending shards of pain through her body with any movement.

So much for a good idea.

A shiver raced through her whole body then, reminding her of the fever that would not go away. She still bled as well, her body not healed yet from the birth eight weeks before.

Dying would be one answer to her problems. But she would not leave this life until she found out her bairn's fate. Not yet, she thought, as she shifted her weight to her uninjured hip and tried to pull herself up. Her leg slid on the slippery floor of the cave and she fell hard, forcing the breath from her body in a loud whoosh. Her head hit the wall and, as Eva watched, everything around her grew dark.

When next she opened her eyes, Eva could see a shape moving in the shadows. A fire burned somewhere close, and a huge creature skulked along the path inside the cave where she'd tried to hide. Oh, Dear God in Heaven! Had she unknowingly fallen into the cave of some dangerous animal? Mayhap if she lay quiet and unmoving, it would not hear her? But shivers racked her body and her teeth chattered so loudly she could hear them.

The dark, fur-covered creature rose up to its full height and turned to where she lay hidden among the rocks. It began to growl and…curse? Her fevered mind could not make sense of how an animal could speak in a human voice, but this one did. As it moved along the path and closer to her, she closed her eyes and prayed.

For forgiveness. For her daughter. For her soul.

All was for naught as the huge figure stood only a few paces away from her and stared at her with eyes filled with the glow of hell itself. Could it be a bear? Nay, they had not been seen in centuries here. Some other mythic creature sent to punish her for her disobedience and other sins? Eva reached up and swept her hair away from her face, squinting into the shadows to see what would be her executioner.

At its first step closer, she shook her head and tried to push herself along the slippery floor. With its second, Eva opened her mouth to scream. It would be the only thing she could do against something of this size and strength. She drew in a breath and brought her daughter to mind in that moment of her own death.

'Haud yer wheest!' the creature growled, stopping the coming scream with a hand over her mouth. 'Every noise echoes in this blasted place!'

A hand? Not a paw or claws? A hand, strong and warm across her mouth and cheeks. Eva blinked as the shape released her mouth and reached for its head.

'Are you Eva MacKay?' a man's voice asked. He pushed back the cloak that covered him, and he leaned forward. 'Are you?'

'Aye.' Her voice barely came out of her scratchy, dry throat.

She'd been found. All her attempts to evade her father's men were for naught. She would be dragged back now and forced to marry and leave these lands forever.

Eva fell back, giving up the fight. She was so cold and in so much pain that she could not struggle against her fate any longer. The fever that had plagued her since giving birth continued to rise and fall, sapping her strength.

'Give me your hand,' the man said. 'Give it here.'

Glancing at him once again, she could not get a clear view of his face. There was a torch or fire somewhere close, and it threw shadows across the cave and him. One moment, his face looked like that of an angel and the next like a demon. She swallowed against the dryness of her throat and stared at him.

Then, he held out his hand and motioned to her again. Knowing she would never be able to stand on her leg, she shook her head in refusal.

'Are you naysaying me?' He crossed his arms over his massive chest and gave her a dark glare. 'I said, give me your hand.'

'I cannot stand,' she whispered in fear of both the pain to come and this man. 'My foot, my knee, are...' She pointed to her injured right leg.

The grumbled cursing began anew as he knelt next to her and pushed her cloak aside. His indrawn breath at the trews she wore frightened her, but he ignored everything but her right leg. Lifting it with a gentleness she never expected, he slid his hand over her, pressing lightly around her knee and then on the boot that covered her foot and ankle. She could not help the gasps that escaped with each touch, but she cried out when he squeezed her ankle.

'Your pardon, my lady,' he said quietly. Easing her leg back down to the floor, he stood up. 'I do not think it broken, only bruised badly. But that boot needs to come off so your foot can be seen to.' The man walked a short distance away, back towards the opening of the cave and turned around as though searching for something. 'How did this happen?' he asked.

'I fell...in,' she whispered, glancing up at the opening above and behind her.

His words, filled with all sorts of expletives and unimagined insults, shocked her. And yet, they did not match the ease in his manners when he approached once more and crouched next to her.

''Tis a wonder you did not kill yourself. Or was that your plan?'

'Nay!'

Surprised at his boldness, she realised she had no idea of this man's identity, even though he had clearly been searching for her. Had her father hired mercenaries to keep her disappearance a secret from the clan and from the man coming to marry her? She stared at him, unable to answer his unthinkable query and unwilling to tell him anything.

'Who are you?' she asked. Eva pushed back with her arms, trying to sit up to face him. 'How did you find me?'

'I come from your father,' he said with a shrug. 'But neither of those things are important. A storm is blowing in from the north and this cave will flood very soon. We must get out of here now, for I have no desire to die in a place like this.' His emphasis on *I* made it clear what he thought her intentions were.

Spring brought powerful storms as the winter struggled to keep hold of the lands and seas this far north. The man who suggested this place to her had said it was far enough from the sea's edge to be safe. But now, listening to the sound of approaching waves, she knew the villager had been wrong. If her mouth and throat could grow any drier, they did just then as a wave of choking fear filled her.

'Come,' he said once more, reaching for her. 'Put your hands on my shoulders and let me get you to your feet first.'

This time, she did as he said, reaching up and grabbing hold of his shoulders. He slid his large hands around her at her waist and lifted her, bearing most of her weight as she placed her foot on the floor. When he began to let her stand, her leg gave out and she stumbled. A moment later, she found herself cradled against his chest.

His wide, muscular chest. He barely exerted himself in lifting her. She could feel the strength in his arms as he walked towards the entrance to the cave. As they neared the torch he'd stuck into a crack in the rock wall near the opening, she dared a glance up at his face.

And wished she had not.

The light from the torch caught the auburn in his hair and made it flicker. His brow gathered in a frown that made him look fierce and frightening. His chin and cheeks, not disguised by the beard he wore, seemed carved from the same hard rock of the inside of the cave. She began shivering again and could not control the way her body shook.

'Are you ill?' he asked, carrying her towards the steep path that led to the top of the cliff. 'Christ! You are burning up!' he growled against her head. The anger in his voice made her tremble.

The fever must be back.

Glancing around, she saw the path she'd not seen when trying to reach the cave. Eva had approached the openings in the ceiling of the cave when she'd slipped and fallen in. The only reason she had not died was that she slid most of the way down, hitting her foot and leg on a large rock as she came to stop on the floor. They reached it, and he stopped.

'I cannot carry you up this way and I cannot help you walk up. The path is not wide enough for two of us and I will need my hands on the steeper places.'

Her mind was so dulled by pain and fear that Eva could not come up with a solution. Then he began to lower her feet towards the ground.

'Put your uninjured foot down,' he directed. When she did, he gripped her waist until she steadied. His next action surprised her. He leaned her against the thick bushes there and removed a long length of tartan from around him. Then crouching before her, he said, 'Come now, lady. Climb on.'

If she had thought herself confused before, this confirmed it. Her head ached as she tried to determine what he wanted her to do. Her hesitation was noticed, for he turned and motioned to her with his hand, pointing to his back.

'Carrying you on my back will be safer,' he explained, moving back until he almost touched her legs. 'Hold once more on to my shoulders. Lean against me and give me your injured leg first.'

It took her several attempts and so much pain before she could position herself on his back. His touch was gentle as he guided and supported her leg around his waist and held it steady as she lifted her other one. Eva clutched his shoulders until he gave new orders.

'Slide your arms around me, lady,' he urged as he stood up. 'It will be a more secure hold for you.' She did as he said and she did feel more stable.

He tossed the length of wool around her, pulling it below her and wrapping it snugly around her, tying her to him much as a babe could be worn by a mother. He made several adjustments, uttering vile words when things did not do his bidding. Then, apparently satisfied with her position and the binding holding her there on his back, he took the first step up the path.

Between her exhaustion and pain and the warmth of his very strong body beneath her, Eva found herself drifting off to sleep as he climbed almost effortlessly up the steep trail. She woke to his voice, deep and masculine, calling out curses at the sky as the clouds opened above them. Spring rains were cold and this was just that. Only her head was above the woollen covering to feel it but he was more exposed and was getting soaked.

'Hold on, lady,' he said over his shoulder. 'We are almost at the top.'

He stumbled then and nearly pitched them to the ground, but he somehow regained his balance before they fell. Eva waited for the ear-blistering epithets that she expected would follow his misstep and was surprised when she could hear only his breathing. She began to drift in and out of awareness with each step as the pain flooded her body.

They reached the top and he grunted and stopped. Eva could feel his lungs taking in deep breaths and expelling them hard. As though her body had waited for them to be on level ground and not scrambling up a steep cliff side, the moment he turned his head to look at her and spoke her name, the blackness claimed her.

Rob felt the moment she lost consciousness. He'd heard every gasp and moan as he'd carried her up the cliff. She probably did not even realise she made such sounds, but he heard each of them. And yet, not once did she utter a word of complaint. Strange, that.

Since she was secure wrapped against him as she was, he untangled the reins of the horse he'd borrowed and led the animal along the main road that led back towards the village of Durness. He'd found a small unused cottage there for his use during this search and he would take her there.

As the winds howled around him now, he wondered

no longer why everyone here spoke often about the weather and the storms. The blacksmith had warned him about a coming storm when he asked about borrowing a horse. The innkeeper had, as well. And the miller, when he'd arranged for the cottage on his land. And, as if the mere thought of it made it happen, the rain became a wind-driven tempest, knocking him back and off balance.

Fighting against it, he made his way to the small dwelling and, after tying the horse behind it, Rob took the lady within. Crouching down to sit on the pallet, he untied the woollen fabric and eased her back onto it. He'd not realised how hot she was until he moved her off his back. Touching her cheek with the back of his hand, Rob felt the heat of a fever there and realised the danger of it.

His sister was the healer and she would know immediately what to do. He searched his memory of the times he'd watched her care for kith and kin, whether in the village or when they'd sought refuge in the mountains. Margaret was very succinct in her directions, and he smiled as he heard them in his mind now.

'Warm the chill. Cool the heat.'

'Watered ale throughout. Broth when hungry.'

Even a simpleton, or a man, could follow those directions, she'd told him once. He'd laughed then but not now, as the dangers of a fever were too real. Glancing around the cottage at the supplies he'd brought, he knew he did not have enough to last more than this night. Rob had not planned to stay here, only to use it as a place to sleep. After lighting a fire in the small hearth, he knew that now supplies were the most pressing need.

The lady yet slept, so he decided it would be best to go now and fetch the needed items from the village or from the miller. Her garments, the scandalous trews she wore, as well as her cloak and tunic, were soaked through, so Rob knew he must remove them and the short boots she wore, too. He drew his *sgian dubh* to slice the seam of the boot open so he could take it off without injuring her ankle more than it was.

Rob pressed along the arch of her foot and the curve of her ankle but could find no broken bones. Good. He watched her face to see if she reacted and found none. That could not be a good thing. He untied her cloak and eased it from around her. Her hair, woven into a long braid, was tucked inside her tunic. Placing the cloak near the growing fire to dry, he turned his attention to her garments.

He tried not to notice the womanly curves visible because of those trews. He loosened the ties at her waist and slid them down, finding her shift tucked within. Drawing it down as he moved the trews, it gave her some measure of cover, though he held his breath as he noticed the thin fabric did not truly cover much at all. Then he gathered up the tunic and removed it over her head, lifting her as he eased it off. Another surprise waited for him there.

She'd bound her breasts to play the part of a boy.

Rob frowned at this revelation. She was set against marriage to him so much that she left her home and belongings behind, disguised herself as a boy and hid in a cave, nearly killing herself. She shivered just then, and he knew he must put aside his irritation and sense of insult and deal with all that later.

He would need something to wrap her ankle, so he

lifted the thin shift and, with care, sliced one side of the bindings. Tugging them slowly, he removed them and tried not to notice the indentation of her breasts in the fabric. Or notice the way she sighed deeply in her sleep as though his action had brought some kind of relief. Rob moved down to her feet, shaking the strips of linen to separate them.

Her ankle swelled now that it was out of the confines of her boot, so he swaddled it with layers of linen, wrapped snugly but not too tight. He leaned back on his ankles and looked it over when he finished. It would do for now.

The howling winds reminded him of what he needed to do sooner rather than later, so Rob stood and tossed a dry plaid over her still form. He tucked it around her and then gathered what he needed—some coins and a leather sack.

The MacKay had given his leave for Rob to use his name, and it would ease his way once more but a coin or two was even more effective at gaining co-operation and information. He'd found the cave by sprinkling a few palms. Now, he would do what he needed to get the necessary supplies. With a final glance at the woman he hoped would be worth such trouble and embarrassment, he opened the door and stepped out into the storm.

Chapter Four

A war waged within her.

The forces of good and evil were surely battling over some prize—her soul mayhap?—leaving her battered and bruised. Every place on her body ached. She could not even lift her hand to wipe the sweat from her brow and eyes. Waves of pain began in her foot and sent tremors through her whole body.

But, she had given birth already. She should not feel this much pain now. Had she not? Or was this all a terrible, dark dream, and she was yet labouring to push her child out?

Nay! Her child, her daughter, was alive. She'd birthed her weeks and weeks ago. Eva struggled to open her eyes. She needed to find her...

'Hush now, lass.'

The voice came once more. Not a woman's soft tones but the deep masculine tones of a man. Not her father, surely. She tried to force her eyes open, but they would not obey her.

'Do not struggle,' he said. 'You've been ill and need

to rest.' A soft caress of her cheek was followed by something blessedly cool on her brow.

She wanted to offer her thanks, but no words would come out. Eva stopped fighting and let her body and thoughts drift, as he'd said. The next hours and days melded into a blurred time of pain and relief, heat and chill, dreams and emptiness.

When she was hot, cool touches eased it. When she shivered with cold, warmth surrounded her. When she called out in fear, a soothing voice urged her on. On and on, over and over, days blended into nights until suddenly Eva woke. She glanced around to discover she was no longer in the cave she remembered. Lifting her head caused so much dizziness that she did not try it again.

Across the small chamber, the door opened, letting in light and a man. A fresh wind blew through the room, bringing the smells of spring inside and banishing some of the staleness. Her dry throat tightened as she tried to speak. He was next to her in a moment.

'Here. Try a sip of this before you try to speak. I doubt you have much of a voice left by now.'

He placed a cup at her mouth and lifted her head a tiny bit to help her drink. The watered ale tasted better than any fine wine or spirits she'd ever drunk. After one more sip, he took the cup and she tried to reach for it. When she settled back, Eva looked closely at the man as he moved back and sat on the floor next to the pallet on which she lay.

No kith or kin she remembered. But his face was familiar to her. Something flashed through her mind, a memory of someone or something, then darkness again. Had he been sent by her father to find and bring her back?

'Who are you?' she asked in a voice barely above a whisper. 'What is this place?'

'I wondered how much you would remember,' he said. 'You have been ill for days. I found you in the cave and brought you to this cottage.' He stared at her, clearly expecting her to remember.

She remembered shadows moving around the cave and something approaching her. A large beast-like creature. Then he'd spoken.

'I thought you a bear from long-ago times,' she admitted. 'I do not remember much else.'

'I have been called worse, lady,' he said with a chuckle. 'You mistook my plaid and furs for the beast.' He nodded towards the corner where he'd draped several cloaks and then at her, or rather the pallet beneath her where his furs now were. 'The dirt floor was damp, and I feared it would make you sicker.'

Only then did she realise that she lay naked on those furs! Her garments, even her shift, were gone, and the woollen plaid was her only cover.

'Your garments were soaked with water and sweat. They are dry now,' he said, once more nodding to the corner.

Eva had been here for days. She'd been sick and unconscious, and this man had been with her. Who was he?

'Are you my father's man?' she whispered, still not certain of what had happened. She remembered seeking the cave and falling into it. Then...nothing more.

'He sent me.'

This man held his tongue well, never saying too

much. Mayhap he would hold that tongue if she paid him? If he was a hired man and not kin, it was not an insult to offer him coins for his silence.

'You took care of me and I am grateful. I would know your name,' she said.

He must have noticed her hoarseness again, for he came closer with the cup. Each sip was like a soothing balm as it slid over her tongue and down her throat. Why was she so hoarse?

'Rob,' he said, offering her another sip.

'I would pay you for your time and service, Rob,' she said. 'I have coin.'

He seemed to choke on whatever he wanted to say. Instead, he reached inside his tunic and took out a small flask. After drinking a few mouthfuls of what she thought must be strong spirits, he returned it and looked at her.

'And to return to your father without you, lady?'

His words were spoken evenly, but there was so much anger within his tone. Nothing in his gaze or manner gave her any clue of the reason for it, so she thought she must have insulted him in some way. When she would have offered words of apology, her body began to fail her. A yawn escaped when she would have spoken instead.

'You are still weak and need to rest,' he said, standing now. 'Sleep. We can speak later.'

In spite of her efforts to prove him wrong, her eyes closed and she lost herself in a deep sleep.

The lady's eyes had barely closed before he stormed out of the cottage. He needed some air and some space, or he would have said things he knew he would regret later. He'd learned early in life that words could damage as deeply as the sharpest blade, and he'd sworn not to make the same mistake that his father had.

Rob walked around the cottage, saying all the things he wanted to say to her to himself and adding a few choice words he would never say to a woman. She thought him a mercenary, ready and willing to take whatever coin offered him!

She so wanted to avoid marriage to him that she offered him money to walk away. Even not knowing who he truly was, she'd suggested that money could buy her way out of this.

He turned his face into the winds and closed his eyes. Margaret had warned him about his temper, and he'd fought to keep it under control. But this, this insult burned. Was he again not good enough, not high enough, not close enough to noble blood, for this lady to consider him worthy? Was that why she'd run, with no consideration for her own safety or life? Would marriage to him be such a terrible thing to risk so much?

The storm had blown itself out, its power seeping away as it crossed from the sea onto the land. Now, the sun shone as though it had not been dark and squalling for the last three days. In a way, the rainstorm had served a purpose, for the lady would never have been able to travel in her condition. As it was, she would not be strong enough for at least another two days.

It was one matter to be with her so intimately when she was sick and unconscious. But to be in such small quarters with her awake and staring at him with those sky-blue eyes and that lush mouth would be torture. And knowing what curves lay hidden beneath either

her garments or the plaid blanket that covered her made him restless.

And so he walked.

As he passed the door of the cottage, he noticed the young woman approaching along the road. The miller's daughter had been a godsend to him, seeing to Eva's more personal needs and care each day.

'Good morrow, Brita,' he said. 'I thank you again for your help.'

'Good morn, sir,' she replied with a slight curtsy. 'I am glad to help the lady. And my father thanks you for your coins.'

'She was awake for a short while just now. I gave her some ale.' He walked along with the woman.

'A good sign, then. The fever has broken. My mam said she will be calling for food very soon now.' Brita lifted the basket she carried so he could see in it. 'She said to begin with the broth and then the stew if she keeps it down. There is bread, as well.'

Rob reached out to take the basket for her. She smiled at his offer but shook her head.

'I can carry it, sir.'

'I will leave you to your ministrations then, lass,' he said, stepping out of her way. 'Call if you have need of help.'

Brita reached the doorway and turned to face him.

'My mam also sent something more filling along for you, sir. She said a man cannot survive on broth and bread.'

The miller and his wife had been most helpful. Aye, he had paid them well, but they seemed to genuinely want to. With a few exceptions that he needed to send to the village for, they'd provided the food and ale and blankets for the lady. Once they knew she was the MacKay's daughter, they did whatever he'd asked them to do. Even if they did look askew at a man seeing to her care.

Deciding that a ride might do them both good, Rob told Brita he would return shortly and went to get the horse. He wanted to see the cave in the light of day and see if she'd left anything behind. When she woke next, he had questions for her.

Such as who was the Mairead that she called out for in her fevered state.

The young woman's arrival both answered a question that loomed in her mind and allowed her to see to her personal needs without having to ask…him. Brita, as she was called, was the miller's daughter and had apparently been helping her each day during her illness. The girl had a pleasant way about her and her quiet chatter made things much less embarrassing than they might have been.

Within a short time of waking, Eva found herself washed and in a clean shift. The miller's wife had sent some broth for her when she felt ready to try it. And a loaf of bread. But Eva had more questions than hunger at this point, so she asked about the man who'd rescued her from the cave and stood as her guard and caretaker these last days.

'Do you know Rob?' she asked as Brita helped her to sit. The girl wanted to see to her hair.

'Nay, lady,' Brita said as she took the braid and loosened the ties holding it. 'He is from the MacKay, your father, and brought you here.'

'So, you've not seen him before? Not when my father visits here?' Eva could not remember even seeing him.

'Nay, lady. Just when he came to our house a sennight ago.'

'Last week? He has been here a week?' Eva found it exhausting just to sit up, so trying to figure out his identity tired her even more.

'Aye,' Brita said. 'He asked to rent this cottage. Said the laird set him to the task of finding you.'

She sat in silence as the girl tended to her hair. She desperately needed to wash it, but just having it brushed was a pleasure. Brita finished the tasks she'd been sent to carry out and curtsied when she was leaving. She stopped at the door, just before opening it.

'My mam said you should know that your bleeding stopped two days ago. She was the first one to tend to you, lady.' The girl's face filled with a blush as she said such a thing. 'She said she thought you would want to know.'

Eva smiled and nodded, feeling both relief and sorrow. The fever and bleeding had been happening together since she'd given birth. Fearing childbed fever and death, Eva knew it had continued too long. But her mother had refused to speak of the birth at all, so there had been no one she could seek advice from. Everyone at Castle Varrich had been forbidden to speak to her about those months she'd spent away, *visiting kin in the west* was the explanation.

Brita left, and Eva remained sitting up, leaning against the wall with several blankets behind her. Rob would return shortly, according to the girl, and it would do her good to move a bit. But, she feared the first time she would put her weight on her injured ankle. Even now, wrapped tightly, it throbbed from just moving it around as she washed and dressed.

A few minutes later, the door opened and *he* walked in.

The first thing she noticed was that his auburn hair was windblown and wild. She must be feeling better if she was taking in such details now. He seemed more alive than when he'd left. He pushed the door, and she heard the latch catch.

'I found this in the cave,' he said, tossing the small bag to her. He was angry. Again.

She opened it and found the few things she'd managed to take with her when she'd run off in the middle of the night. A small purse filled with coins. A small *sgian dubh* made to fit a woman's hand. A comb. An extra shift. Her prayer beads. And the skin of water she carried.

'You left the safety of your father's keep with only this?' he asked. 'What was so terrible that you would risk your life to get away?' His hands fisted and released, and she could feel waves of ire pouring off him. 'Why did you run?'

Something was terribly wrong here. If she'd suspected it before, Eva knew it now. This man had no right to speak to her like this. Or to be in the same chamber as she. Or to demand help and supplies on behalf of her father. Who was he?

A sick feeling roiled through her stomach then. It had nothing to do with her illness and everything to do with the man standing before her.

If he'd been paid to do this by her father, he would have sent word for someone to come for her in her condition. A mercenary would not even worry over her illness, he would be paid for finding her.

A mercenary would not give a moment's thought to why she'd run or what she'd taken. He would not have done most of the things this man had in caring for her.

A sinking feeling filled her, and she could feel the blood draining from her face and head. It took all of her courage to ask the question that now spun out in the space between them, but she must. The answer, which she suspected she already knew, would explain so much.

'You are not my father's man.' She asked, her voice trembling with each word, 'You are the Mackintosh's counsellor and cousin, are you not?'

He crossed his arms over his chest and nodded. If his face grew any darker with anger, it would explode.

'Robert Mackintosh,' he said as though introducing himself to her for the first time. 'Your betrothed husband.'

She gasped at his declaration. 'Betrothed?' she asked, shaking her head wildly. 'We were not betrothed.'

'Aye, lady, we were. Your father and I signed the documents before he gave me his blessing and sent me off to look for his runaway daughter.'

'Nay!' she cried out, trying to get to her feet in spite of her injuries and continued weakness. 'I cannot marry you. You cannot force this on me!'

He took her by her arms and pulled her up to him, their faces but inches apart. He stared at her, searching there for something.

'In the eyes of the Church and by the laws of this land, we are married, lady. The vows can be spoken when we return to Castle Varrich. The rest can wait until we arrive in Glenlui.'

The rest? The rest! Eva would never share with any man what she'd given to Eirik.

She balled up her hands and pushed against his chest with them, trying to force herself free. He simply held her tighter, giving her no chance to get away. Because he was so much taller and stronger than she was, her feet did not even touch the ground.

'You do not understand,' she began to plead. 'I cannot marry you. I...'

'Are you pledged to someone else already?' he demanded. 'Tell me why you cannot marry me.'

She could not reveal the truth to him. Her father would be furious if she continued to fight this marriage. He was the only one who knew where her baby was and, if she did not do as told, the wee bairn would pay the price. Ramsey MacKay was a cold-hearted and ruthless man when it came to getting his own way. No one opposed him—not his wife, his daughter, his kith or kin—and not suffer for such defiance.

'And tell me who Mairead is,' he said, in a quiet but no less dangerous voice. 'Who is she?'

He could have hit her and it would not have hurt as much as hearing her daughter's name on his lips. The shock rippled through her and in the next moment, as he called out her own name, Eva fainted.

Chapter Five

'Eva!'

Rob swore aloud, but she did not even react to the coarse words he'd said. The mention of that name had caused this. Her eyes had been glaring at him one moment and then they rolled up into her head the next. Cursing her, her father, her mother, his friend and anyone else he could bring to mind in that second, Rob carried her to the pallet and laid her there, being careful of her injured leg and foot.

She did not rouse. He tapped on her cheek, saying her name in as calm a tone as he could, but there was no sign of her coming around. Stalking as far away from her as he could get within the cottage, he watched her.

Bloody hell! Damn this woman to perdition!

She'd run from him. Refused to marry him. Worse, she placed herself in immeasurable danger because of her wilfulness. It was a miracle he'd found her in that cave before the storm blew in and flooded it. It was a miracle that she had not been attacked by ruffians or outlaws in the forests and on the roads between her father's keep and this place. A miracle.

He let out a loud breath then, releasing some of the pent-up anger within him. Walking back to her side, he knelt down and touched her cheek. Thank the Almighty— no fever. When she did not move or wake, he sought out the cloth and water and touched the rag to her head and cheeks and then along her neck. Rob repeated it several times before her eyes began to flutter open.

Rob brought over the cup of ale and held it out when she looked at him. Without a word, she pushed up to lean on her elbows and took the cup. She averted her gaze and sipped several times before handing it back to him. As he watched, those blue eyes filled with tears that began to spill down her cheeks. The lady turned away, tucking her face into the pillow and sobbing silently.

He felt sick to his stomach. He'd wanted to force a reaction from her and he got one, just not the one he was hoping for. He wanted truth, but realised he'd lied to her from the first, too. Oh, his words about their betrothal were true, for he'd made certain she was his before setting out. Now he wondered over the wisdom of his course of action.

And still she cried. The sound of it was filled with despair and grief, and it shook him in a way he did not wish to acknowledge. At least not the part he played in it. Standing, he sought out the basket of food and took out the broth and bread from Brita's mother. He poured some in a cup and placed it to warm near the flames. A glance over his shoulder told him that her weeping eased a bit.

He carried on preparing the food, not ignoring her, God, there was no way to do that, but just trying to allow her some time. Finding the meat pie wrapped

in cloth, he placed it in a bowl and broke it apart with
a spoon. It took its place next to her broth, warming
slowly there. Soon, the enticing aroma of the food
wafted through the cottage. His own stomach growled
in anticipation of the taste, for Brita's mother, Helga,
was a superb cook.

Testing the heat of both the cup and bowl, Rob removed them and placed them on the small stool he'd
been using as a table next to her. He tore two chunks
of bread from the loaf and put them there, too. After
watering some ale for her, he filled his cup with the
stronger spirits from his flask. And then he sat down,
cross-legged, waiting for her own hunger and thirst to
bring her there.

It did not take long.

He tried to focus on his food, but he could not help
but watch her. First she leaned up and found the damp
rag and used it on her eyes and face. Using the edge of
the plaid to dry herself, she pushed up to sit, her breathing yet ragged and loud. Rob sensed that helping her
now would cause her to crumble again, so he waited
for her to move or to ask for help.

She would not meet his gaze. Even when she managed to sit up and lean against the wall, she would not
look at him. He did not force her to, he only slid the
table closer so she could reach the cup, if she wanted
it. And, after a few minutes of laboured breathing, she
did. Rob tore the chunks of bread into smaller pieces
and moved them closer.

They ate in an awkward and yet somehow companionable silence. It took her some time to finish just the
cup of broth, but she did, dipping some of the bread in
it to sop up the liquid. He did the same with the meat

pasty—a hearty mix of chunks of beef and root vegetables and broth. Helga was unsurpassed in her dishes, no matter that he'd eaten at palaces and castles of the noble and the royal kind over the last few months.

The lady placed her empty cup on the stool and leaned back, tugging the plaid higher and holding it against her. As he watched, her eyes closed and he knew she was almost asleep. A shiver brought her to wakefulness.

'Your tunic is dry now, if you are chilled,' he offered.

'The furs keep me warm enough,' she whispered back.

He jutted his chin. 'Then go to sleep. My sister says it's the best thing for most illnesses.'

'You have a sister?' she asked, leaning away from the wall and sliding herself down under the blankets.

'You do not have to say it with such disbelief in your voice. Aye, I have a sister. Margaret. She serves the clan as a healer at Glenlui.'

'I meant no disrespect, sir,' she offered. 'I know nothing about you or the Mackintoshes.' She spoke with closed eyes and each word came out slower than the one before it. She was falling asleep in the middle of a conversation.

'Then none is taken. Sleep, lady. We will have time to talk.'

And she was gone, deeply asleep in moments.

Rob stood and cleaned up from their meal, going out to wash the cups, bowl and spoons with water from the bucket outside. The sun had set and the air grew chilled. He closed the door tightly and dropped the latch and then did the same thing with the wooden shutters to keep out the winds.

Soon, the cottage was prepared for the night...but he was not. After adding some more peat to the fire, he lit a few candles and picked up her sack. Surely, there must be more inside than just the few items he'd seen when he opened it at the cave.

Sitting on the floor near her, he turned the sack inside out and watched as the few things fell before him.

A small *sgian dubh*, more suited for eating or mending tasks than for defence or attack. And she did not wear it in her boot where she could reach it quickly.

A leather purse holding some gold and silver coins. Not enough to live on for long, but enough to present a temptation to any thief along the road.

Another shift.

A set of prayer beads, carved out of some black stones. Well, she might appreciate the book he'd brought for her if she was a godly woman. But a godly woman knew her place and obeyed her father and then her husband. Eva MacKay did not know the first thing about obedience or her proper place if what she'd done so far was the measure used.

Rob laid the things aside and shook his head, watching her sleep there. What kind of woman would run away when given the news of an impending marriage? Especially a marriage that would hold benefits for both families involved.

She shifted on the furs and mumbled some words in her sleep. Though he could blame some of her restlessness in sleep on her illness and fever, she never seemed to be at peace when she slept. She called out names, mostly the one, throughout the time when sleep claimed her.

Something was wrong here. Very wrong.

If she did not know him or the Mackintoshes, then they could not be the reason for her refusal to accept the marriage. Yet, she did the unthinkable and left the safety and protection of her father's keep to avoid it. Was it just maidenly fear or something more? Though clearly fear was not something that seemed to rule her life if she was brave enough to do what she'd done.

Rob stared at her, trying to decipher her actions and her intentions. If she did not want to marry him and had a good reason for her objections—one that would satisfy Brodie and Arabella—he would see that the betrothal was broken. He'd not expected a love match at all, but he would be damned before he married an unwilling woman.

If she would only explain herself...

The winds howled then, rattling the wooden walls of the cottage and sending cool air through the cracks. The low flames of the peat fire danced in the current. It would grow much colder before the sun rose in the morn.

Eva shivered then, curling herself into a tight ball under the blankets. He was tempted to wake her and give her the tunic she'd refused earlier, but he would not disturb whatever rest she could get. On the morrow, he would send word to her father that he'd found her, and they would begin the journey back to Castle Varrich a day or two after that.

For now, he did what he'd done these last three nights—he took off his boots and tunic and lay down next to her, sharing his body's warmth with her. She startled a moment and then moved back nearer to him, as she did each time he shared the pallet with her. Then he pulled the extra blanket over both of them.

Although she sank into a deep sleep, it evaded him for hours. The riddle that Eva MacKay was haunted him all night. At some moment, he realised that she was awake next to him. So, he decided to ask her for her reasons.

'Have you need of anything, lady?' he asked first. 'Do you thirst?' Helga had told him he should give her as much to drink as possible.

'Nay,' she whispered back.

Silence reigned for a long minute or two before she spoke again.

'You have slept like this each night, then?' she asked.

'Aye.' Then he explained further, 'At first there was no sleeping, you were that ill with fever. Then, I found that you were cold more than hot, so lying this way seemed to keep you warm.'

'And you knew of the betrothal, so there was nothing wrong in the eyes of God or the law in doing that.' Her words were more a declaration than a question, but there was something buried within them.

'Just so.'

The lady began to say something more but paused and held her words behind her teeth. A minute later, she did the same thing—began and paused. When she did it for a third time, he spoke instead.

'Just speak your mind, lady. Between us. Tell me what you wish to say.'

'I mean no insult, sir. I have no intention to embarrass or insult your laird and chief. I just cannot marry you.' He could hear her trying to remain calm and failing as her voice hitched on the words.

'Is there someone else, lady?' he asked. 'Or do you have some other objection? Give me some reason that I can understand, for I have no wish to marry an unwilling bride.' And he did not.

'I cannot marry you,' she repeated.

'Mayhap if you'd remained in your father's house and discussed this before the betrothal, we could have made an agreeable arrangement. Now, though...' he said.

'Nay, pray do not say it is too late now?' she asked, turning to face him. The grimace of pain told that she'd forgotten that injury in moving.

'The betrothal is legal and sound. I fear it is too late.'

Rob waited, waited for tears, waited for angry words, waited for some emotional reaction from her. None came. All he heard was the sound of her ragged breathing. Once more she turned away from him, tucking her face into the pillow.

A thought occurred to him in the night some time later, as they both yet lay awake in the dark.

He'd not wanted this marriage. She wanted it not. So, why would he force this? It spoke of a disaster in the making. And problems and conflicts every step of the way. He would not even have a marriage of convenience, he would have a marriage of catastrophe.

'I will speak to your father when we return. 'Tis clear to me that we do not suit. My laird will offer suitable compensation for breaking the betrothal contract and handle the issue.'

'Truly?' she asked, her voice now filled with hope. And that stung worse than any of her words so far.

'Aye. I want no unwilling wife.'

Then silence filled the cottage, broken only by the occasional crackle of the fire or burst of wind outside. He thought she might have fallen asleep as he still tried to do.

'I thank you, sir. I will always be grateful for the mercy and good will you have shown me when you have every right to treat me otherwise,' she whispered.

Again, her words stung him. However, he'd spoken the truth. It would be easier to return to her father and his laird with a specific reason for breaking the contract, but Rob knew Brodie would have his back in this...or in anything he asked him to.

He rolled to his side and found himself drifting to sleep.

At some time in those last few hours before dawn, she turned to him and he slipped his arm over her, drawing her closer. He drifted in and out of sleep until the sound of swords being drawn got his attention.

Opening his eyes, he found Ramsey MacKay and six of his warriors standing around the pallet where he and Eva lay.

Where the MacKay's daughter lay naked in the arms of her betrothed husband. Where Eva MacKay sighed his name before opening her eyes to find her father standing above them.

Her reaction—a loud, shrill scream that filled the cottage and made him squint—was something Rob could understand. But it was the MacKay's soft words that bothered him more.

'Well, I guess ye have no objections to taking my daughter as yer wife after all, Mackintosh. Welcome to the family.'

Chapter Six

The door to her chambers slammed open and the maid helping her with her bath let out a shriek. With a nod of his head, her father ordered the maid out and closed the door behind her. Eva knew there would be a reckoning, and it appeared to be at hand.

'You are quite bold for someone with so much to lose,' he said quietly. Too quietly. 'I told you what would happen if you did not do as I said. 'Tis the little bastard who will pay for your sins, daughter. All I have to do is send the word, and she will die.'

Eva grasped the sides of the tub, unable to breathe or reply.

He stood next to the large wooden tub and glared at her. There was no way to hide herself or to leave the tub. Her ankle was much improved but would not hold her weight yet. So, she was trapped here until he left and the maid returned.

''Tis a good thing he is willing to overlook your disobedience and stupidity and wilfulness,' he began. 'And a good thing he does not know you are nothing but a lying, ungrateful slut who does not know when to keep her mouth or her legs closed.'

She made the mistake of opening her mouth then, determined to find out what he'd done with her child, but he slapped her with the back of his hand. Her head bounced back against the side of the tub.

'God knows, I have been too lenient with you. 'Tis your mother's fault—she coddled you and allowed you too much say,' he said, grabbing her by her hair and dragging her over the side of the tub. Unable to stand, she tried to crawl away, but he grabbed her arm and pushed her to the floor.

'You dare demand that I tell you what you want to know? You dare threaten to reveal it to the Mackintosh's man if I do not?' He held her down with one strong hand on her back, and she could not move from his hold.

'Mayhap if you'd been strapped well when I found out about that boy and what you'd been doing, you would have lost it and saved me such trouble.' Only then did she see the long leather strap in his hand.

Eva tried to grab for some covering, but she was too far from the bed and from the stool where the drying cloths lay. He did not wait before striking her, laying it hard on her back and buttocks. She screamed against such pain, but it had no effect on him.

'I have him where I want him. You will not speak of this to him,' he said in a lower voice. 'Or your child will not live to see the first anniversary of her birth.'

The threat took away her breath then, against Mairead and against Rob. She tried to bear it in silence but could not and screamed with each blow. Four lashes delivered with a heavy hand and he'd reared back to hit her again, when the door opened. Already out of breath, her father called out over his shoulder rather than stop.

'I'm seeing to my daughter. Get out now,' he called.

'She is my wife.'

Rob.

Eva could only curl up in a ball there on the floor. The pain in her back and her buttocks took her breath away.

'Then learn from my mistakes, Mackintosh. She needs to be taught obedience. She only understands the strap. Used often and used well.' Her father swung once more, wrenching another cry from her.

Eva wanted to die then. Humiliated before the man who would control her life, she could not raise her head to look at him. It seemed that every time he came into her life, she was helpless. Now, worse than helpless, for she was naked on the floor being beaten by her father.

'Then I will see to it,' he said to her father.

The tension in the chamber heightened as she waited to see what her father would do. Ramsey MacKay was not used to interference with his wishes or to being ordered about, so she held little hope that he would cease now. Eva dared a glance to see what would happen.

'I agreed to the betrothal. I agreed to the marriage. She is mine, to do with as I please and no longer under your authority, MacKay. Or do I tell Brodie Mackintosh that you reneged on the contract?'

When she dared to peek, Rob had crossed his arms over his chest in a frightful pose. His face grew dark and threatening, and Eva was not certain who was most in danger: her or her father. She shivered at the sight.

'Very well,' her father said, relenting. He tossed the

strap to Rob and crossed the room to the door. Staring at her, he began, 'Do not allow her disobedience to go unanswered. You will rue the day you did not make certain she knows who is in control of her.'

Eva dipped her head again, unable to look at his face and see his hatred of her. She cried now, unable to control her tears in the face of the pain and humiliation.

'Give me your hand,' Rob said.

'Please, I pray you leave,' she whimpered.

'I said give me your hand.'

Eva pushed herself up and held out her hand as he'd ordered. Her hair dripped on the floor and was a tangled mess over her face and shoulders. It was long but not long enough to hide the rest of her from his sight. She was not certain what he planned to do, for he had reason to continue the punishment for her sins against him.

He took her hand and then helped her to her feet, careful to keep her weight on one foot. Then he lifted her up and carried her to the tub. Placing her in the still-warm water, he stepped away, never looking at her. Eva held herself away from the side of the tub, not resting back now, but hugging her knees.

'I will send your maid to you so you can finish your bath, lady,' he said. 'We will speak our vows before the evening meal and leave in the morning.'

She nodded, surprised at his gentle touch and treatment.

'I have to say I am confused.' He reached for the latch on the door and turned back to face her. 'You want to refuse marriage to me and remain here with your father, knowing what will happen to you. What would keep you here, Eva, rather than taking the chance with a man who has done nothing to harm you? I think it must be something very important indeed.'

He paused then, and she wanted to tell him. She wanted to explain that this had nothing to do with him. That she needed to be here to seek out her daughter before her father moved her so far from her reach that she would never find her. The words were there—she owed him at least that. She struggled to keep the words within her. Eva just could not take the chance that her father would hurt her child…as he already had Eirik.

She looked down at the water that swirled around her and said nothing.

When she looked up, he was gone. Shuddering from the pain and humiliation, Eva rocked in the water. Her father would kill her daughter, she doubted it not. But what had he meant about Rob?

She remembered Rob's promise to end this betrothal, a promise made in the dark of night just before her father had found them. However, with her lying naked and next to him on the pallet, there was no way to talk their way out of it. The marriage was a fait accompli because of those circumstances, with the witnesses and those who would swear to what they'd seen.

And the villagers who would tell that Rob had cared for her for days alone.

Had Ramsey MacKay arranged it all, then? To trap Rob into having no choice? For surely a report back to his laird that he'd compromised the MacKay's daughter would result in the marriage going forward. No MacKay would speak to an outsider about last year's *incident* and her disappearance for several months. A bit of hysterical laughter escaped her then, echoing around the chamber.

It would not surprise her at all, for he was a master at manipulation and deceit.

A soft knock on the door warned her of her maid-servant's arrival. The girl approached slowly and then gasped.

'Oh, my lady,' she said. 'Let me get some ointment for your back,' Nessa said. 'And a cool cloth for your face.'

Her face was the least of it, with her back and buttocks burning in pain from his blows. She accepted the cloth and held it to her face as Nessa saw to her injuries.

Did she have any choice in this at all? If she spoke of it to Rob, her father would deny it and punish her through her daughter. If Rob backed out of the contract over it, there could even be war between their clans, or the Mackintosh could seek retribution in some other way.

And what of her daughter's fate?

Her father had sworn that she was some place safe and would be raised well. Eva might never see her again, but she would be safe. Mayhap that was the price she would have to pay for her sins?

Running away had not worked. Eva was in exactly the same position she'd tried to avoid by escaping her father.

Seeking her daughter on her own had not worked. Her heart broke as she knew she'd failed.

Trying to protect the man she loved from her father's wrath had been a terrible mistake and had ended horribly, a cost her soul must bear forever.

Eva hissed when Nessa washed her back, no matter that the girl had a light touch in the task. The pain brought her back to her predicament.

'Just see to my hair now, Nessa,' she said. 'You can see to those when I dress.'

As the efficient maid washed her hair, Eva faced the unspeakable realisation that her only way out of this was to protect her daughter. She would have to take her father's word that he would not harm Mairead if she did as he ordered. And it meant forcing the Mackintosh's man into a marriage he did not want.

Between the devil and the deep sea, Eva made her decision in that moment.

After shaving and dressing in his finest shirt and plaid, Rob strode down to the hall, needing something to drink after the scene in Eva's chambers. His hands shook in fury as the image of Ramsey taking a strap to Eva repeated in his mind. He wanted to strangle the man for such a callous act. Especially now that Eva was Rob's.

He stopped. Buffeted by the servants and others in the corridor who were not expecting him to do so, he leaned against the wall, out of the way.

When the hell had he decided she was his?

Thinking back over the last days, Rob realised that when he'd rescued her from the cave and took her to the cottage, he began to accept the idea of it. That was why her pleading words to escape him bothered him so much.

The idea of being forced in to marriage had angered and repelled him at first. Just as it clearly had Eva.

It took him the weeks of travel here to begin to accept it as his fate. Eva had not.

It took days for him to accept her. From what he'd

just witnessed and heard…and not heard, it would take her much longer, if she ever would.

Yet, in spite of his actions and treatment of her and in spite of her father's, she seemed disinclined to marry him.

Had she set her sights higher, then?

As the reality struck him and the old wounds of pride surfaced, he knew he needed a drink. He pushed off the wall and made his way to the hall. Expecting something to mark the occasion of the wedding of the laird's daughter, instead he found the hall as it had been during other meals.

Although he would sit at the high table, he searched for a servant and asked for something stronger than either the ale or wine he usually drank. He drank the first bit down and held out the cup for more…and twice more. He waved the man away then, for a drunken groom would just give wagging tongues something else to pass around.

Rob moved aside and watched as the hall filled and the priest arrived. The portly man almost waddled as he walked, making his way to the table at the front of the hall and greeting several MacKays along his path. From what Rob could see, the priest seemed good-natured and well liked among those here. When the lord and lady arrived and took their seats, he knew it was time, both to make his way there and to take this step that would change his life forever.

The laird greeted him and introduced him to Father Darach before sitting and motioning for them to sit. The lady conversed quietly with the priest at her side and the laird nodded to those at this and the other tables.

Nothing in his words or manners gave any sign of

the scene above stairs a short time ago. No clue to what the man truly felt or was about. Rob's gut told him something was going on here, but outwardly all seemed well enough. When silence filled the room, he looked up and saw that everyone's gaze was turned to the stairway in the corner.

Eva MacKay had arrived in the hall.

He was on his feet before he knew it and on his way to escort her before he could think of it. A blank expression momentarily changed as their eyes met, and Rob watched as surprise gave way to a glimmer of fear. Even that disappeared and the neutral countenance was back in place.

Rob stopped several paces from her and took his first true look at the woman who was his bride. The simple but elegant gown outlined her lush curves, and he noticed the way her long, unbound hair fell over her breasts and ended just above her hips. His mouth went dry even while his palms grew sweaty. Her hair was pulled away from her face with only a few curling tendrils outlining her face, and the graceful lines in her jaw and neck were revealed to him.

This woman before him was new to him.

Not the runaway disguised as a boy.

Not the ill woman, pale and wan.

The only signs of her recent illness or injury were the dark circles beneath her ice-blue eyes and the limp.

The limp. He strode to her side and bowed.

'Lady Eva,' he began. 'Should you be walking on that ankle without help?'

A blush rose in her cheeks, giving her more colour than he'd seen there before. Even when she sat naked in her bath. Rob tried to forget the images of her creamy skin and feminine curves as he offered his arm to her now. How she had managed to make it this far, he knew not, but he knew she was trembling and in pain. Far more than just her ankle now.

Though he'd tried not to look at her back when he'd stormed into the room at the sound of her screams, he had. It was all he could do not to tear Ramsey MacKay apart with his bare hands. The welts were wide and deep.

'Here,' he said, placing his arms behind her with a care to those areas struck and lifting her from her feet.

She did not resist him. She did not say anything. Eva just sat in his arms, unmoving, as he carried her forward. If he was not mistaken, some of the women watching sighed as they passed. Although done for another reason, if it would smooth things over, that was good, too.

Rob stopped near the table and placed her on her feet, never letting go of her completely. He nodded to the priest who walked towards them and then glanced down at the woman at his side.

And in that moment, he realised his life was about to change in ways he probably could not even dream of. More than his decision to support Brodie. More than his work or position in the clan now that they had been successful and ended the threat to it.

More than any step he'd taken in his life up to this moment.

So why was his gut telling him to turn and walk away?

Chapter Seven

For whatever reason, the priest's words about their marriage contract eased his concerns. Rob listened to the details of the agreement reached between the MacKay and Brodie and calmed with each bit spoken. He'd not known about her dowry or the amount Brodie was giving him until the priest said it, and the wealth he would gain surprised him.

Any sane man would leap at the chance to take Lady Eva MacKay to wife.

Any sane man...

The silence startled him, and Rob realised they waited on his words. His vow. Words that would tie him—body, soul and possessions—to the woman who stood at his side now.

Who stood trembling at his side.

Rob glanced down, now noticing the paleness of her face and the way she held her mouth closed tightly. And how she shook as she waited on him to speak. Did she harbour a hope that he would yet disavow this arrangement?

He opened his mouth and spoke the words the priest had asked for—*I will.*

I will, a second time.

And then, the words he'd always imagined he'd speak at some point in his life, but not now and never in this way.

'I, Robert Alexander Mackintosh, take you, Eva MacKay, as my wedded wife, to have and to hold from this day forward, for better, for worse, for richer and for poorer, in sickness and in health, to love and to cherish, till death us depart, according to God's holy ordinance; and thereto I plight thee my troth.'

Father Darach turned to Eva and waited, even as Rob did, for her response. Rob did not dare to look at her, but he felt the shudder that tore through her then and wondered if this would be the moment when she refused him. When the moment expanded to several seconds, he thought it might be.

'I...' she began, so low that he doubted anyone but he could hear her. 'I...'

Eva pulled against his hold, trying to move away, though with her injured ankle and foot, she would never be able to do so. When he did glance at her, he recognised the expression in her eyes—sheer and utter panic. That turned into terror when her father took a step in their direction.

'Courage now, lass,' he whispered, sliding his arm back around her. 'You surely have faced greater dangers these last weeks than anything you face from me.'

Why he'd felt the need to assure her, he knew not, but one look at her haunted eyes and he'd been unable to stop himself. Something terrified her. Something or someone. As he motioned for her father to step back, Rob suspected the latter. And it seemed more than just the simple strapping her father delivered.

It took a few more seconds before she stood up straighter and nodded at Father Darach. Another second and she began to repeat the words he offered her, giving her consent to this marriage. Rob let out the breath he'd been holding as she did so. Not many could hear her words, but her voice grew stronger with each word. Then it was her turn to say the words that would join them.

'I, Eva Morag MacKay, take you, Robert Alexander Mackintosh, as my wedded husband, to have and to hold from this day forward, for better, for worse, for richer and for poorer, in sickness and in health, to love, cherish and obey, till death us depart, according to God's holy ordinance; and thereto I plight thee my troth.'

Father Darach nodded and smiled at them and then held out the prayer book where Rob had earlier placed his mother's wedding ring. Brodie had offered to have one made, but Rob wanted his wife, any wife of his, to wear the one his mother had worn when she'd pledged her heart and life to his father. Rob eased his arm away from Eva and took the ring before turning to face her. She did not resist when he took her hand in his and held the ring above her fourth finger.

'With this ring, I thee wed,' he said, watching her face as he slid the ring onto her finger. Moving it a bit lower with each phrase, he continued, 'With my body, I thee worship, and with all my worldly goods, I thee endow. In the name of the Father, and of the Son, and of the Holy Ghost. Amen.'

As those around them raised their hands to bless themselves and the priest declared them by their words and consent husband and wife, Rob watched as the terror and fear left her face. But instead of whatever emotion he thought to see there, he saw an expression of abject hopelessness in her eyes. She closed her fingers into a fist and looked away, staring into the distance as tears trickled down her cheeks.

Shocked by it, he could not feign joy when the MacKay and his wife approached to offer their felicitations or when Father Darach made some comment about nervous brides. Nor when they went to their seats and cups were raised in their honour. He drank deeply of the cup of rich, red wine and held it to be filled again.

Servants poured out of the kitchens and pantry to carry platters of food to the table. Within minutes, every sort of delicacy and treat sat before him...and his new bride. But every bit he put in his mouth tasted like dirt. Eva, he noticed, took little to eat, but also finished her cup of wine.

He remembered little of the rest of the meal or anything said to him. Eva sat motionless at his side, barely replying to wishes offered them and flinching every time their hands touched or their legs brushed against the other's under the table. Soon, the meal, such as it was, was done, and it was time for them to retire... together.

Rob remembered telling her that he would not avail himself of that part until they returned to Glenlui, and that was his plan. Until he could decipher what was happening here, to them, between them, he would not take her to his bed. So, this night would be one of rest before their journey on the morrow. At ease with his choice, he stood and held out his hand to her. She pushed up from her chair and balanced more on her uninjured foot as he prepared to pick her up.

'We have a special chamber prepared for you,' Lady Morag called out. 'For your first night together as man and wife.' She smiled, and Rob could almost believe she meant it sincerely. Almost. Right in this moment, he would not trust any of them to be telling the truth, his new wife included.

'A kiss!' someone yelled out from the back of the hall. Iain, he thought.

'A kiss!' someone else called out. And then another and another until the hall echoed with the sound of it. All of them urging, nay, ordering him to kiss his new wife.

Eva glanced up at him. Clearly, she'd not thought that this would happen. He'd be lying if he tried to say he'd not thought about tasting that lush mouth of hers, so he shrugged at her and leaned over.

What trouble could one kiss be between them now that they were man and wife?

At the first touch of his mouth to hers, he discovered the answer was not the one he'd thought it would be.

Eva tried to tell herself it was the wine. Or the pain and exhaustion that yet plagued her. Or the crowd shouting their names. Any of those things could be the reason for the way her heart pounded as his mouth touched hers.

Taller than her, he'd leaned down to meet her as she looked up at him. His lips were firm as they touched hers, but he canted his head and pressed more fully against her mouth. She lost her breath. He took advantage of that moment and slid his tongue over her lips, teasing them to open for him. Eva did, though why, she knew not, and everyone and everything else in the hall disappeared when he dipped into her mouth and tasted her.

She wobbled then, fighting the urge to reach up and grab him for support as he relentlessly plundered her mouth with his. As he thrust his tongue deeper, she touched it with hers and he growled, sucking it back into his mouth. Before Eva could reach up, his strong fingers entangled in her hair, pulling, holding her closer to him. He released her for a scant moment, allowing her to draw a ragged breath as he did, and then he kissed her again.

And again.

And once more.

Thoughts scattered. Her body awakened as it had not for months and months, her heated blood rushing and filling places she'd not felt since…Eirik had loved her.

Eirik.

With a push, she freed herself and leaned back against the table, breathing hard and trying to gather the wits she'd clearly lost at his touch. Rob looked just as surprised as she felt. Truth be told, he looked worse. Those watching still cheered loudly, banging their cups and spoons on the wooden tables, calling out for more.

'Twas expected at a wedding feast, but hers, theirs was not the usual marriage or feast. He blinked several times and then looked at those calling out to them. He leaned down once more, and she thought he would kiss her again. Instead, he lifted her into his arms and nodded to a servant to show him the way to the chamber her mother had mentioned. He carried her with a tenderness she did not deserve from him.

Eva wanted to put her head down and hide, but that would mean touching more of him than she wished to. So, she let her body relax as he climbed the steps and took her away from the cheering and yelling of those in the hall. She did not fool herself into believing that they were actually happy for her—Eva knew quite well that they were happy to be rid of her and the shame she'd threatened to bring on their clan with her behaviour.

The MacKays rid themselves of her and got a wonderful new treaty with the powerful and wealthy Mackintosh clan, all with just a few words uttered and a few secrets hidden. On the morrow when they left, her father would rejoice in his newfound friend, the Mackintosh, and in seeing his biggest problem on her way out of his gates forever.

She had not realised she'd moaned out in pain and misery until he first cursed under his breath and then whispered some words of comfort to her as he carried her down the corridor. After tomorrow, she would lose her daughter forever.

And her new husband had no idea.

The servant girl opened the door to the chamber, stepped out of the way as Rob carried her inside and then closed it softly after they'd entered. When he stopped, Eva looked around the room.

A fire burned in the hearth in the corner and candles lit the chamber. The large bed was covered with plump pillows and blankets and the linens lay turned back, ready for someone to rest beneath them. A pitcher and cups sat on a tray on the small table near the bed, along with a bowl of fruit and cheese.

The chamber looked as it would for an honoured

guest's arrival. Certainly, Robert Mackintosh was that. He carried her to that bed and set her down with her legs over one side. She sank into the feather-filled mattress on the rope-strung bed. Before she could say a word, he walked to the door, lifted the latch and left.

Surprised by his actions, she wondered about what he meant to do. To sleep elsewhere this night would be an insult that she was sure not even her father would allow to go unmet. Eva pushed herself back a bit and wondered what she should do. It took only moments, lying on the soft, warm bed to fall asleep.

It could not have been long before she woke to someone saying her name.

'Lady? Eva?' He stood over her, peering down with a serious gaze and a frown. 'Are you well?'

She struggled to sit up, her gown and chemise rubbing over her sore skin. He held his hand out and she took it. 'Your pardon, I fell asleep.' He stepped back and 'twas then she saw her maid behind him.

'Here now, Nessa,' he said, as he helped her to move to the edge of the bed. 'See to your lady's needs. Did you bring the unguent for her injuries?'

'Aye, sir,' Nessa said, moving to his side. 'And some of the healer's brew to help with the pain. And a fresh shift to… To sleep…' The young woman blushed fiercely and could not meet her gaze then. Everyone knew what they should be doing this night, and it should involve little or no sleep.

'Just so, lass,' Rob said as he stepped away. 'I will return soon.' He'd reached the door, and still she was unable to speak. He surprised her at every turn, and she could not predict his next word or action. And then, he was gone.

Nessa did not waste time, moving a stool close to the bedside and helping her to sit on it. The maid's movements were steady and quick, removing the gown and her other garments. Nessa spread the soothing ointment on the welts on her back and covered them with clean linen bandages.

Nessa offered her the healer's brew; however, Eva waved it off. She would not seek solace in an herb's grasp again, no matter the pain involved. The last time... Eva shuddered at those memories. Nessa took the potion away and brought her some ale instead, which she sipped as the young woman loosened her hair and brushed it in long, soothing strokes. Her eyes drifted shut, and soon the crackling noises made by the fire were the only sounds in the chamber.

When he'd opened the door, she knew not, but one moment he wasn't present and the next he was, staring at her as Nessa drew the brush down the length of her hair. He might have hissed, or Eva might have misheard the sound. It mattered not, for now he had the right to enter her chamber whenever he wished and whether or not she wished him to be there. She saw the steaming bucket he carried and chided herself for misjudging him again.

'What is wrong?' he asked, placing the bucket near her on the floor.

'Nothing, sir,' Eva answered, as the girl stopped tending to her hair and gathered up a few other supplies. 'Just some confused thoughts.'

Nessa spread a drying cloth and other linens there and then poured a thick liquid into the water. A lovely scent filled the chamber and Eva inhaled it. Then, Nessa curtsied to her and, with a nod to her husband, left. Rob knelt on the floor next to her and reached out for her injured foot.

'You walked too much this day. It is swelling again,' he said as he lifted it and placed it on his own leg.

He found the end of the strip binding her foot and tugged it free. She could only watch as he tended her ankle and foot. Once the bindings were removed, he moved the bucket closer and guided her to place her foot into it. She could not help the sighing sound she made as the warmth of the water with its appealing scent eased the pain in her foot. After only a few minutes of soaking, she could move her foot without much pain.

'What did Nessa put in it?' she asked. 'It smells lovely.'

'Promise not to be angry if I tell you?' He smiled just then, and she glimpsed a completely different side of this man for a moment. A very appealing, handsome one at that.

'Aye,' she said, nodding. 'What would there be to anger me over such as this?'

'It is a concoction of some kind of oil and other ingredients that my sister makes. It is especially helpful in treating injuries…to our…horses.'

'Horses? You are treating me with horse liniment?' She tried to sound aggrieved, but the unexpected laugh that burst out ruined that attempt. 'It does smell good,' she said. 'And it feels even better.' She wiggled her toes in the water to show him the range of comfortable motion in her foot now. 'I will have to forgive you for the insult, since it works.'

He leaned back on his heels and crossed his arms over his chest, studying her face with a serious expression in his eyes.

'You are a pragmatic woman, my lady. Accepting such a thing because it works is not the reaction most women would have. My own sister would be chiding me for using it on my wife's foot.'

This man did not go in for the flowery praise of courtiers. She could hear the compliment in the tone of his words and she smiled, saying nothing in reply. This was the first time he'd called her *wife,* and it made her unsettled inside. He did not seem to wait on a reply, so she sat in silence as he tended to her.

He lifted her foot and dried it. With sure movements, he wrapped the fresh strips of cloth around her foot and ankle. The over and under of it soothed her somehow, as did the obvious carefulness of his touch. Then, the task finished, he knelt there, so close to her she could feel the heat of his large body. Her breath caught as he leaned over, staring at her mouth as though his intention was to repeat the kisses shared in the hall.

Eva fought an inexplicable and traitorous need to lean into him and kiss him back. Her body urged her forward, as his seemed to do for a scant second. Only inches separated their lips as he stared at her mouth and then licked his lips. Something deep within her tightened and ached. She must resist this pull.

She must. She must, she chanted to herself.

In the end, he pulled back and sat on his heels, his breathing shallow and fast. His gaze moved to her eyes then, and she saw the same confusion in the deep brown of his that must reside in her own. Pushing back and standing before her, he gathered up the soiled and wet linens and now cooled water and carried them to the door.

'We should seek our rest,' he said as he placed the

bucket outside the door and closed it. 'The journey will be difficult even without considering your injury.' She swallowed and then again as he nodded to the bed before speaking. 'Let me help you,' he offered, his usual even tone deeper.

The kiss had affected him, too, though he clearly did not wish it so. It took but a moment for him to pull down the bedcovers and place her in it...

And step away.

Much of what he'd said or she'd said during her illness in the cave and then in the cottage remained a blur. The fever had seen to that. So when she thought she remembered him saying he would not see to *this* part of the marriage until they arrived at his home, Eva simply did not know if he had said it or not. Now that the time was here to...*see to those matters*, she waited and watched him.

But it was his words that chilled her to her very soul.

'This should be no surprise to you, lady,' he said, walking around the bed and nodding to it. 'It should be almost commonplace when you think about it.'

Fear pierced her at his words, and she felt as though she would faint.

Did he know the truth? Did he know she was no virgin and had given birth recently? Tempted to utter one of his curses, Eva waited for his next action.

Chapter Eight

He watched the colour drain from her face at what he thought was a simple observation. They had slept next to each other for all the nights since he'd discovered her in the cave, with the exception of last night. Granted, she'd been ill or nearly unconscious most of those nights, but he'd never once taken advantage of her nearness or body.

Not that his body had not wanted to.

Rob noticed the fear was back as terror turned her pale blue eyes a darker colour. She clenched her mouth closed as though struggling against a scream. What the hell was going on here? Did she fear he would just take her as was his right? Did she think he would use his strength and his body to overcome whatever objections she yet held to their match?

Christ Almighty! What did she think he was? A ravening beast with no regard for her? Or someone so beneath her that this marriage was an affront to her position? A lady brought low by a simple warrior and not worthy of her?

'Have no worries, lady,' he said from between gritted teeth. 'I have no plans to force myself on you.' He reached out and took several blankets from the bed, planning to sleep on the floor. 'I meant only that we have slept next to each other before.'

Even uttering the words of explanation tasted bitter to his tongue. But the touch of her hand on his stopped him.

'Wait, I pray you. And once more, I must beg your pardon, sir,' she whispered. 'I have never properly thanked you for your care while I was injured and ill.' He remained still, her hand on his. 'My memories of that time are confused and blurry.' She met his gaze then. 'I remember only the most recent morning and knew not how we came to be in such a...state.'

He felt like a cad then, reacting in anger and misinterpreting her words. Neither of them wanted this marriage and neither knew the other. Aye, other marriages had begun in this same manner. Others had begun with a fuller knowledge and ease with the other. No matter how it had begun—they were married and must acclimate themselves to the other. Instead of trying to explain, he showed her, having a care for her innocent sensibilities as he did.

Rob shook out the blankets, tossing them across the bed and across her legs. Then he walked around the chamber blowing out the candles and banking the fire. Standing away from the bed and facing the hearth, he undressed, loosening his belt and dropping his plaid to the floor. Tugging his tunic off, he folded it and the plaid and placed them on the trunk in the corner.

She gasped as he approached and their eyes met. He knew that the shadows hid most of him, but not all... or, from her shocked expression, not enough. Worse, the randy bits began to rise under her continued regard. He lifted the top layer of blanket and slid beneath it, leaving several *protective* layers between them. Only when he was covered did she lie down at his side.

After a short, tense silent time, he turned on his side and leaned his head up to look at her. Eva lay as she'd lain, moving not a muscle or other body part. She surprised him when she spoke.

'So this is how we slept all those nights?' she asked.

'Aye. Your virtue was ever safe even though we were legally betrothed.'

Rob watched as she startled at his words. Would everything he said always bother her in some way? He rolled away, turning on his other side, facing the hearth and the wall. Better that way, he told himself, trying to believe it was for her benefit and not his own. The wee laddie under the covers was intrigued by the body lying with them. Rob wanted to get some sleep, so he tried to ignore the feminine sounds she made.

And tried to forget the sight of her naked in that bath or on those nights when he cared for her.

She was not tall, she reached only his chest, but her body was filled with womanly curves and softness. Her breasts were not more than his hand would hold, but then he had large hands. Her hips would cradle him nicely when they …

Bloody hell! He was making things much worse by thinking of her body and how she would feel as he drove his flesh deep between her legs to find release.

Rob reached up and ran his hand across his forehead, checking for a fever. That was the only explanation for his wayward thoughts and desires. He had not wanted a wife and had only begun to accept the match when he'd arrived here. Then, when she'd begged to be free of him, he'd accepted that they would not wed after all.

Then, circumstances changed once more and led to this—him hard and erect, trying not to think about his attractive wife. The one who lay next to him. The one who did not want him.

He began to count his breaths, hoping to distract himself from the rest of it. When he reached a score and he was still hard as rock, he gave up on that. Then the woman at the centre of his difficulties spoke and took his attention from his wanton flesh.

'Tell me the journey,' she said. Though she did not move, things did seem less tense as she continued. 'Tell me of your kith and kin.'

'I had thought to travel by boat down the west coast, but with the intensity of the storms, I think it best to go south by horse,' he explained. 'Your father has offered a small travelling group, so we'll have three of his men and a wagon to carry your belongings.' He glanced over at her, his erection easing. 'I can tell you of the Mackintoshes on our journey.'

'And the dowry?' Considering the distance between his home and hers, her father had offered it in gold. Though he would carry some of it, the rest would be brought south when the MacKay attended a larger gathering of the Chattan Confederation and their allies later in the summer.

'It has been handled,' he said. 'Your father also arranged to have your inheritance put into my control.'

Rob had never felt good about that part. Again, 'twas his right, but it was her wealth and something he'd not expected in this bargain. He waited on her response, but none came. Wondering if she'd fallen asleep—and he'd witnessed her do that from one moment to the next—he turned over and looked at her. She watched him with a veiled gaze as though trying to assess him and his plans.

'Have you questions about that, lady?' he asked. She must have used up whatever coins she'd saved during her escape and during the weeks when she had to fend for herself. How much had her escapade cost her?

'I would like an amount put into my own hands, to spend on my own needs and purposes.' Her words were clear and forthright. He only worried about her intentions.

'Do you plan to run away again?' he asked. Rob studied her face as she answered him.

'I had not planned to, sir. But I cannot say it will never enter my thoughts.'

He laughed then, enjoying her honesty, though he should have been reprimanding her for her audacity.

'I suppose that every woman, every wife, should have some coins for her own purposes. My sister would certainly agree with you on that,' he said. Margaret believed every woman should be able to survive on her own, though he wondered what she would say to Eva's idea on the same issue.

'You sound as though you respect your sister's opinion on matters.'

'Aye, I do. Partly because she makes sense and partly because she'll cut off my bollocks if I do not!' He laughed then.

Though many men did, he'd never felt threatened by a woman's strength of personality or will. Some men were—Eva's father clearly was, or he would not strike out at the strong-mindedness of his daughter or his wife's suggestions. Some of the women in his clan had helped save lives and the clan itself through their strengths. And Arabella, in spite of her fair looks, had a spine of steel and, when it came to a battle of wills with Brodie, she won as often as she lost.

'I think I may like your sister's methods.'

'And I will remember not to let the two of you do too much plotting together.' Rob remembered something he wanted to ask her, to offer her, rather.

'With your father's permission, I would have no objection if you would want to ask Nessa or another to accompany us home.'

Of all the things he could have said, Eva would never have dreamed it would be this. She could see his face, watching her as they spoke. She knew he was hiding his maleness from her sight and that he had desires and needs he would want seen to, as any husband would. And yet, through it all, he did not force her to it and even now considered her needs.

'Truly? You would allow such a thing?' she asked.

'Our clans are not at war. You do not arrive as an enemy bride. You may bring or invite whomever you wish to come to visit or to make their home at Glenlui,' he explained. The tears came unbidden on his words.

If only…

If only she had met this man first…

If only he had been the one…

He watched her in silence then, not touching her or saying anything. The desire to explain it all to him pressed from deep within her, but she knew it was not to be done. He would never forgive her this deception, and her father would carry out his threats. Better to keep the secret in silence and try to find a way back to her daughter once out of her father's rule.

'I thank you again, sir,' she said. 'For now, I would like to ask if Nessa would be willing to come with me.'

'Rob.' He took her hand in his and just held it. 'I expect you to call me by my given name now that we are married.' He smiled at her then. 'Or Robbie as some do.'

'Why are you being this way?' she blurted out. She could protect herself better if she understood his motives and his methods. She'd long ago learned her father's and it had helped her...to a certain point. 'You were so angry at the cottage.'

'Lady,' he began, still holding on to her hand. 'Neither of us wanted this. Neither of us truly controlled our own lives and choices. Yet, here we are, forced in some way to give our consent and exchange vows in a marriage we never thought would happen.'

All true, but not the explanation she needed to hear.

'I am angry over being forced to accept this arrangement. When you arrive in Glenlui, I am certain that someone will report to you the words I used when I was told of it.' He frowned then and met her eyes. 'You will probably be as happy then as I was when I learned that you'd run away rather than marry me.'

She grimaced at his words and tried to move away. Eva heard a glimmer of that anger and hurt beneath the even tone he tried to speak with. He tugged her back towards him, closer than she had been before.

'None of it matters now though, does it? The marriage is a fact, our vows exchanged and we leave on the morrow. The only thing we can control is what we do now. Of the two of us, you have the lesser of the bargain. I end up with a beautiful, wealthy noblewoman as my wife and you end up with me—a simple warrior and kinsman to the chief. If either of us deserves our right to anger, it would be you, my lady.' He lifted her hand to his mouth and kissed the top of it as in salutation.

Releasing her, he turned back on his other side, and she tried to sleep. But too many thoughts and worries plagued her, and the pain in her back prevented her from finding the rest she needed before morning. She'd not slept with a man willingly or knowingly for many months, and those times sleep was not their aim. Finding a comfortable position next to this man took some time.

Only when the light of dawn crept into the chamber and she woke, did she realise she must have slept. She lay close to him, his arm clasped around her waist as it had that night in the cottage. Her new husband snored, she discovered. The sounds of the keep and its inhabitants rising to a new day began to grow louder and more frequent, and Eva knew the moment she dreaded was at hand.

She would leave everything and everyone and every place she had ever known and rarely, if ever, return here. Never had she felt as low as she did now. Any chance she had of finding Mairead involved being close enough to search for her. Every mile away would mean less and less chance for success.

Eva heard the soft knock and watched as the door opened a slight bit. Nessa nodded and looked away quickly, bringing some fresh water for washing and clean cloths. The girl had not lived at the keep last year, so she did not know the truth. No one else here would expect to find blood on the sheets as they would with a virgin bride.

As her husband would when he decided it was time to bed her.

Just as the door latch dropped behind Nessa, Rob began to shift and turn. The sharp, masculine angles of his face were no longer hidden under a growth of beard, and she studied them as she did the rest of him.

The bedcovers barely covered him now, exposing his strong legs and chest to her view. He was, as she'd seen last night, a huge man. A strong, tall man with long legs and muscular arms. Curls the same auburn as his hair covered his chest and disappeared under the edge of the bedcovers below his waist. Even his thighs bore hair the same colour, and her hand itched to see if those were soft or scratchy. She lifted her hand, tempted to find out, but stopped when he opened his eyes and met hers.

'Give me a few moments and then call your maid,' he said in the gruff voice of morning. She should turn away or at least avert her gaze as he left the bed, but Eva found she could not.

In the light of day, his body was even more impressive than the glimpses she had stolen in the night. Or just now. He stood and stretched his arms over his head, nearly touching the ceiling of the chamber. He rolled his shoulders and then reached over for his tunic, giving her a full look at his back and buttocks…and more when he bent over.

She lost her breath when he turned, only half turned, but enough for her to see all of him. A virgin would have swooned at the sight, but she was not one and with an unseemly curiosity she watched his every move.

'The randy lad will rise if you do not cease staring,' he warned without looking at her. 'And he likes those noises, too.' Had she made noises? Panting like the wanton her father called her, mayhap?

'Twas past time for her to get out of the bed, so she tried to ignore him as she pushed herself to the edge and eased down to the floor. Gingerly, she put some weight on the injured foot and ankle and found she could bear it.

'Here now,' he called out as he rounded the bed and reached her, now fully dressed. 'Do not stand on it completely yet,' he urged. He slipped an arm around her waist and helped her to move to the stool near the bed.

'It feels much better this morn,' she said, holding it out and wiggling it. 'Your sister's ointment was a wonder.'

'Remember, that is between us. She cannot know,' he said, winking at her as he passed her to approach the bed.

He tugged the top layers back, exposing the sheets. Before she could guess his intentions, he'd drawn his small dagger, pulled back his sleeve and sliced the skin just below the inside of his elbow.

'Rob!' she said, standing to go to him. Only when he held the bleeding wound out over the middle of the bed did she realise what he was doing—marking the bed with blood.

'I wish no questions asked about what happens between us, lady.'

He spilled blood because a virgin bride would shed on her wedding night.

He thought to shield her from any embarrassing questions of nonconsummation, while this action would simply humiliate him when he discovered the truth. And it would give him one more reason to hate her when the truth was out. Eva sat back down, unable to stop him without explaining the real consequences of presenting this sheet to her father.

Clasping her hands on her lap, she waited as he allowed several drops to mar the whiteness and then he covered the wound with his hand and walked to the corner where Nessa had left the fresh water. She did not have to turn to see what he was doing—he tore a strip from one of the cloths and then used the rest to staunch the bleeding. After dropping it in the bowl, he held the strip out to her and walked closer.

Without a word, he knelt next to her and held out his arm. Taking the strip, she wordlessly bound the wound so that no one would see it. Inwardly, she wanted to cry at his actions…again on her behalf. And Eva knew that she must do something to keep him from being the object of derision and laughter.

'I will see to our arrangements before breaking our fast. Wait here for me,' he said, pulling his sleeve back into place. 'Remember to ask Nessa, and I will speak to your father.' He glanced at her mouth as though considering whether or not to kiss her, but he turned and left instead.

Eva sat for a few moments before standing and limping to the bed. When a knock came, she blocked the view of it with her body and called to enter. Nessa opened the door and entered, carrying garments for her and this time curtsying before going about her tasks. As she moved around the bed, the girl noticed the bloody stain and gasped.

'Are you well, my lady?' she asked. 'Can I get you anything?'

'I am quite well, Nessa. So much so that we need not speak of that again,' Eva said firmly. 'Will you stoke the fire for me? I feel a chill in here.' Eva forced a shiver and waited for the girl to do it.

'Oh, aye, my lady,' Nessa said. She knelt before the hearth and cleared away some of the ashes before kindling a new flame. Once it took, she added a few more logs. Once the flames took, she moved away. 'I forgot, my lady. Your husband told me to bring something to you and I left it in your old chamber. Let me get it now.'

Eva nodded, not believing her good luck in this. As soon as the girl left, Eva pulled the sheet free and balled it up. With halting steps, she made it across the chamber and tossed the sheet to the back of the hearth where it caught fire and flared up as it burned. She stood there, even when Nessa returned, watching it be destroyed. Then she faced the young woman and invited her to serve her in her new home.

Nessa's reaction was the best thing to come of all of this mess. The joy and excitement at the girl's desire to travel past the borders of Tongue and to see other places and meet other people was almost catching. And it took the girl's attention off the sheet. Sending her off to pack, Eva finished dressing and waited for Rob to return.

She noticed the stick lying on the bed as she leaned against it. Nessa had brought it back but had been so taken aback by the invitation that she'd forgotten it once more.

'I thought it might help you walk until your ankle and foot heal completely.'

He'd done it again. Surprised her with a kindness she did not deserve. Her list of sins grew with each passing day, and she knew she would pay for each and every one of them.

'And once more I thank you,' she said, turning to face him as she gathered her nerve.

'The sheet?' he asked as he looked past her to the bed.

'Seen to,' she answered quickly. Placing the stick in her right hand, she leaned to test it. 'Oh, Nessa would like to accept your invitation. She seemed quite pleased about it as she ran off.'

'I saw her as I returned from the stables. I may regret it at some point, but she will be good company for you on the journey,' he said, offering his arm to her. 'Come let us break our fast and begin the journey while the sun shines.'

The next hours passed in a whirlwind as they made their final preparations and then took leave of Castle Varrich and Tongue...and everything she'd ever known.

Though Rob tried to engage her in conversation as they made their way down the hill from the keep and then along the edge of the kyle, all Eva could do was look back and pray that the Almighty would look after her bairn now that she would not.

Her heart broke a little with each passing mile until Eva was certain there was not one left within her.

Chapter Nine

Try as he might, she sank into a melancholy mood with each passing hour and day. His wife was not belligerent or unpleasant, for she answered any question put to her and accepted any task he asked of her along their journey. But the quiet despair he'd witnessed several times in her gaze kept its growing hold over her.

The maid, Nessa, was quite the opposite. Her excitement over the journey and her attempts to learn more about her new home were filled with a joy and enthusiasm he wished Eva felt.

The only query Eva made was to ask about their distance from Tongue and Durness. And then she would turn and stare behind them with a sadness that made even his heart hurt. Was this what Arabella meant when she'd said that he would not face leaving his home as women did? He'd not given much thought to it before now, before watching it affect someone in his life. Especially when he was the reason for it. So, he used every bit of patience he had within himself in dealing with her during their travels.

Rob knew his forbearance surprised her—it had surprised him. After the anger of finding her alone, disguised, injured and ill in the cave and those few days in the cottage, most of it had seeped away. Certain it would return when he discovered the truth about whatever she held hidden from him, he let it be for now.

Secrets were kept for many reasons, he knew, but mostly to protect yourself or someone else. There was certainly no love lost between Eva and her parents. Her father wanted her gone, and her mother was clearly estranged from her, most likely at Ramsey's behest. But what mother would not do whatever was necessary to protect her child?

As they set up camp on their fifth day on the road south to Glenlui, Rob watched her yet again trying to gain some sense of what bothered her. Someone so young and sheltered should have no cares in the world. Yet she carried something inside that seemed to be as heavy as the weight of the keep from which she came.

A clue came from the maid when she whispered a wish to her lady as they prepared the plain meal over a fire. The girl hoped that she would find a fine husband among the Mackintoshes so she could remain at Glenlui forever. Nessa's expression as she spoke was filled with the wistfulness of a young woman wanting to be in love.

He stumbled at the realisation.

Was Eva in love with someone in Tongue? Or Durness where he'd found her? It made sense. Her resistance to marry him. Her escape might not have been to avoid the marriage but to find her lover? Ramsey MacKay would never have allowed someone to get in the way of his arrangements. Had he sent the man away, and then Eva sought him when word came of their own match?

It made sense and explained much of her behaviour and her father's. Mayhap the man was not high enough or connected by blood or marriage to a clan Ramsey wished to align himself with? Or the older man simply had another objection to him?

Eva passed him by then, seeking something in the wagon, and he watched her with the knowledge of this new realisation. It made so much sense. Her disappearance. Her resistance. Her surprise at the way her body reacted to his kiss. She'd not been inexperienced, she'd been surprised.

His wife loved another man.

Rob's stomach rolled at the thought of it. Not that he loved her or even liked her, but taking another man's cast-off lover did not sit well with him. Had she run to him, and he refused to take on her father and claim her? Had the man turned his back on her?

That did not sit well with him, either. Though never pledged to another, indeed having never loved a woman, Rob did not claim to understand the intricate emotions involved. But as a matter of honour, he knew what should have happened.

That, that was the very choice he'd faced with her. A sane man would have listened to his gut and walked away. A smart man would have turned and left when faced with the reality that she'd disappeared of her own volition for any reason. An honourable man stood by his words and pledge and did what he must do. At her approach, he glanced down at her face and eyes. Other than sadness, he saw nothing else there.

'You did not hear Nessa call you to supper,' she said, holding out a bowl to him. 'Such as it is.'

Meals on the journey were plain and simple and most times not hot. Oatcakes, cheese, nuts, dried fruit or meat. Porridge in the mornings. But they'd passed by a small village and had been able to buy some stew and fresh bread from the innkeeper. The smell of it made his mouth water as he accepted it.

'Have you eaten yet?' he asked, dipping the spoon and stirring it to cool.

'Mine is over there,' she said. She pointed to where the others had gathered, close to the fire.

Rob followed her back and stood next to the log on which she sat. She was using the walking stick less and less and was not favouring her right leg any longer. The swelling was down, but Rob still offered to bind it for support before they mounted up each day.

Though the days were growing longer and they could have travelled further each day, Rob chose not to push too hard. The paleness of her skin and the dark circles around her eyes told him she had not yet recovered from the fever that had plagued her. Nessa had told him, when Eva was not near, that the lady had been sick before she left home weeks ago. But the girl did not know the origin of the fever or type of illness.

So, each day when he saw her begin to grow tired, he called a halt and set up camp. He did not think that arriving back in Glenlui and presenting a half-dead wife to his laird would be a good thing to do. That was the reason he gave to the men and to her and he tried to make himself believe it, but he cared even now more than he should. Once she finished eating, he took her bowl over to Nessa, who handled cleaning up after their meals.

'Lady?' he asked. 'Would you like to walk a bit? There is a stream just over the hill. You could wash there?' There had been little time or place for the usual care of herself, and yet she did not complain as most women, most ladies, would in similar circumstances.

Though she looked as if her first reply would be no, she paused and, meeting his gaze, she nodded. With his help, she rose and then walked at his side away from the others. He kept a slow pace, knowing his legs covered twice as much ground in one step as hers did. Soon, they reached the crest of the hill and could see and hear the stream.

She smiled for the first time in days.

When the hell had he begun keeping track of her smiles?

It was not deep or fast-running, but the water meandered at a nice flow. He walked her to the edge, seeking a dry, level place, and found it several paces upstream. She would be able to kneel and reach the water there. He took her hand and held her arm, guiding her to her knees and watching as she rearranged her skirts closer to her on the ground. Rob drew his dagger at the sound of someone approaching.

'My lady,' Nessa called out. 'I brought you a cloth and some soap.'

Rob took them and waved the girl off before she could offer to help. He wanted a measure of privacy with this woman he'd married. He had questions that he knew he must ask. There was no surety that he would like the answers he got, but they would gnaw at his insides until he did ask.

He crouched next to her and offered her the cloth. She moved with a certain feminine grace that could not be disguised, not even by the garments of a lad.

'Did you think your disguise would work?' he asked.

Eva stopped and looked at him, startled by the topic. She dipped the cloth in the water before answering him.

'I stayed off the roads during the day and travelled mostly at nights. It worked when I needed it to,' she said. Shaking out the cloth, she pressed it to her face and neck.

The thought of her on the roads at night…alone… with no protection nearly drove him back to the anger. It must have shown in his face, for she sat back on her heels and watched him for a long moment before speaking.

'I know, it was a foolish thing to do. I know terrible things could have happened to me, and some bad things did happen. And I could have ended up much worse if you had not found me when you did. As I told you, I believed I had no other choice.'

Her words showed she understood now the foolishness of her act, but the reason for it was another question. It burned his mouth trying to escape and be spoken. Rob knew no good could come of it, yet he asked anyway.

'Were you truly running from me or were you running to someone else, lady?'

She gasped at his words and then pushed herself to stand, tossing the cloth to the ground. A myriad of emotions crossed her face as he watched. And then, she turned and ran. In her shock or fear or anger, she did not realise that he would not even have to run to catch her. Uncertain what he would say or do when he did, he followed her, but staying a good distance from her.

He listened as she ran through the bushes and low branches. The sound of her breathing could be heard in the silence of the woods. Rob followed her easily and, when the sounds of her movements stopped ahead, he slowed his pace and listened.

'Lady?' he called out as he approached a clearing. Glancing quickly, he found her sitting at the base of a tree, leaning against it and breathing heavily. 'Are you well?' Walking to her, he looked at her leg. 'Have you hurt your leg again?' He crouched down next to her, but she swatted his hands away when he reached out to check her ankle.

'It is not injured,' she said. 'I just needed to…'

'Run away?' he finished.

'Nay, not run away. Just…' she glanced at him and then away '…away.'

'From me?'

'From your questions.'

'Why not just answer them? Surely, the truth cannot be worse than all the possible lies that I am thinking?' He stood and took a pace back, giving her some space. 'Running away never helps.'

'Spoken like a man with choices,' she muttered. 'Would running away from or running to make a difference? I ran, sir. I ran.'

When put that way, Rob wondered if it did matter. Running from was a personal insult to him. Running *to* meant her heart and possibly her body were filled with someone else. Either way, one of them suffered more than the other.

'Nay, lady.' He shook his head and walked away.

He needed to get back to Glenlui, where he understood the people and the rules. Where the effect she was already having on him would be minimised, and he would have tasks to see to, diverting his attention and his thoughts from her.

He needed to return to what and who he knew.

Rob did not abandon her, but if she would not answer his questions, he did not want to speak to her, either. He walked halfway back to the clearing near the stream and waited until he saw her stand and begin to move towards him. When she did not limp, he walked the rest of the way and waited there.

Eva wanted to answer him, to give him something, but whatever she said would only lead to more questions that she could not and would not answer. Though her leg and ankle hurt, it did not feel injured again as she followed him down the pathway. It was just unused to such activity, and she knew it would ache this night.

She deserved it by the look in his eyes when he asked her that damn question. He had no idea about the bairn. He thought she was running to a lover, to another man. Though he would deny it, she could tell by the way he held himself that he braced himself to discover his wife had a lover.

Why? Why would it bother him so? It should not. They had just met. They were otherwise strangers. She watched other married couples, and as long as the wife did as she was told and was in her husband's bed when he demanded it, there was no trouble. He was different, and she needed to offer him something in repayment for all the patience he'd shown her.

Eva noticed he'd stopped near the clearing. She continued on, not knowing what else to do. She owed him something—for in other circumstances, this marriage would be a welcomed relief from life under her father's control. He'd worn her mother down, and he would do the same to her, if he could. If not for... She stopped before him and took several deep breaths to regain her sense of calm before saying anything.

'Sir,' she said.

'Rob.' He ground his teeth when angry, she noticed. His mouth barely moved as he spoke. 'I asked you to call me by my given name.'

'Rob, I pray you, give me some time to accustom myself to this marriage. I have left behind my home, my people, everything I've ever known.' She stepped closer, forcing her to look up to watch his face.

'It would not have mattered who stood before my father as part of the marriage he arranged. I would have run no matter.' She reached up and touched his hand. 'I ran from the impending marriage.'

His answer was a sound rather than a word. Something softer than a grunt or snort, she'd heard this quick, shallow exhalation from him before. Almost as though he was saying he would consider her words. The nod he gave then eased her worries a bit.

'Do you wish to finish washing?' he asked a moment or two later. 'The sun will set soon and we should return to the others before dark.'

Not wanting to diminish his gesture of bringing her to the stream, she nodded and walked back to the water's edge. Kneeling once more, she made quick work of washing her hands and face and all the places she could reach without undressing. The frigid water made her shiver, but it felt good to be clean of the dust of the road.

When she finished, she held the cloth and soap out to him. Eva thought he would refuse it, but he surprised her and stepped to where she knelt and accepted it. His lower face and neck were covered with several days' growth of beard, she noticed then. He'd shaved before their wedding, unlike her father, but not since. She suspected that he preferred to be clean-shaven when not travelling.

'How much longer before we arrive at your home, Rob?' She yet tripped over the use of his name, but she would try.

'Three more days, if the weather holds,' he said without looking at her. He put the cover back over the small bowl of soap and twisted the cloth to remove the excess water before standing and reaching for her hand. 'Four if the storms of your northlands follow us.'

She held on to his arm this time, her legs tired and unsteady. He walked to match her steps. A small thing, but she noticed it. They were almost back down the hill when he drew to a stop, facing her.

'I have a request of you, lady.'

He stammered a few times, and she feared what he would ask of her.

'When we arrive in Glenlui, I do not wish word of your action to be spread amongst my kith and kin.'

'My action?' she asked.

'That you ran away rather than marry…me. Some would not understand. My sister…'

She nodded. 'It is my shameful behaviour, but if it would please you, I will keep it between us.' A small thing after all and one she could manage.

'And the girl? Would you instruct her?'

'Nessa?' He nodded. 'Certainly.'

'My thanks, lady,' he said, as he began walking once more.

They reached the others and set about their usual tasks to prepare for the night. She and Nessa slept in the wagon, nestled between the crates and boxes, while Rob and the men slept around the fire. She did as he asked, trying to make it more about exposing her to derision than at his request, and Nessa seemed to take it seriously. The girl dearly wanted to remain in Glenlui, so Eva knew she would obey.

The terrible storms of spring did not follow them south and, three days later, just before nightfall, they arrived in Glenlui, the home of the Mackintoshes. As they rode down the mountainside opposite of the keep, Eva could see the village spread out below them. Larger than Tongue, it was closer to the keep than their village was. Drumlui Keep rose to the height of several storeys and was enclosed by wide yards and high walls.

But as they rode through the village, Rob took the reins of her horse and motioned for the others to ride on. He guided them down one of the paths branching off the road and stopped before a modest cottage there. Before they could dismount, the door opened and a woman came out, peering up at both of them before letting out a scream.

'My sister, Margaret,' he said. 'God help us both.'

Chapter Ten

'Robbie!' Margaret called out after she stopped screaming.

There was a strong resemblance between the two that marked them as siblings. She stood tall for a woman, but did not come close to his height. Their colouring was the same—auburn hair and brown eyes. His eyes were much lighter than hers, for there were small flecks of gold in his that Eva did not see in Margaret's.

Holy heavens, she was noticing his eyes now! When had that happened? When he had gone from bear to man or man to husband? She shook her head, not wanting to consider what this meant.

'Forgive me, my lady. I did not mean to startle the horses,' his sister said as she approached. 'I am Margaret Mackintosh, Robbie's sister.'

Pushing her disturbing reverie aside, Eva looked down at the woman standing beside her now. Lucky for her, the training of her childhood and position as the heir of the MacKay asserted itself, since the illness and exhaustion had certainly muddled her wits and made her forget even the simplest of polite behaviour.

'Margaret, I am pleased to meet you. I am Eva, daughter of the MacKay,' she introduced herself as she had always been called.

Rob had dismounted and now reached up to help her down. His hands spanned her waist, and he lifted her easily to her feet. He did not release her for several seconds, allowing her legs and foot to adjust to standing after hours of riding. Margaret's sigh, loud enough to be heard by her and the small, gathering crowd, misread the situation but somehow made this easier.

They thought Rob held on to her as any newly married man would his wife. Eva knew why he did it. Once she felt steady, he stepped away and stood at her side.

'Rob had told me much about you on our journey, Margaret. I am glad to finally meet you.' She held out her hand to the woman in greeting and was surprised to find herself pulled close to Rob's sister and wrapped in a strong hug.

'Well, he hasna told me a thing about ye, my lady,' Margaret said, shooting a dangerous glare at her brother. 'So, once yer settled in, we must have a chat.'

A glance at Rob made her want to laugh. He looked at his sister with such love and caring, but a dash of fear and nausea entered his gaze at her invitation. He did not want her to speak to Margaret. What could she learn about her new husband in a chat with his sister?

'We are sisters by marriage now, Margaret,' she said, stepping back from the embrace. 'You must call me by my given name. Eva.'

Margaret searched her face, taking a closer look at her features, and then glanced over her, head to toes.

'You have been ill, my l… Eva?' she asked. Glaring once more at Rob, she continued, 'Was there a fever?'

How had she known? Ah, she was a healer, familiar with such things.

'Margaret, there is no time for this now. I have not yet introduced her to Brodie, so let it be.' Rob turned to Eva. 'I wanted you to meet her first, lady,' he explained in a whisper. 'I thought it would ease your arrival here to meet family.'

'I thank you for your consideration,' she said in the same tone. 'Margaret, I look forward to making your further acquaintance, but my husband must see to his duties.' Leaning over to his sister, she whispered, 'I was ill. A fever. But I am well now.'

Looking placated, Margaret hugged her once more and then nodded at Rob before moving aside to allow them room to mount. Only as Rob walked to his horse did she see the exchange of glances between brother and sister. Odd those, it was as if they were speaking in some silent language only they understood. And, from their expressions, not all of the exchange was happy.

Margaret Mackintosh would have some choice words for her brother when they were alone, Eva could tell, and she looked forward to such disclosures. She nodded to Rob and urged her horse to follow his towards the keep.

'Will your laird be insulted that we stopped to greet Margaret before him?' she asked when they were away from listening ears.

'Nay,' he said, nodding to someone who greeted him as they rode past. 'Brodie knows better. Margaret served him well and faithfully in his fight to protect the clan. So, he will understand.'

Strange, that.

Her father would punish any slight or insult, perceived or real, with a firm and sometimes ruthless hand. The slap she'd got in her bath, even the strapping, was not the first time her father raised his hand or a belt to her. Or to anyone who served him. The way of things, the way of things between nobles, demanded that her husband present her to the laird first. Not kith or kin and certainly not to a woman.

She rode the rest of the way in silence, taking in the sights and sounds of this village and clan. Many men, and women, called out words of greeting as they passed, nodding in respect to her. Eva wished she'd had time to wash and change her gown before arriving, but with night coming quickly, it was more important to finish their journey than worry over appearance. Rob assured her that Brodie and Lady Mackintosh would take no offence over it.

They passed through the gates and thick wall and into the yard that surrounded the keep. Almost as big as the village without, it was filled with people going about their duties. Seeing their wagon and the others ahead, they rode on. Nessa's face lit with delight at everything she saw.

That should be her. She should be thrilled to be here, newly married with a husband who stood high in his laird's regard and concern. Instead she'd counted every mile crossed with sadness and despair. Nessa's excitement simply made her sadder for her failure to feel it, too.

'Rob!' a loud, deep voice called out.

Glancing up, she watched as a man who could only be the new laird of the Mackintosh Clan strode down the steps and pulled Rob from his horse. They tussled like boys would for a few moments and then exchanged some serious words. All of that ended with them staring at her.

Rob seemed to remember she needed help and walked to her side, lifting her once more to the ground and holding her while she got her balance. The laird missed nothing but stood with his arms crossed watching everything they, she, did.

'Her leg was injured…' Rob began.

'I hurt my leg…' she also began to say.

'So that was the cause of your delayed return, then?' the Mackintosh asked.

'Nay,' Rob said.

'Aye, my lord,' she started. 'Nay.' Brodie Mackintosh looked from one to the other as he heard what she had—an attempt to come up with something to say and failing.

'So what caused the delay? We expected you over a week ago, and Arabella wanted to send me north to find you,' he said.

'The weather, my lord. The spring storms were earlier than expected and slowed travel,' she said smoothly. Rob had cursed often and virulently about the weather and the constant conversation about it. It seemed the right thing to say now. His barking laugh confirmed it. The chieftain's dark eyes brightened and he laughed, too, surely sensing the lie but allowing it to pass.

'Well, whatever the reason, you are here now. Come inside or my lady will have my bollocks for keeping you from her,' he said.

Eva realised her gaffe and curtsied before him then, afraid that he would be angry over such an affront to his dignity and title. Strong hands took her by her shoulders and drew her up straight.

'You are kin now, lady,' he said. 'And neither Robbie nor his wife will ever bow to me.'

There was such warmth and welcome in his voice for her and such respect for her new husband that she almost burst into tears then. She felt Rob's arm around her waist and allowed him to assist her on the steps. The laird led the way into the keep and into a huge hall.

Half again as large as her father's hall, it was decorated with large tapestries and banners along each wall. Eva looked to the front and saw a large raised dais with a table that ran from one side to the other. A huge hearth covered the back wall behind the dais and heated the whole chamber. As they approached the dais and climbed the steps to the table, she also noticed a small grouping of some chairs in one corner, near the hearth.

A woman sat in one chair with her legs supported by a cushioned stool. Brodie walked to her and crouched to speak to her. Only then did Eva realise that the woman was sleeping. The huge warrior raised his hand and stroked the woman's cheek until she woke. The laird stood and held out his hand, helping the lady, obviously his wife, to her feet.

Arabella Cameron, the woman called the most beautiful woman in Scotland, took her husband's hand and walked with him to the table. Eva was caught unaware at the sight of the lady's huge, pregnant belly. Before she could stop herself, her own hand went to her belly, remembering the feel of carrying a bairn within. She dropped it quickly, hoping no one had noticed the gesture.

Now she felt completely unprepared as the lady approached. Though heavily pregnant, the lady was stunning in appearance. Her blonde hair was intricately arranged and her gowns were of the highest quality. The lady's skin and face were glowing and not sallow and swollen as her own had been at that point in carrying. While Eva had suffered through the pregnancy, Lady Arabella clearly thrived through it.

'Arabella, may I present my wife, the Lady Eva MacKay to you?'

She began to curtsy before the lady, since she held a higher position as Lady Mackintosh, the wife of the chieftain, than Eva did as daughter to one. This woman would also control her life, for as lady of the house, she would see to the women living there. The lady stepped to her and pulled her up. Their gazes met, and all Eva saw in her eyes was warmth.

'Welcome to Drumlui Keep, Lady Eva,' she said. ''Tis about time Rob brought a wife here.'

'Arabella!' both men whispered. The lady looked at each of them and then back at Eva.

''Tis the truth! If we had not forced his hand, we might never see him married and settled.' Something in the lady's tone told her that this was the truth, but a genuine concern for him, as well.

'The same could be said about you, Arabella,' Rob countered. 'If we had not kidnapped you, you would have married another.'

'And I thank the Almighty every night that you did, Rob.' What Rob had meant as a teasing remark grew serious then as the three shared some remembered thought. 'And I am glad you are here. Safe and sound?'

'The lady injured her leg before I arrived in Tongue. It slowed our journey here, Arabella.'

'Has Margaret been called? She will be here for the

feast on the morrow, but you should seek her out if you are in pain, Lady Eva.'

'We saw Margaret on our way through the village. I expect she will come in the morning.'

'God help you both!' Brodie said under his breath. The same thing Rob had said. Margaret must truly be a force to be reckoned with among this clan.

'Come. Sit. We have prepared food for you and the others. Something plain and filling. Then you can rest after your journey,' the lady said. 'We will have a feast to celebrate your marriage and the alliance on the morrow.'

'A feast?' Eva asked. She touched her gown.

'Worry not. We can see to all that once you've rested.'

Rob escorted Eva to the table where platters of roasted meats and other foods had been placed. The men who'd travelled with them and Nessa were directed to a table below them covered with the same fare. She waited until the lady and laird had taken their seats before sitting herself.

Food was served. Wine was served. Other than listening to Rob speak with his laird, who did most of the talking, Eva did little else. The lady sat on the other side of her own husband, adding a comment or question for Rob here and there. She was more tired than hungry, so she ate a little and then found herself drifting off even as she sat there.

'Lady?'

She startled at Rob's voice. Opening her eyes, she realised she had fallen asleep and now rested against him. Straightening up, she began to apologise.

'Men!' Lady Arabella pushed her chair back and lifted her bulky body to her feet. Several men, including her own husband and the lady's, jumped and moved to help her. 'You can continue this in the morn. Can you not see the lady is exhausted and needs to seek her bed?' Arabella looked at her. 'Your maid?'

'Nessa.'

'Nessa,' Arabella called out to the lower table. 'See to your lady.' With a nod and a few gestures, other servants rose to see to her needs. Nessa went ahead with another woman.

'My chamber is not that way,' Rob said, as he watched as the servants were led to one corner and down a corridor there.

'Your chamber is not suitable for a wife. I had your things moved to the larger chamber in the western tower.' Arabella could be quite the commander, and Eva found herself enjoying the way the woman had everything, and everyone, under her control. Then the lady pulled her into an embrace and patted her back.

'I know that I am not his true sister, Lady Eva,' she whispered. 'But he is like a brother to me. I wish you both much happiness.'

Brodie watched Bella's face as Rob took his wife to their chambers. The expression there on her face did not please him, for it spoke of worry and concern. She walked back to the table, and he knew his own expression concerned her, too. Though he would deny it, he was worried, too.

'She is not what I expected,' she said, sitting down on his lap.

With her body growing this way and that with each passing day, she found him to be more comfortable than any chair, and he liked having her close. He slid his hands around her girth and placed them on her belly. The bairn within calmed as he did that and he smiled.

'How so?' he asked, as he nuzzled her neck.

'I cannot decide, but something is wrong.'

'With the lady?'

'Aye. And something is wrong between them.'

'They only met weeks ago and were married within days. They are not accustomed to each other yet, Arabella.'

She thought on that part of it, and he knew it made sense, even if she did not wish to accept it. But he also knew that something else bothered her. 'Tell me what you are thinking.'

'He does not touch her.'

Brodie did not answer, but that was only because he was considering her words. He did not like to speak rashly, so he kept his own counsel until it suited him to say something.

'He held her as he helped her from her horse. He held her as they climbed the steps.'

'Brodie,' she whined. 'He did not touch her hand while they sat there. He did not kiss her. He did not try to kiss her.'

He could think of nothing to say, but he understood what she meant.

'He is always touching some woman or another. He has slept with almost every woman available to him here and any place he travels. His bed is never empty.'

'I think it unseemly that my wife knows the habits of my cousin so well,' he said.

'Oh, Brodie. His *habits* as you say are known to all. Two of the laundry maids had a competition to see which of them he would bed first!' She leaned back and met his gaze. 'And he took them both to his bed. The man's appetite for that sort of thing is insatiable and known to all.'

He slid his hand around and rubbed her back, a place he knew bothered her during this pregnancy. She moaned as he pressed against a tight muscle low in her spine until it eased. Arabella should not be worrying about anything right now, not as the day of giving birth approached. Margaret and the midwife had both urged her to take on fewer tasks and rest more, but his wife, his Arabella, could never resist worrying over her kith and especially her new kin.

'Give them some time to settle in together, Bella. Welcome Lady Eva and make certain the others do. And then give them time to learn each other as man and wife.'

'But…' He put his hand over her lips.

'Time, Bella. All they need is some time to adjust to their new marriage.' Kissing her quickly, he watched as her eyes darkened. 'Mayhap he is just being considerate of her? As I am of you?'

'You are?' She sat up straighter on his lap and turned to him. 'This is why you have not…?' She was angry now, for she pushed out of his lap and stood by him. 'I thought you found me too…big.'

Women. How could they so misinterpret a man's actions?

'God in Heaven, Arabella!' he said, pulling her back to him. 'I thought you were too tired. Or feeling ill. Or that I would harm the bairn. I did not want to bother you if you did not…'

'Brodie!' Her voice echoed through the hall and caught the attention of anyone yet remaining there.

Those few now scattered. 'I do not wish you to be considerate,' she whispered now, not allowing anyone but him to hear her words. Her breath on his ear and neck made him harden in seconds. 'You need not be considerate, husband.'

'I love the way your body has changed, Bella,' he whispered back. 'The fullness of your breasts. The way your nipples have darkened and harden when in my mouth. Feeling the bairn within you as I lick down to your...'

Her breaths were shallow and fast now, and he knew she was wet. As wet as he was hard.

Brodie stroked down her leg and slid his hand under her gown, having a care that no one could see. He stroked up her leg and slipped his hand between her legs. When their gazes met, he held hers and watched her expression as he moved closer, inch by inch, to the place he wanted to touch.

And lick. And taste. And fill.

Then he stopped and waited until she gave him a sign of willingness. When she thrust her hips towards his hand, pushing his fingers where he wanted them, he nearly begged her for more.

'So I do not have to be considerate?' Brodie sat up and pulled her to him with his other hand. He kissed her over and over, even while moving his fingers within the folds of flesh between her legs.

'Margaret and the midwife...said all is well...and that we...we...we can still...' She did not have to say the rest. He understood now. He stroked her and circled the spot there that would drive her mad, even as watching her face as her arousal grew was driving him mad.

'So, wife, I can have you when I want?' He practically growled the words, so great was his need for her right now.

'Only if I can have you,' she whispered.

Looking up, Brodie noticed that every person and every servant had left the hall, giving them a measure of privacy. But he wanted more than no watching eyes, for he planned to be very inconsiderate this night and pleasure his wife relentlessly to make up for his inattention lately.

She hissed when he removed his hand and his own flesh throbbed in reaction. Quickly, he pushed the chair back and lifted her in his arms. Aye, she could walk, but this would be faster and easier.

He climbed the stairs two at a time and reached the top storey where their chamber was. Mayhap if he kept her occupied, she would forget to worry over Rob and his new wife? And mayhap there would be nothing to worry over after all?

At the sight of them, the two remaining servants took their leave without a word. Brodie kicked the door closed and carried her to their bed.

Then, for a long night, neither the laird nor the lady worried about much at all.

Chapter Eleven

Rob eased from the bed as dawn crept over the horizon, sending its pale light into their chamber. Glancing over at the other side of the bed, he realised that Eva had not moved since she fell asleep last night.

And she'd fallen asleep when her head lay on the pillow there. Before undressing. Before the hot bath the lady sent up to their chamber. Before he could thank her for what she'd said and done in front of his sister and Brodie and Arabella.

He rolled carefully away from her, realising that his sleep had been deep, too. The comfort of the bed, the warmth of the chamber and the good food filling his belly all conspired to send him to sleep. But now, he had things to do and tasks to see to, as he took up his usual life in Glenlui.

He climbed from the bed and dressed quickly, wanting to allow the lady to sleep as long as necessary this morn. He'd given those instructions to Nessa so he knew no one would bother Eva before she woke on her own. Brodie would be waiting on his report about the MacKay, so he left the chamber and went down to the hall.

He made his way to the room off the great hall that Brodie used for the records and other documents for clan business and was surprised to find the room empty. When his stomach grumbled, Rob decided to seek out some food and wait for Brodie in the hall instead.

It was some time before the laird showed his face and when he did, he looked exhausted. Happy but exhausted.

'My wife would say it is not a good sign that you are here, awake and eating, before me this morn, Rob.'

Rob shrugged. What could he say?

'Did you expect otherwise? 'Tis not a love match.'

Brodie waited until the serving girl put a bowl of porridge before him, filled his cup with ale and left before speaking.

'You are still angry over this?' he asked.

'Bloody hell, Brodie! Aye, I am still angry at being forced to this.' Rob drank some of his ale and lowered his cup. ''Tis a damned debacle, that's what it is.'

'She seems nice enough. From what I remember of her father, 'tis saying much.'

Rob could only glare at him across the table. More servants and people were entering the hall and he did not wish tales of his words to be spread through the clan.

'Can we do this somewhere more private?'

Brodie stood and nodded. 'Not now. I told Arabella the same thing I will tell you, Rob. You and the lady need some time to be accustomed to this marriage.'

'Time, is it?'

Leaning closer, Brodie spoke in a very quiet voice, one Rob had learned long ago to be wary of.

'Did you sign the papers?' At his nod, Brodie continued, 'And say the vows before a priest?' Another nod. 'And consummate the vows?'

'There were bloodied sheets in the morning, aye.' Rob glanced away then.

'Then you are married, and that is not easily undone. Accustom yourself to this and move on. We will speak about the MacKay on my return.'

Then he was gone, heading towards the stables. Brodie kept to a routine each day and it began with a ride through the village and out to the fields and the cattle. More often than not, Rob accompanied him, but not this morn.

When he realised he'd not unpacked the wagon, he asked their steward where it had been stored and went to find it. With help he sorted out the crates and trunks and arranging for their delivery where they needed to be. He asked that his trunk and the lady's several be placed in the alcove near their chambers until she rose. The maid's he had delivered to the small room where she would stay down the corridor from theirs.

Fergus took the chest with the gold and the contracts to his storage room where all the valuables were locked in strongboxes. Rob could retrieve them when Brodie returned.

Once that was settled, he noticed that the men were gathering to train in the yard. It had been weeks since he'd battled with anyone but Lady Eva, and he itched for a good fight of the physical kind. He called out to Magnus, who had just arrived from the village, and challenged him to a bout with the quarterstaff. He lost the first two fights with Magnus, beating him only when they changed to swords.

The hours passed as one man challenged grew to two, and then others joined in their mock battles. Rob and Magnus worked with the others to show them how to use their weapons more effectively. The session ended when Brodie entered the yard and Rob wore himself out fighting the chieftain, who was a wicked fighter with or without weapons. He could feel the tension in his muscles and body being released and a lightness in his mood that came from this kind of challenge.

But would it help the other challenge who yet slept in his bed?

Eva waited while Nessa knocked on the solar door and opened it. Entering the chamber, she saw Lady Arabella sitting in a large chair in the corner and walked to her. When the lady tried to rise, Eva rushed there to stop her.

'I pray you, do not rise.' The laird's wife smiled and rested back. But there were circles under the woman's eyes.

'Did you not sleep well, my lady?' she asked. The last months were the most uncomfortable, she knew, when finding a position that allowed sleep was impossible.

'I, ah…' Lady Arabella stammered. A red blush rose into the lady's cheeks, making her even more attractive. A telling blush that spoke of lost sleep for another reason.

'Since the laird is in the village, mayhap you should rest now?' she asked, unable to stop herself from teasing the woman who was so obviously in love with her husband. It almost hurt to watch it there in her eyes.

'I told Brodie that I was going to like you, Lady Eva,' the lady began. 'Truth be told, we have too much to do for me to go back to bed.'

'Lady, there is no need to…' Eva stopped when the lady held up her hand.

'There is every need to welcome you properly to our family. Not only are you Rob's wife, but the treaty signed by your father and Brodie is advantageous and beneficial to all our clans. Such a thing is to be celebrated.' The lady looked very happy when Eva nodded her assent.

'Good. Now, we must find you a gown suitable for this evening's feast. My aunt Gillie has a good eye for such things, but she is visiting her relations now. Ailean? What say you? The lady and I are, were, of a similar size. Which of my gowns could be altered for her?'

Once again, the lady proved the effective commander of troops, and Eva found herself trying on all sorts and colours of gowns under the critical eye of Arabella Cameron. Although she claimed her aunt was a better judge of such things, one did not gain the reputation she had for beauty and grace and womanly appearance without having some herself. Only the arrival of Rob's sister, Margaret, slowed down the relentless Lady Arabella on her quest to find the perfect gown for the new wife of Rob Mackintosh.

'Margaret!' Lady Arabella called out when the servant opened the solar's door. 'Come, we could use your help. Have you met Rob's wife yet?'

'How do ye fare this morning, Eva?' Margaret came over and sat next to her. Arabella looked a bit annoyed not to be the centre of Margaret's concern until Rob's sister turned to her. 'And you, Arabella? Has the bairn dropped lower yet?'

Eva could barely stand the pain of hearing questions about the bairn. It was too soon. Her own pain too deep and fresh. She took in a halting breath, trying to hide her distress. Margaret took her hand then.

'Ye have been ill? Tell me what happened?'

'Ill? I thought you had injured your leg?' the lady asked.

Eva knew she needed a simple story that would satisfy these two women. So, she stayed with the truth as much as she could. She must remember to tell Rob.

'Nothing exciting. Truly, the story just demonstrates my lack of grace, Arabella.' She took a breath and wove together all the bits of it. 'Rob was delayed in his arrival and my father gave permission to visit my cousin. On my way back, I slipped on the muddy ground and twisted my knee and ankle.'

'You did not break anything?' Margaret asked, glancing down at Eva's leg and foot. Eva held it up and rotated her foot to show it had healed.

'Nay. Rob had come to meet me and he bound it well. He said he learned from you,' she added.

Margaret made the same, soft huff sound that Rob did when he was thinking on something, further identifying them as siblings. 'I wish he'd had some of the ointment I use to help reduce the swelling. It would have had you out of pain and stronger faster than just binding,' Margaret added.

The devil stood on Eva's shoulder then, urging her to tell Margaret what Rob had used. Something about being with women who cared and who wanted to help, made her want to be part of this camaraderie. She'd never felt at home what these women made her feel within minutes of meeting them. They cared deeply and were cared about just as deeply. Looking at the concern in their gazes, she smiled.

'Rob did use a liniment on my ankle and foot, Margaret. He said you'd made it. It smelled of an herb and mayhap mint?'

Margaret started to say something and then stopped, clearly thinking on which liniment Rob could have had with him. Then her mouth dropped open and she shook her head.

'Pray you, tell me he did not?'

All Eva could do was laugh as Margaret realised the truth. Margaret explained it to the lady, who laughed, as well.

'Our Rob sorely needs his wooing skills improved,' the lady said when she finally could speak. Wiping tears from her eyes, she said, 'His ease with women has clearly made him forget how to do it correctly.'

Ease with women?

Eva was no fool, she'd seen the glances thrown his way both in the village and here in the keep. And, she'd seen his body and melted under just his kiss and knew he would draw willing, available women like bees to flowers.

And, if she told herself the truth, the way he had a care for people was enticing, too.

'Well, then,' she said. ''Tis a good thing he did not need to woo a wife, then.'

Eva knew she'd misspoken when her words were greeted with silence. Ah, these two knew Rob had not wanted the marriage. Considering his penchant for expletives and his admission that he'd shared his feelings about not wanting to marry, 'twould make sense of course. She changed their topic, directing them off the subject of her marriage.

'The healer at Varrich thought I might have fallen because of the fever,' she explained. 'That the dizziness made me lose my balance.' Though the healer had not seen to her, Eva believed the fever had caused her fall.

'Puir lass,' Margaret whispered, touching her hand. 'To be ill and then injured and have to journey here. Why did Rob not wait?'

So many reasons, Eva thought.

'Once the fever broke and I felt better, we wed. Rob saw to my leg on the journey, and it is healed now.'

She looked up then and found Lady Arabella blinking quickly and moving her mouth like a fish did. Margaret did not speak, but she did mumble words under her breath that Eva decided she did not wish to hear.

Lucky for her, the sound of cheering outside drew their attention. She stood and walked to the large shuttered window and opened it to see the yard. She gasped when she saw the men below. Margaret helped the lady to her feet and they joined her to see.

There was some sort of challenge or fight going on below. Eva picked Rob out immediately—his height and colouring made it easy. He was on the attack, swinging his sword at his opponent, forcing him back and back until the fence stopped their movement.

His opponent was darker, of the same height, and it took little time to recognise the laird. Arabella gasped as he tripped and went down on one knee, confirming his identity.

The third man, pale haired but taller and wider than any she'd seen before, stood nearby, watching, it would seem. Then, he attacked Rob when he was not looking. Now it was her turn to gasp as the two, strong warriors fought Rob at the same time. Eva did not know she'd clenched her fists until Margaret took hold of one and spread her fingers.

''Tis but a practice, Eva. Brodie and Magnus will not harm him.'

She turned and glanced at Margaret. The way her voice softened on the other warrior's name was telling. Then, a roar went up from those watching as Rob knocked Magnus to the ground and flung the man's sword away. Now, it was just him and his laird.

'Do not fret, Margaret. I do not think Rob injured Magnus,' the lady said. Once more the tone of the words spoke of something between Rob's sister and the warrior who now climbed to his feet but did not re-enter the fray.

'Easing a man's aches is not the worst way to spend a night, Arabella.'

The lady burst into laughter and went back to her chair. 'Nay, 'tis not the worst way at all.'

Eva stared at one and then the other. These women enjoyed their men without shame or fear. Her mother's marriage had never been like this. She'd often spoke of the burdens and pain of the marriage bed, warning Eva that she would simply have to bear up under it.

And even though her time with Eirik had been

thrilling and exciting, Eva had wondered if part of the enjoyment had been the thrill of the forbidden. With another glance out the window at her husband, she wondered what it would be like with him.

'Ah, here is Ailean with the gown now,' the lady called out.

It took little time to try it on. The lady's maid had excellent skills with needle and thread and the gown fit as though made for her. Her body had changed since... and most of her gowns no longer fit well. Mayhap she would ask Ailean's assistance in fixing hers.

'That colour is lovely against your skin and hair, Lady Eva.'

'You must call me Eva, lady.'

'If you cease calling me lady.'

She nodded and turned as Arabella motioned for her. Both women and even the maid seemed pleased with the results. Eva slid her hands over the costly fabric and enjoyed the way the gown flowed and moved as she did.

'Margaret? The scarf you gave her? The colour would look beautiful if woven through her hair,' Arabella motioned with her hands to show how it should be done.

All Eva could think was *what* scarf?

'I hope you liked it?' Margaret asked. 'Rob had no idea of the appropriate gift. Arabella, you sent a book?'

Eva tried to keep her smile firmly in place, but her heart sank. She'd received no gifts from her new husband. Had she expected to, truly? What man would present gifts to a woman who scorned his offer of marriage and humiliated him by running from it? Taking in a breath, she nodded.

'You were both generous in giving those to me. The scarf is beautiful, Margaret. And, the book was more than I could have expected.'

'We wanted you to feel welcomed. Under the circumstances...'

'And I do.'

A thick silence filled the chamber until, once more, the commander issued her orders.

'You must be tired from all this,' Arabella said. 'I have sent a hot bath to your chambers, and then you should rest. I will send Ailean to help your maid with the dress and your hair.'

Knowing how difficult this feast was going to be for her, acting and playing the part of the bride to their favoured kinsman, Eva did as Arabella ordered.

The feast came much too quickly.

Chapter Twelve

How could his sister be bitterly reprimanding him all the while wearing the smile of an angel?

Margaret had charged him when he'd entered the hall the same way Magnus had charged him in the yard earlier this day. The only difference was that Magnus used a sword to try to skewer him, while Margaret used only her sharp tongue.

'You did not give her the gifts, did you, brother?' Margaret accused. 'The scarf? Arabella's book?'

'I… I…'

He really could not come up with an excuse, at least not one he could share. The day of and morning after their wedding, he was not feeling very kindly towards the woman who'd run and hidden from him. Even risked her own life to get away from this marriage.

'She is not wearing it. She said you had packed it away for the journey and she knew not where it was.'

Nay, he had not only not given her the gifts, he'd buried them deep in his trunk with no intention of giving them to her. Now though, just thinking on it made it feel mean to him.

She nodded at his wife, who sat next to Arabella at table. He should be at her side, but Margaret had pulled him away before he could. Margaret turned away, so Eva could not see her face now.

'And you used horse liniment on her leg? Dear God, Rob, did I not raise you right?'

His older sister had raised him when their parents died and when she was little more than a girl herself. The interesting part of this was that Margaret was disgruntled in Eva's stead.

'She said it helped. And it did, Margaret.' Rob glanced up at Eva now. 'She also promised not to tell you. But what can I expect from a woman who did not wish to marry me?' She winced at his words and shook her head.

'And did you want to marry her?' Margaret asked.

Rob shrugged at his sister. 'She knows that, Margaret. Believe me, there are no false hopes existing between the lady and me.'

'Daft man!' she whispered furiously at him. 'She lied to protect you to us. Lied to me and Arabella.'

She walked off then before he could say another word, muttering some choice words under her breath. Inventive suggestions about what he should do to and with various parts of his body. Now, he winced.

He stood where he was, watching Eva talking to Arabella. She wore something that resembled the false smile that Bella had worn on her first visits to this hall. Polite but one that did not reach her eyes or make her cheeks move. The obvious look of a woman doing what was expected of her in the situation in which she found herself.

No wonder Brodie hated that expression so much.

The man himself approached and handed him a cup of wine before taking a position next to him against the wall.

'You did not come to speak to me this morn.'

'I turned everything, the documents and the gold, over to Fergus. It's in your strongboxes when you wish to examine it all.' Rob drank deeply from the cup, avoiding Brodie's gaze.

His friend knew how to use silence as a weapon to force others to speak and sometimes to speak too much. That was the true reason he'd avoided speaking in private to him.

'You did not come to speak to me,' Brodie repeated, in that damnable calm tone of his.

Finally, Rob accepted the inevitable. He would have to say something to explain his behaviour and his inexcusable failure to obey Brodie's call.

'I would rather avoid my laird than lie to my friend.'

They stood there after his declaration as the servants began moving the tables aside and making a place where they could dance. But more words pushed forward, as he felt the need to give his friend more.

'I suspect she loves another.'

There. Though he had no claim over her affections, and though some of her actions were worse than others towards him, that was the worst. For a reason he could not explain to himself or his friend. Brodie nodded and stepped away, looking at the table where their wives sat.

'And yet, she lied for you to my wife and your sister to keep you in their good graces.'

Rob opened his mouth to argue the point, but he could not. Brodie walked quickly along the path next to the tables to the front, greeting his wife with a fierce kiss. From the sidelong glances at him, he knew he should return to Eva and make an attempt to present himself as a happily married man. Or, at the least, a man at peace with this marriage.

Eva watched as he walked in that languid, easy gait, stretching his long legs to cover the distance from where he stood to the table where she sat in fewer strides than most men here would need. She had always been close to him and only today and now had she had the chance to observe him from further away.

The sight of him fighting Brodie and Magnus in the yard had taken her breath away. Not so much because she thought him in danger, but because he fought in only his trews. His long hair was tied back to keep it from his face and hung down past his shoulders. His chest and arms and back were like finely sculpted statues, glistening in the sun, as he moved with his sword. Oh, the other two men had taken off their tunics as well, but seeing him and knowing how the contours of his muscles looked up close, made her lose her breath.

Even now, her body reacted to the memory of seeing him naked in their chamber.

Shaking her head, she had only to bring her father's words to mind to break Rob's hold over her thoughts— only sluts and whores sought a man's touch for pleasure. A lady accepted the duty expected of her and accepted her husband's touch when he so wished.

Mayhap that was the lesson here? By disregarding her father's instructions and lusting after Eirik, she had lost everything. Home. Family. Love. All lost because she followed her own heart and desires. And now, here she sat among strangers, married to a man who did not want to be married to her. Who held her in such low regard that he did not even wish to sit with her at table, escaping as soon as was seemly to do so.

'Are you well, Eva?' Arabella whispered, touching her hand to Eva's cheek. 'You are pale.'

'I am well, my lady.' At Arabella's glare, she smiled. 'I am well, Arabella.'

'You look beautiful. That dress does look good on you,' Arabella said. 'Brodie? I think she looks better in that gown than I ever did. What think you?'

'Bella,' he growled. Eva almost fell sorry for the man put in such an uncomfortable position by his wife. But he was a man in love, and he rose to the challenge. 'I think that you both grace the gown with loveliness in a different way.'

Eva laughed then at the words of a well-trained husband. When Brodie leaned over to kiss his wife, again and again, she had to look away.

They did not hide their passion away. They seemed to allow it to show whenever they were together. He was kissing her or touching her or holding her hand whenever she was at his side. And when she was not, he sought her out and made it so.

Rob reached the table and took his seat on the other side, away from Arabella, who was still kissing Brodie and noticing little if anything else.

'Have you need of anything, lady?'

'Nay, I am well,' she replied in a pleasant tone. 'The feast was more than I could have expected, especially at such short notice.'

He glanced over at her, examining her hair and gown.

'You have probably seen this on Arabella. She graciously had it fitted for me just today.' She smoothed it down over the legs. 'Ailean is so talented with the needle and thread and promised to help me repair my gowns.'

Her hair, he noticed, was decorated with silk ribbons that both held her curls in place and made the blonde undertones of her hair shine. The gown borrowed from Arabella was of a colour that the scarf from Margaret would match perfectly.

The scarf that lay hidden away in his trunk.

His stomach soured as he realised how petty his actions were. Especially in the light of her efforts to defend him to his sister. He stared at her until she met his gaze. He noticed the tears gathering in her eyes.

'I see how lovely you look in this gown, lady.' She blinked several times, glancing away until the tears disappeared.

'And you look very handsome, Rob.' She nodded at his tunic and plaid, gathered over his shoulder. 'You did not wear this at Varrich.'

''Tis our ceremonial garb, lady. For special occasions and such.'

Eva did not reply, but only glanced around the hall at the other men garbed the same way.

'Lady?' he said softly so only she could hear. When she did not look at him, he took her hand in his and stroked her palm until she did. He moved his gaze to her hair and then back to her eyes.

'I am sorry.'

He watched as she turned away and swallowed several times. Then only with a slight nod did she acknowledge his apology for the slight he'd dealt her.

Before he could say or do anything else, a clamour

arose from those below. Banging cups and stamping feet made such a noise but when they began calling out, Rob knew what they wanted. He sensed she was fragile in that moment and a repeat of what they'd done at Varrich was not what she wanted.

He raised their joined hands so all could see and then leaned over and kissed her mouth gently. She did not resist but she did not participate. The crowd was not pleased, and several people called out to them.

'I thought ye kenned how to kiss a woman, Robbie!' called one man. 'I can show her how 'tis done if ye canna!'

'Haud yer wheest!' he answered back. A hint of a smile played on her mouth now.

'Kiss the girl, Robbie! Show her how the Mackintoshes do it!'

'Loch Moigh! Loch Moigh!' Brodie shouted in reply.

As they always did when their chieftain yelled the clan's battle cry, everyone stood and answered.

'Loch Moigh! Loch Moigh!' Then they changed the words but continued chanting, loudly, as they clapped and stamped their feet on the floor. 'A kiss! A kiss! A kiss!'

Rob pulled Eva up to him, lifted her off her feet and kissed her. He kissed her as the crowd wanted him to.

He kissed her the way he wanted to.

Deeply. Fully.

Relentlessly.

He tilted his head and captured her mouth, pressing his tongue against her lips until she opened and then taking her. Her breasts rubbed against his chest and their hips met. His flesh hardened and throbbed against her.

She held back for what seemed an eternity and then kissed him back. He could feel her hands on his shoulders, clutching at his plaid as he thrust deep, tasting all that she was. Suddenly aware of the silence around them, he lifted his mouth from hers and glanced around.

He should stop. He should stop this farce, for it was only a kiss for show.

And he would have if she had not looked at him through passion-glazed eyes and slid the tip of her tongue across her kiss-bruised lips.

Eva read his intention in his eyes but could not stop him. He held her up higher and slid his hand up along the back of her neck into her hair. His fingers entangled there held her mouth to his as he claimed her once more.

She told herself this was just a pretend kiss, one meant to satisfy those clamouring for such a show from the newly married couple. Even as her breasts swelled and she grew wet in that place between her legs, she told herself this meant nothing. But when his other hand slid beneath her bottom and pressed her against the ridge of flesh, she wondered if there wasn't more this time.

Using her grasp on his shoulders to push herself free of his mouth, she found an intensity in his dark eyes that frightened her. She did not fear harm from him; nay, she feared her own response to him. She shivered then, before succumbing to yet another kiss.

The shouting reached a crescendo and then burst as everyone shouted wishes for their happiness. Rob finally released her, and she slid back to her feet, trying to steady her shaking hands as she reached up to check her hair. When she dared to glance at him, he held out the blue silk ribbon that Ailean had woven through her hair.

If that kiss in front of everyone had not embarrassed her, this did. Her hair tumbled down over her shoulders without the ribbon to hold it in place. She turned to leave when he grabbed her shoulders to make her stay.

'Dear God in Heaven!' Rob swore.

Lifting her chin to bring her gaze to his, he took in the swollen lips and her heaving breaths. Then he followed the length of her curls that ended around her hips. Though he'd thought her hair was light brown, now, these riotous locks caught every flicker of light in the hall and showed shades of blonde and gold and brown and more.

She was a beauty.

Seeing her at her best for the first time, he cursed himself for never realising it before. Even her form had changed over the weeks since they'd met in that damnable cave. From ill to recovering to something closer to health, she was stunning this evening. Arabella knew, for she'd chosen exactly the right gown to show it off.

His body urged him to finish this. To steal her away now and take her the rest of the way. To make her his and his alone, by claiming her body and making it answer to his touch only.

And his mouth.

And his prick.

He could do it if he wanted. Plant himself deep in her flesh and spill his seed. Mark her so that no one who'd come before would matter any longer.

No matter which man had been there first.

A flicker of fear rippled through her eyes then, stopping him. What did she fear? Not the act, surely? The way her body reacted was not the way an innocent's would. But did she fear him knowing it for a fact rather than just suspecting it?

'I pray you,' she whispered then. 'Nay.'

The passion fled at the word. He released her and stepped back, reaching for his cup and hers. When she accepted it, he drank his dry and held it out to one of the servants for more.

'Let us move on to the real entertainment now that we have given you ours!' he called out. Brodie nodded to the musicians, who had gathered below, and they began to play. Soon voices joined in, singing the songs of the family and of bravery and more.

He sat back down at Eva's side and wondered if her reticence might have saved him from making a huge blunder. He studied her profile as the others, and she, watched the musicians. The one thing he'd not considered about their situation now raised its head.

She'd not bled since the day he'd found her. She'd never complained or mentioned her monthly arriving. Even if she'd not speak of it to him, he'd seen no evidence of her dealing with such things on the road, though he knew from other comments overheard that the maid had.

What if she carried some man's babe? Though the words burned to be spoken, he would not ask her this question. The answer would be clear soon enough. Clamping his teeth together, he knew not to speak at all right now. For what he could ever say to her now? Arabella saved him in that regard.

'Eva, how is your leg faring? Is it still bothering you?' she asked.

'Does it pain you, lady?' he asked. She'd not mentioned it when he'd spoken to her briefly earlier in the day. But he'd not asked her about it, either.

'It is sore, I fear.' She lied. He read it in her eyes. She wanted to escape him, at least for the moment.

'Mayhap we should both retire and leave the others to dance?' Arabella pushed her chair back and stood. Brodie helped her and nodded to Ailean. Nessa followed Arabella's maid to the table.

'See to your ladies,' Brodie ordered them both.

'Do you need help getting to our chamber, lady?' he asked.

'I can manage my way back, sir,' she said blandly. *Sir* again? 'Nessa will see to me.'

Rob stepped back and watched them leave. Brodie did not last much longer once his wife had gone. They'd left the table and sat below where their kin danced to the music. One or two songs later and Brodie took his leave.

Margaret and Magnus danced several times, and he was pleased to see them together openly. The man was a wicked fighter and honourable. Margaret would not find a better man than him, and he whispered his good wishes to her before they left for the village.

Others joined him, some of the men he'd fought with and lived with in the mountains during their worst times. A few of the women he'd shared a bed and some good times with spoke to him, letting him know with and without words that he was welcome to return if he so wished.

Even Fiona's furtive heated kiss on his neck and the insistent grope of her hot hands in the corridor as he left the hall did not rouse his interest as much as it did the randy lad under his plaid. His flesh reacted to some of the memories of those times, but when it came to accepting an offer from his most recent lover, he just could not.

So, after drinking too much ale and other spirits than he probably should have, he sent her away and sought his chamber. He must be drunker than he thought he was, for the chamber was dark and cold. Climbing into the bed, he was asleep faster than he thought possible.

Only as he sank into sleep's grasp did he realise that Eva was not in the bed with him.

Chapter Thirteen

She snapped at Nessa, causing the girl to cry after the third time.

Eva tried to figure out the reason for it, and it all led back to him. She discovered an empty bed when morning finally arrived and no sign that Rob had ever returned here after the feast. When she added that to feminine attentions he'd received at the feast and his obvious disdain for the marriage he'd been forced to, it could mean one thing.

She told herself she could not be surprised and could not complain. He was a lusty man, from the tales told and from his desires shown her already. His invitation to share passion was right there in his eyes, clear enough to her that she spoke her refusal. Men often sought comfort in the beds of other women, and married or not, Rob had no lack of offers. A few of the women had been bold enough to whisper it loud enough so that she would hear it.

No matter her body's reaction to his kisses, her heart could not bear to accept him in her bed. She did fear his reaction when he discovered what he most likely suspected—her virtue was gone. As he would whenever he decided to exert his rights to her body. That time would come, it must, but she would delay it as long as she could.

If it meant that he would seek relief and pleasure elsewhere, she would have to learn to accept it. As her mother had when her father had brought his leman into the keep for his pleasure. She thought it might have been relief on her mother's part, but the humiliation in her mother's eyes as he gave his leman a place that belonged to her mother would never be forgotten.

Eva took pity on Nessa and sent her on some errand and saw to her own dressing. She bound her hair in a long tight braid and decided that it was time to see the rest of the keep and village. Her leg felt good, not painful as she'd told Rob last night. Aye, she'd used it for an excuse and should feel guilty but did not.

Leaving word with one of the maids about her plans, Eva decided the village would be her first destination. Thick clouds covered the sun, but it did not feel like rain. Making her way out of the keep and through the yard, she glanced over at the yard where men practised, thinking she might see Rob there.

Then chiding herself for that, she walked out through the gates, nodding to the guards who knew her by name. A long trail of people walked the road to and from the village as the usual chores and tasks called them on. She followed the smells of baking bread to a large building near the centre of the village.

She'd been so intent on getting out before she encountered Rob, she'd not taken time to eat anything and her stomach grumbled loudly, letting her know its displeasure. Deciding to buy a small loaf to appease it, Eva next realised she had no coins with her.

'Lady Eva, good morrow to you,' the baker called out to her.

'Good morrow,' she said back, walking closer to where loaves sat on the windowsills cooling. 'Your bread smells delicious.'

'Would you have a loaf?' the baker asked, pointing to several already-cooled ones. 'The miller grinds my flour very fine, lady. 'Tis the finest around and you'll find no bits or stones in my loaves.' He walked over to her and smiled. 'Why, the Lady Arabella herself asked me to help bake for the feast last night!'

'I did not bring coins with me…'

'Tomas be my name, lady.'

'I will come on the morrow prepared to buy some,' she promised.

'Here now, lady. I cannot have you walking off empty-handed. What will people think?' he asked as he pressed a warm, aromatic loaf into her hands. 'Consider this a small gift on the occasion of your wedding to our Robbie.'

After thanking him, Eva continued through the village, eating chunks of the bread that turned out to be as good as its maker promised. Soon, others greeted her as warmly and presented her with tiny treasures to mark her wedding. Their gifts meant much to her, a complete stranger, but it was their words that meant more.

Eva knew that Rob was highly regarded, but until she heard the stories of these people, she'd had no idea of how much so. She'd not paid heed to anything about the man she'd married when her father spoke of him. Now though, each of the villagers she met praised his loyalty to the clan and his deeds of courage during the dark times of the last years.

Before she knew it, she carried a round of cheese, more bread, a small jar of soap, a length of plaid that matched the one Rob had worn at the feast and other surprises. Realising she was not going to be able to carry them as she held them, she paused by the well to wrap them in the plaid.

'Ye kissed him.'

The voice was so soft she nearly missed it. Turning around, she found a little girl there watching her.

'Ye kissed Robbie,' the girl said again.

'Were you in the hall last evening, then?' Eva asked her. The girl nodded her answer. 'What is your name?'

'I am called Fia.'

'I am Eva.'

'Lady Eva, Mam said,' Fia answered. 'She said that Robbie married a great lady from the north.' She pushed her brown curls out of her face and squinted at Eva. 'Why are ye a great lady?'

Eva laughed then. She'd never been asked such a thing. 'I suppose because my father is the MacKay, the head of a powerful clan in the north.' She watched as the girl considered the reason and then shrugged.

'Why did ye marry Robbie?' Fia asked, moving closer and helping Eva arrange the things within the plaid.

'My father and your laird thought it would be a good idea.' Trying to keep it simple and clear, Eva explained it the best way she could.

'Are ye going to kiss him again, Lady Eva? He likes to kiss women, ye ken? I have seen him kiss Isabel and

Jean and Mairi and Fiona. He must like Fiona the most, for he kissed her more times than any of the others.'

She laughed then, for what else could she do at such a disclosure and from a child at that? What Rob did with others and especially before she arrived here was not her concern, she told herself again. Then Fia leaned closer and whispered.

'Wee Jamie kissed me once, but it was no' good. He tasted like mud,' Fia declared. She followed her words with the funniest expression, sucking and slurping loudly and then spitting on the ground. Eva laughed more.

'Well, Fia, I think you will think differently about kisses when you are older.'

'Lady Arabella said I can come to the keep and work as her maid when I am older. She liked the way I helped her wash her hair.'

'I will remember that if I need help with washing my hair,' Eva promised.

'Fia!' The girl's eyes widened at the woman's call. 'I have been waiting on ye, lass.'

'My mam,' Fia whispered, nodding her head in the direction of the approaching woman. 'I was to fill the bucket and bring it back to the house.' The forgotten bucket lay on one side of the path.

'Lady Eva,' the woman said. 'Good day to ye!'

'Good day.' She glanced overhead and realised she'd lost track of the time of day in her wanderings through the village. 'Your pardon if I kept the lass from her chores,' she said.

'No worries on that, lady,' the woman said. 'I think she probably kept ye from yer tasks with her chatter.'

She motioned to Fia to get the bucket. 'I am called Bradana.'

'I will leave you to your chores,' Eva said, gathering up the plaid filled with her presents.

'Visit any time, lady. Ours is the last cottage on this path. And if ye need the lass to run errands, just send word and I'll send her to ye.'

Eva took her leave and had only walked several paces from the well when she saw him sitting on his horse, watching her every move. His expression gave no hint as to his mood or purpose there. She nodded and continued walking by him and towards the road to the keep.

'Margaret said she had not seen you this morn.'

''Tis true—I have not seen her this day,' she said, over her shoulder.

He guided his horse behind her. 'Where are you going now?'

Eva turned back and stared at him. 'Where do you think I am going?' she asked him back.

'What is in your bundle there?' he asked, never giving her a reply.

'Bread. Cheese. Some soap. A few trinkets and such,' she answered, holding it out for his inspection.

'Almost like you're readying for a journey.' Even watching him as he spoke did not give her a sign of whether he was jesting or serious. 'All you need is a place to go and some gold and you would be ready.'

'You think I am running away?' she asked.

'Do I have any reason to think that?' he added. They stared at one another for several long, tense, silent seconds, and then she shook her head.

'I am... You can go to... Wherever you need to go.'

Several foul suggestions had lain on her tongue just then. Mayhap she was developing his habitual use of such words after being around him these last weeks? She ignored him and walked on.

'Lady,' he said. She turned just in time to catch the sack he threw to her.

'What is this?' It felt like coins, but why would he give her those when he'd just accused her of fleeing him if she had these?

'You said you wanted coins for your own use. Those are some of the amount set aside for your use.'

She stopped then and looked at him. Aye, she'd said that, but she never dreamed he would allow it. Oh, aye, a household account when, if, she ran their household, but coins for whatever she wanted? Nay, she'd never expected him to do it.

'I will take you to Fergus, Brodie's steward, so you know how to get more when you need it,' he explained.

'I am returning to the keep now,' she said, answering the first question he'd asked her again.

His actions in giving her the money had surprised her. She had scraped and hidden her few coins away over weeks, never wanting her father or mother to become suspicious of them. Eva stared at him and tried to remember what had even become of the belongings she'd taken when she'd run away and could not.

'Give me your hand and put your left foot here on mine,' he instructed. In a matter of seconds, she found herself sitting on his lap. He shifted, moving her between his legs, and then touched his heels to the horse's side. 'This is easier than walking up the hill to Drumlui.'

'I do not want to take you away from your duties,'

she said, trying not to rest back on his wide chest. His hair, she noticed, was damp and he smelled clean. So, he'd bathed somewhere this morn. Mayhap wherever he'd slept?

'Seeing to my wife is my duty,' he said softly in her ear. 'Or so I have been told this morning.' Rob felt her stiffen in his arms, her back going straight and her shoulders rigid.

One of Arabella's maids gave him the message that she'd left but could remember no more than that. When he returned to their chamber earlier, Nessa mumbled something about Eva's cross mood, but the only thing that was clear was that his wife had lashed out at her maid several times.

Arabella herself gave him a tongue lashing over the matter of her gift and his abandonment of his bride. A good husband or a fool trying to be one should have followed her back to their chambers immediately and not remained below as though still a bachelor, she'd said. Brodie stood at her side, silent as usual, while she berated him. Then, when she burst into tears and fell into his arms, Brodie motioned to her belly and he waved Rob out of the chamber.

It was only as he walked through the yard and watched people coming and going through the open gates that the idea that she had run occurred to him. It stopped him in his stride and he stumbled before regaining his balance.

The thought that she would try to run from him a second time hit him in the gut. And since his stomach still suffered the effects of too much ale and other spirits, it took little time before he knew he could not remain in the keep and see if she came back.

Margaret's response to him was a loud, long, bent-over-at-her-waist laugh that drew Magnus out of the cottage. Others in the village were more helpful, and soon he found himself following her route as she moved through the paths there. He'd heard Fia's talk of kissing and wondered if that had been the cause.

Had Eva got word of his encounter with Fiona in the corridor? He did not think they were seen, but he'd had so much drink in him he could not be certain. The horse misstepped and she shifted against him then. Still stiff. He let out an irritated breath and shifted his arms.

'Here now, lean back for the steep part of the path,' he instructed. Eva leaned back but did not soften against him.

This being married was more difficult than he'd imagined it would be. More difficult than it might have been with a willing bride. But, as Brodie had counselled, they would both have to adjust to each other and it would take time.

He felt her let out a sigh as the horse walked up the pathway that led to the gate and keep.

'Was it Margaret or Arabella who spoke of your duties to me?' she finally asked.

'Arabella,' he said. 'For Margaret had her say last night at the feast.'

'I thought your face looked a bit exasperated while she was talking.'

'She raised me after our parents died. She is used to giving me lessons,' he admitted. Margaret had been little older than he when she took over his care. 'She forgets I am grown.'

Eva snorted in reply. Oh, it was a very feminine, soft

snort but, one none the less. They rode up the trail, approaching the gate, and entered.

'Arabella asked that you seek her out on your return, lady. She will be in her chambers,' he said as they drew to a halt and a young boy rushed to hold the reins.

Rob swung his leg over and jumped from the horse. Then he reached up for the lady. Once more she stiffened under his touch.

Was this to be their pattern of life? He would do or say something stupid and then need to apologise? He cursed even feeling the need to do so. When her feet touched the ground, he still kept his hold on her waist, waiting for her to raise her eyes to him.

'Brodie counsels me that it might take us more time to accommodate ourselves to this marriage. Especially considering our less than fortuitous beginning,' he said softly, so that only she could hear.

'The laird knows?' she asked. 'You told him?'

'I spoke only of a difficult meeting. He urged patience,' he explained. 'I am not accustomed to answering to a woman, to a wife, about my behaviour or accounting my time to one. For years, I have answered only to the laird.'

She watched him with suspicion in her blue eyes, as though waiting for a blow to fall. When he lifted his hand to wipe across his face, he would swear she flinched before regaining control.

'I indulged too much last night. After that kiss...' he forced his eyes not to look at her mouth as he continued '...and everything else I did wrong, I sought comfort in my cup.'

'And not in the bed of the lovely Fiona?' she asked. How could she speak the words without any inflection or emotion? Ah. She cared not if he swived other women, as long as he did not bed her.

'Nay.' He shook his head. 'I mistakenly went back to my old chamber and slept there. I was so drunk I did not realise it until morn.' Rob waited for a reaction, some reaction. None came. Still, he needed to say the rest of it, for his behaviour and apparent disregard for her had been witnessed. 'I will try not to embarrass myself or my wife in such a manner again.'

The last words made her tremble for some reason. Worse, he watched her mouth. Her lower lip quivered, and he so wanted to lick it and suck it into his own mouth.

'I appreciate your candour and your words, sir,' she whispered. 'I comprehend that you have the right to do as you please, especially in a marriage such as ours,' she began. 'If I can beg only for discretion that is what I would ask.'

Now it was his turn to react to words. She asked only discretion? She truly cared not. The lady must have realised she'd erred, for she stepped back from him.

'I only meant that I married you because my father believed your connection through blood and loyalty to the Mackintosh was advantageous. You married me because your laird wanted the same from my father. I think if we try to see more than that between us, we will never have peace.'

The reminders that he was nothing more than a means to an end for his laird and hers stung again. Unfortunately, what she said was the truth.

'Just so,' he said, realising there was no other choice in this matter between them.

Rob watched as she walked into the keep, leaving him behind without a backward glance. The lady was correct. He knew that. He tried to tell himself that. Through each moment of that day. As he went about his duties to his laird and clan. But the words that echoed in his thoughts were not quite as generous as those.

Damn her and this marriage to hell!

Chapter Fourteen

Eva approached the door and stopped before knocking.

Every day became more and more difficult, and she had to force herself to accept the lady's invitation here. Arabella made her feel welcomed when she did not have to. She pulled her into the clan and introduced her to life in Drumlui Keep. She made her…feel wanted.

And yet, it took every bit of her self-control not to throw herself to the floor weeping at the sight of the very pregnant Lady Mackintosh.

And it took every remembered punishment for not behaving appropriately as the MacKay's daughter to keep herself returning to this chamber each day.

But would it be worse when the bairn was born?

That thought struck her like a blow, and she nearly fell to her knees with pain. Only the sound of footsteps on the other side of the door forced herself to draw it all back within herself and stand tall. She reached out towards the door so it would look as though she was about to knock.

'Oh, here she is, my lady,' Ailean said, with a warm smile. 'She was worrying that you were not coming.'

Eva took a deep breath, put a smile on her face and entered the place where she would suffer until given leave to go. Arabella's greeting and hug told Eva that the lady would never have invited her had she known how painful it was for her. But, that would mean exposing her deepest secret, and Eva would not do that.

'How are you feeling this morn, Arabella?' she asked as she sat in the chair offered her, at the lady's side. Eva clenched her teeth as she watched Arabella's reaction.

'I feel well,' she said. She slid her hands over her large belly, outlining the shape of the still-growing bairn there. Worse, when the lady pressed on the side of her belly, movement could be seen there as the bairn responded to its mother's touch.

Eva closed her eyes for a moment, remembering the intense joy of feeling that life within her just a few months ago. She grabbed the wooden arms of the chair to keep her hands from stroking her own belly as she used to. She would press when she felt an arm or leg pushing against the skin and then laugh at the feel of the bairn turning and tumbling at her touch.

She would...

The utter silence in the chamber told her she'd been lost in reverie. Eva opened her eyes and found the others watching her. Arabella's keen and clever gaze had not missed a bit of what she'd done.

'As I said, the rains have kept us prisoner long enough, Eva. I have prevailed upon my husband to take us to a place I think you should see.'

'But, Arabella, you should not...' she began.

Arabella held up her hand to stop her from arguing.

'I have had this discussion with my husband, the midwife and every assorted person here in Drumlui Keep and Glenlui village, and I am done with it. I want to have a last outing before I am shut up in this keep to give birth.' The lady stood, so she did, as well. 'The day is warm and sunny. My husband has agreed to take me there on his horse.'

No one argued with the lady, for her steely stubbornness was honed to a fine edge by the pregnancy. Eva smiled and nodded instead.

'Where is this place?' she asked. 'The one you wish me to see.'

Arabella walked to the window and pointed towards the hills. 'There.'

She joined the lady and looked in the direction she'd indicated. Across this distance she could see what looked to be a small gap in the trees.

''Tis deceiving from here. Once you see it, you will understand,' Arabella assured her. 'In that clearing, Brodie first explained how he'd rather have received more cattle or horses than me in the marriage negotiations between our clans.'

'Pray you tell me he did not!' Eva covered her mouth in shock at what the lady said.

'Oh, aye, he did,' Arabella said, nodding her head.

'And you married him?' she asked.

'Well, when we got to that part of it, there was truly no other choice.' Arabella's sigh then hurt Eva's heart in its poignancy. She'd heard pieces of their story from Nessa, who was an accomplished gossip.

They'd been in love when they married. Enemy clans who would be united through a marriage. Treachery and vengeance were finally defeated by loyalty and strength and love. A tale nearly unbelievable except for the fact that the proof of it was before her nearly every hour of every day since Eva had met them both.

Even this concession to Arabella's desire to escape the keep for a short time spoke of the laird's love for his wife. Now it was Eva's turn to sigh, but hers was filled with a bit of envy and wistfulness over what would never be. A knock on the door drew their attention.

'Shall we go then, Arabella?' the Mackintosh asked in a soft voice. 'As I said...'

'Only an hour. Only with you carrying me in your arms. Only with my maid and Eva. Aye, husband, I understand your conditions.'

The husband in question let out an exasperated breath and nodded. Stepping back, he held out his arm for the lady to take. Which she did without hesitation. Within minutes it seemed, they were mounted and heading out the gates. The small group moved at a slow and even pace along the road and to the trail that led up the mountainside.

Eva marvelled at the hills and the lands, so very different from the ones where she'd lived. The strong winds of the north coast prevented most of the lands there from having tall trees like those that grew here in the Highlands. She had not noticed much of the scenery as they'd travelled south, so this was her first true look at it all.

Although Arabella urged her husband to move faster, he would not relent. Even the lady's complaints that she could have walked up the hill faster than they were travelling caused no change in their pace. The weather held and they soon arrived at the turn in the road that Arabella had pointed out as the entrance to the clearing.

It was as spectacular a view as Arabella had promised. She drew her horse to a halt and waited as the guard who had accompanied them came to help her down. The laird held his wife close and somehow managed to leap to the ground without jostling her at all. A soft kiss between them made Eva turn away. Soon Arabella walked to Eva's side and began pointing out places and landmarks.

Brodie joined his wife and detailed the width and breadth of their lands and identified the lochs and hills that they could see. Arabella grew silent and then glared at him.

'Brodie. You promised,' she said to him, ignoring his matching glare.

'Arabella.'

'Brodie.'

Eva watched this contest of wills with interest. Her mother would never have dared question or second-guess her father. The retribution for such defiance, especially with others watching, would be terrible. Holding her breath, she waited for this tension to break.

'Fine!' he shouted, not at his wife but into the sky. 'An hour, Bella. And Iain will be at the turn of the road. That is all I will allow. And I will not be swayed in this more than that.'

Arabella did not smile until he'd kissed her hard on the mouth and motioned for the guard to follow him out of the clearing. Once they could not hear the sound of the men riding away, they stood in the silence and Eva stared off into the distance at the loch there.

It was peaceful, and she closed her eyes, enjoying it for the moment.

Eva did not fool herself—there was an alternate purpose to this little excursion. She steeled her control for the coming interrogation. When the lady sent her maid off to see how far down the path the guard was, Eva knew it was at hand.

'Will you remain in the keep, Eva?' the lady asked, pacing across a short distance near the edge of the clearing.

'I do not understand, Arabella. Where else would I live?' The lady's curse, not dissimilar to ones her own husband favoured, told her that something was amiss here.

'Did he not ask you?' Eva shrugged at the question. 'No, certainly the daft man did not!' Arabella answered her own query. 'Brodie offered a cottage for you and Rob in the village, if you preferred that to living in the keep.' Before she could reply, a strange expression spread across Arabella's face.

Eva walked to her and examined her face closely. 'Are you well?' A fine sheen of perspiration sat on the lady's forehead and her upper lip.

''Tis nothing, truly,' Arabella said, turning away. 'I did not sleep well last night and my back hurts a bit.' She laughed then, sliding her hand from her belly to her hip and back. 'I suspect I will not be comfortable for some time.'

Eva had a bad feeling about this. Her own labour had begun in the same way—vague pains in her back— but had lasted several days before the true pains struck.

'When is the bairn due, Arabella?'

Instead of answering, the lady leaned over and

grasped her knees, gasping in short, forceful breaths. Then, Arabella grabbed her belly and shook her head as a puddle appeared on the ground at her feet.

'I think the bairn is coming now, Eva.'

Eva let out a curse worthy of her husband and ran to the edge of the clearing. A glance down the road showed no sign of Ailean or the guard.

'She won't be there,' Arabella called to her. 'They... they...'

Are lovers. The words did not have to be spoken for Eva to realise the truth. Arabella allowed her maid to tryst with her lover, the guard assigned them. If anything untoward happened to the lady or the coming bairn, Brodie Mackintosh would have their heads.

Eva ran back and assisted Arabella to sit on a log there, trying to think of how much time had passed. The laird would return in an hour, but would the lady last that long? And if the bairn was turned or other problems existed, what would happen? A low moan echoed across the clearing, telling Eva that things were progressing at an alarming rate.

'Arabella, I am going to run down the trail and find Ailean and the guard. They must get Brodie—' Her words were cut off as Arabella grabbed her arm with an alarming strength and pulled her close.

'You cannot leave me, Eva,' she ordered through clenched teeth. 'Stay. I pray you, stay!'

The terrible hours of fear and pain flooded into her, and Eva shuddered at the thought of what was to come. And how would she survive watching this woman give birth when her own experience still tore her apart, heart and soul? One glance at Arabella's face and the fear filling her eyes gave Eva the answer—she must.

'I will not leave you, Arabella. I am here,' she promised, repeating the words silently to herself.

Though she prayed that these initial signs of an impending birth were simply the earliest ones with hours and possibly days ahead before the bairn arrived, the next minutes proved her hopes false ones. Pain after pain racked the lady's body, and her breathing grew shallow and quick.

After gathering their cloaks and blankets into a pile, she helped Arabella to the ground there, making her as comfortable as possible for the shorter intervals between pains. Surely, the impatient laird would return before his impatient babe arrived? Although she knew it was not yet an hour since the lady's first pain and loss of water, suddenly Arabella called out that she had to push. Not believing it possible, Eva lifted Arabella's skirts and, after gaining permission, gently reached up to check.

Sweet Jesus, the bairn's head was already out!

'Arabella, the babe is coming now,' she said, gathering the lady's garments up and guiding her legs apart and her feet flat on the ground.

With but a few pushes, the bairn slid free of her mother's body. Wrapping the woollen blanket around the small one, Eva wiped the blood and mucous out of her eyes and mouth. A sweet little girl. She didn't know she wept until Arabella spoke.

'Is the bairn well? Is something wrong, Eva? Tell me!' Arabella insisted. Eva shook her head and tried to smile to reassure Arabella.

'Nay, lady. All is well with this one,' Eva said, holding out the bundle to her. ''Tis a girl. A lovely perfect little girl.'

Arabella cried out in joy, and soon both were crying as she gathered the baby to her and kissed her cheeks. 'She is perfect, Eva.' Arabella touched Eva's hand. 'I thank you, friend, for staying at my side.'

Eva could not speak, and the sight of the newborn tore her heart apart bit by bit so she stood away and nodded. 'I will check the road for any sign of Ailean or the laird.' Her throat was thick and words hurt to force them out.

She walked away, keeping her eyes on the road and not on the new bairn or the mother who loved her. She spied the maid and the guard down the road, walking towards her, and called for them. Eva returned to Arabella's side and found her in discomfort again.

'The afterbirth must come out, lady,' she explained.

Eva knelt down in front of Arabella and was preparing to help when Ailean and the guard ran into the clearing. The maid took one look at the situation and fainted. The guard stood open-mouthed in shock at the sight of his lady and the newborn child. At least, he did until Eva ordered him to seek out the laird and get help. Ailean would have to lie where she fell, for the lady's condition was more serious.

'Just let it happen, Arabella,' she urged. 'Do not fight it now.' When the baby cried out, Eva took her and held her close, allowing the lady to follow her body's inclinations without fear for her daughter.

For a moment when she held the bairn, it was as though the months of separation had not happened. For a moment, this was her babe, Mairead. She leaned down and rubbed her head, drawing the edge of the blanket forward and removing more of the fluid and mucous from her. She rubbed her finger down the tender skin of the baby's cheek.

'Mairead,' she whispered. 'My Mairead.'

And she looked up into the eyes of the baby's mother.

The very knowing eyes of Arabella Mackintosh.

Eva drew in a shaking breath and tore herself free from the memories of her own delivery, glancing away from Arabella. Sounds on the road drew her attention then, and suddenly Brodie rode in on the massive black horse.

'What in the name of God is going on here, Bella?' he roared as he leaped down and landed at his wife's feet. He stared first at the lady, and then his gaze moved slowly to Eva. She held out the bairn.

'A daughter, Brodie,' Arabella said. 'That is your daughter.'

For once, the man was stunned. His eyes filled with tears as he let Eva place the precious bundle in his arms. She knew she must get away. She must regain control and get away from the bairn, who looked so much like her own that it was driving her mad.

Eva wanted to weep when Brodie knelt at Arabella's side and huddled close to her, the babe between them. Whispered words of love and surprise tore at her again. She'd never heard those words. Eirik had never seen his daughter. The pain of it burned through her, leaving her empty and aching. She did not realise she'd actually moved away until Brodie's voice called her back into the clearing.

'Eva,' he said, calling her closer. 'I've sent Iain for help. Rob's sister will be here soon, but can you tend to Arabella until she does?'

'Of course,' Eva said.

'Brodie.' He turned at the sound of his wife's call. 'She had tended to me. She delivered our child.'

'I only meant…' He shrugged, and she wanted to laugh. The brave, fierce, always-in-charge laird who now looked helpless. Who was…

'I have not tended to births before, laird,' Eva said. 'But I think Arabella is doing well. As is the babe. I will remain with her while mayhap you see to arrangements to get her back to the keep?'

His reaction at being given a task made even Arabella smile. The woman would clearly bear children with ease, and Eva silently marvelled at her while trying not to think too much about her own experiences.

And while trying not to stare at the newborn bairn now being held by her mother. Eva's arms shook with emptiness with every glance. Luckily, the tense quiet in the clearing was soon filled with the arrival of many others.

Margaret rode in alone, ahead of the rest of those approaching, and was at Arabella's side in scant seconds, relieving Eva of her duties. With a few direct questions and a quick examination of mother and child, the clan's healer declared all was well. It was as though everyone let out their held breath and relaxed then. As Margaret saw to the lady, the laird approached her now.

'I cannot thank you enough for what you have done for my wife and…daughter.' His voice shook with emotion at the words. 'If you have any need of my help, you have but to ask, lady.' Eva shivered at the intensity of his words, almost as though hearing something that had yet to happen or words yet to be spoken. Margaret called to him, and he strode to his wife's side.

Soon, with the efficiency of a commander in the midst of a battle, Margaret had Arabella and the babe placed in a well-padded wagon for the journey back to the keep. Before Brodie called for them to leave, Arabella motioned her over. Taking hold of her hand, she tugged Eva closer so none would hear their words.

'I am forever in your debt, Eva,' Arabella whispered. Meeting her gaze and holding it, the lady continued, 'We will speak later.'

'Lady…' she began, shaking her head. 'There is nothing to—'

'There is everything, Eva. Be at peace for now though,' Arabella said. Brodie called out to her, and the lady released her hand, allowing her to retreat.

The wagon began to move, and just when Eva thought she would survive this trail, the world around her crashed to the ground. Arabella, under Margaret's direction, loosened the ties of the gown and tugged it down, placing the babe at her breast.

As though at her own, Eva swore she could feel the soft, gentle mouth on her own nipple. Her breasts swelled and once again it felt as though they filled with milk. Crossing her arms over her chest, Eva pressed against the sensation. Mairead was gone by the time her milk had come in, so she'd never had the chance to nurse her bairn as Arabella did now.

Barely able to withstand the need to weep, Eva allowed one of the guards to help her on to her horse and she followed the group blindly back to Drumlui. Every second forced her closer to a complete loss of control and overwhelming grief. Eva waited only until the lady was moved inside to seek out her chamber. Sending Nessa away, she stood in the middle of the empty room and struggled against the tide of emotions flooding into her.

When she realised that the blood on her own gown was not the lady's but her own and that her menses was begun, she lost every shred of control. Eva made it over to the corner before collapsing to her knees and sobbing out her grief and loss. When her tears ran out, she lay exhausted and empty there on the floor.

She never heard the door open or knew that Rob had entered.

Chapter Fifteen

It had taken every bit of Rob's self-control not to tear open the door to their chamber at the sounds coming from within it.

He'd returned from a trip to the other side of the village to find the keep and its people in an uproar. News of Arabella's sudden delivery spread through the keep, as did his wife's part in the birth. Words of praise met his every step as he sought out Brodie above stairs to find out what had happened. The bairn was not due for weeks, and an early arrival could mean problems in addition to the usual dangers of childbirth.

Brodie smiled more than Rob had ever seen him smile before, but that was not surprising in this situation. He allowed Rob a quick peek at the babe before returning to his wife in their chambers and a word to Rob about Eva's help in the birth. Which sent him seeking her out. Which brought him here, to their door.

The sounds coming from within reminded him of a wounded animal, not a person. An animal in pain.

He'd witnessed Eva crying before—while she was ill in the cottage, when her father beat her—but this sounded as though her soul was being rent in two. His own heart pounded at such a sound, and his instinct was to tear the door off its hinges and somehow stop her from crying. Rob had his hand on the door when the sobbing stopped.

Easing the door open, he peered into the dark chamber and nearly stumbled at the sight before him.

Eva lay curled up in the corner, her arms wrapped around her as she slowly rocked to and fro. The terrible wailing had become a soft whimpering, and then silence reigned.

What was going on here? What had happened to her? Had the shock of assisting Arabella in the birth sent her into such an emotional state as this? And, as much as he told himself she would not appreciate his interference, he found he very much wanted to do something to help her.

But what?

Standing there, he decided to make his presence known and give her the opportunity to regain control of herself. Stepping back quietly, he closed the door and then knocked on it, saying her name aloud.

'Lady Eva? Are you within?' His query was met with continuing silence. He waited several seconds and then knocked again, calling her name. 'Eva?'

Now, Rob opened the door and entered. She sat on the edge of the bed, facing away from him. A furtive wipe of her cheeks followed before she spoke.

'Aye?'

'Are you well? Brodie said you helped Arabella with the bairn.' He walked closer, but stopped when her whole body stiffened at his approach.

'I do not feel well,' she whispered back, clutching her belly yet still not facing him.

'Did seeing the birth turn your stomach?' he asked. 'I do not think I would want to witness it,' he admitted. Very few men did and, in his opinion, that was just fine.

'Nay.' She shook but did not turn her head in reply. ''Tis…' She cleared her throat. 'My courses have begun.'

That explained much to him. Both her anguish and her emotional upheaval. He'd known enough women to know that each reacted differently during this time of…

'Margaret is still with Arabella. Let me seek her out for some remedy to ease your discomfort.'

Rob was uncomfortable enough discussing such matters, but considered that it might now be something he faced since he was a married man. If he hurried a bit too much, no man would blame him. And when Eva did not try to stop or slow his departure, he suspected that she was relieved by his absence.

A short while later, he once more stood outside his chambers, leaning against the wall and listening. Now though, Margaret was within and speaking to Eva. The low murmurings continued, back and forth, with Margaret doing most of the talking. As she usually did. He smiled then, knowing that his sister would help Eva. When the door opened, he stood and looked past his sister.

'I gave her something to ease her pains,' Margaret said, nodding back at the woman inside. 'It will help her sleep.'

'What should I do?' Rob asked, running his hands

through his hair and feeling completely out of place. Margaret stared at him as though he'd grown another head and shook hers. Pulling the door closed, she stepped closer.

'When did you become such a daft man?' she asked, poking him in the chest.

'What?'

'There is nothing to be done. Some women have an easy time of it each month and others suffer. Just like childbirth. Eva said hers were the troublesome kind.'

Rob felt a little sick then at this discussion. Knowing these matters went on around him was one thing, talking about them with his sister or his wife was yet another.

'Should I sleep elsewhere this night?' he asked. He did not wish to add to whatever burdened Eva. If she would sleep better alone, he could accommodate her wish to.

Margaret gave him that look once more and then burst out laughing. ''Tis a wonder you have survived as long as you have, Rob. Unless you plan to sleep apart every month of the rest of your married life, I would not suggest you begin now.'

'I do not wish her to suffer.'

The words escaped him then, revealing more than he'd expected to feel and more than he wished to admit. In spite of the fact that neither one of them had entered this marriage willingly or without reservations, he did not want to see her suffer. And something did haunt and hurt her. Something more than the simple monthly aches that women bore. Margaret's expression softened then, and she patted his arm.

'All will be well,' she reassured him. 'I must get

back to Arabella now. Should I check back before I leave the keep?'

'Nay,' he said. 'I will see to her.'

A glimmer of something flashed in his sister's gaze then, but she said nothing else. A nod and she was gone, walking in her purposeful gait away from him.

Rob opened the door and entered. Eva yet sat on the edge of the bed, looking pale and a bit lost.

'Margaret gave you something?' he asked, crouching before her so she would meet his gaze.

When he saw the emptiness and pain there, he found that part of him wanted to reach out and pull her close and tell her everything would be well. No, he wanted to make everything good for her.

'Aye. Something to help the pains and for sleep,' she said, holding out the small bottle she yet held wrapped in her hand.

'If you wish…' he began.

'If you wish…' she said, too.

'Go ahead,' he said, watching her face.

'If you wish me to sleep elsewhere, while my… While I…' She gestured around herself, but he understood. 'I would understand.' Shrugging, she met his gaze. 'I am still not accustomed to sharing a bed with a man and now this.'

Once more, he was reminded of all the changes she faced in marriage—ones he'd never considered before. And Rob realised they'd fallen into a routine that had her abed before he entered the chamber at night over these last weeks. Whether consciously or not, he'd known she was reticent to undress before him and so he waited until she'd settled before entering.

'Since this will be a usual occurrence,' he said softly, 'I see no reason why you should do that.'

'My father...' She shook her head then and shrugged. 'If that is your wish.'

'It is,' he said, standing and stepping back. 'Why not seek your rest now? Should Nessa bring you something to eat or will you come to the hall for supper?' A stricken expression filled her gaze then, and he barely saw it before she hid it.

'I need nothing,' she whispered.

'The hall will be a boisterous place this evening, so if you do not feel well, it might be best if you sought refuge here instead. I will explain to Brodie, if he needs to know.' Rob walked to the door then. 'But, I doubt anything you do will raise any issue with him now. You were there when Arabella needed you and saw her through the birth.'

'They are well?' she asked.

'Aye. Well, hale and hardy. The midwife is amazed at the ease of the birth and the size of the bairn.'

'Was he disappointed?' she asked, turning for the first time to look at him.

'Disappointed?' Rob shook his head. 'His wife survived. The bairn survived. He said he feels blessed.'

Tears filled her eyes then, and she blinked against them. Soon they poured down her cheeks, and he went to her, wiping them away. 'Why do you cry? All is well.'

''Twas not a son. Does not every man want a son rather than a daughter?'

Rob knew that if he ever met up with Ramsey MacKay, the man would not walk away unscathed. In more than physical ways, he'd hurt this woman, his only daughter. Someone should make the man pay for those sins. He found it difficult to answer her just then. Taking in and releasing a breath, he shook his head.

'Oh, aye, Brodie wants a son just like any man does. But, fear not, he will treasure this and any daughter born to him and Bella.'

'I pray you forgive me for my behaviour.' She moved from him and put the bottle on the table next to the bed. 'I think I will retire and wait for it to pass.'

He watched as she poured most of the bottle's contents into a cup and filled it the rest of the way with the wine there in the pitcher. It was more wine than he'd seen her drink before. She lifted it to her mouth and drank it down. In one smooth swallow. Until it was empty. Then she turned to him. Rob could not help the raised eyebrow that greeted her when she did.

'I wish to ease the pain,' she said softly, in explanation.

Rob knew then that she spoke of something more than the simple, usual discomforts of a woman's monthly bleeding. She spoke of a pain that tore a person in two. A pain that could destroy a spirit. He shifted on his feet and nodded.

Instead of learning more about this woman, his wife, each day, Rob suspected that she carried some secrets so deep within her that he doubted they would ever be exposed.

'I will return later. Rest well, Eva.'

Rob left and spent several hours trying to carry out his duties, but his thoughts returned time after time to the woman he married. After making himself useful and seeing to things that Brodie usually would, he made his way to their chambers.

Eva did not move or respond to his words when he spoke her name. With the bedcovers tucked high around her shoulders, all he could see was her face and the long braid of her hair. He undressed and slid in next to her, watching her pale face for any sign of a reaction.

And saw nothing.

Once he settled next to her, Rob adjusted the covers and closed his eyes. He listened to the sound of her breathing, deep and even, next to him while considering the woman there.

Neither Brodie nor anyone who'd witnessed the birth spoke of Eva being distraught or upset during it. Her calm manner and reassuring words had kept Arabella from panic and the babe from harm. Margaret praised her. Brodie praised her. It seemed that only when she reached the privacy of their chambers did she fall apart.

And that would be the way he would describe her condition when he'd returned and found her on the floor.

He shifted onto his side and studied her features. Now, after several weeks of recovery time, her cheeks filled out nicely and her gowns no longer hung like rags on her body. The thing that had not changed was her acceptance of their marriage or him. Since he was not likely to force the issue, he'd not given it much thought.

His life had returned to the way it had been before his marriage to her—he carried out his duties, trained the warriors, consulted with Brodie on clan matters and continued to live in the keep. Other than sleeping in her bed each night and being polite when their paths crossed, it was much like not being married.

Except for the way his body reminded him that they were not truly married. Each morning on rising from bed. During the day when he would hear her voice. When their hands touched during meals or while walking together. Each evening when they shared a bed and yet did not.

He'd been waiting for a sign from her—any sign that she was willing to move on from their sorry beginning and begin to live as man and wife. And he'd found none.

She whimpered then in her sleep, and he watched as her brow gathered in a frown and then her lips formed soundless words.

'Hush now,' he whispered to her. 'All will be well.'

When she moved towards him, shifting her body until she touched his, Rob was stunned. Oh, many morns he found her under his arm or against his back, but he thought he was the one bringing such movement about. As he watched, Eva inched over closer and closer until their bodies touched. Then she sighed and sank back into the silent, deep sleep of the laudanum she'd taken.

How did she trust him when she slept but not while awake? He thought back on those nights together, from the first one in the cottage until this one. At some point, one he did not remember, he'd stopped using the bedcovers as a barrier between them and she'd never noticed it or spoke of it. She must surely trust him. Now if she would do so in the light of day, things might be different between them.

Puzzled by his reactions to her, Rob slid his arm

over her and drew her in to his side. She eased against him, sighing again and then not moving.

When had it become important for him to have a real marriage with her? Certainly not their first weeks, after finding her and returning her to her father's house for the ceremony. And not while they travelled back here to Glenlui. And certainly not when she made it clear she did not want his physical attentions. But somehow, some time in these last days, as his life returned to what he was accustomed to, the hollowness of it bothered him.

Especially as Margaret and Magnus grew closer and his sister spoke of marrying—a step he'd never thought his sister would take after her deep mourning for the loss of her husband. Especially as Brodie and Arabella's happiness at the impending birth of their first child. And most especially, as life in Glenlui and the Clan Mackintosh settled back into the way it was before the great upheaval of the last nearly two years.

'Give her time,' Brodie had counselled him. Thinking on it now, it seemed a good plan, but he would not wait for her to come to him forever. He would not sit around pining for a wife who had no desire for him. She trusted him, at least in her sleep. He would use that as a starting place. If she was truly never willing, he did not know what he would do, for it was a situation he'd never faced before in his life.

He understood duty, and he understood his place in the clan. Personal happiness, as Brodie told him once, was not something that always followed duty. Satisfaction was all one could hope for in carrying out their duty to kith and kin. Even though he knew others valued him only for what they could get or do through him, he wanted it to be different with this woman, his wife. Though it had certainly begun as a political marriage, that did not mean it could not be more or be different.

Watching her now, he wanted more with her. In spite of his words to the contrary, she was brave and strong. She had passion within her and a strong sense of commitment, too. She was pragmatic and did what she needed to do to survive. But, he'd seen the longing in her gaze. And the sadness of loss.

Mayhap if he gave her more time, she would overcome the grief that had her in its grip and she would want more? Mayhap she would want…him?

He chuckled then at such a thought, such a need within him. Robbie Mackintosh, the chief's close friend and confidant. Robbie Mackintosh, leader of the clan's warriors. Robbie Mackintosh, who never knew an empty bed or left a lover unsatisfied.

And now, Robbie Mackintosh, a man who wanted his wife's attentions.

Oh, how far he'd fallen and how sad a man he'd become!

When Eva turned and, pressing her back and bottom against him, settled once more, Rob knew he would find a way to approach her. He must.

The rest of the hours between then and dawn were filled with strategies and plans, all focused on the woman who slumbered unknowing in his arms. She would discover that Robbie Mackintosh was a man who never lost a battle he set out to win.

Chapter Sixteen

She'd lied.

Eva had lied to Margaret about her menses. And about how much pain she was suffering.

She'd done it for one reason—she needed the oblivion of the concoction Margaret would offer her. Though she'd sworn to never again cede control of herself to such a potion, she sought it and savoured it that night to wipe away the memories and the pain. It was the running away that Rob disdained so much, but it had been her only choice. Well, other than fracturing into pieces that could never be put back in their places. Other than losing complete control of herself and revealing everything she could not reveal. So, she'd let Rob call Margaret, and she'd greedily accepted the small bottle. She drank it all, for the elixir offered the blackness she needed so much in that moment.

Now, two days later, Eva knew she must face the lady and her questions.

Pressing her palms on her gown, she smoothed it down as she stood. Nessa had cautiously approached her this morn to help her dress and fix her hair. The girl said she'd been sent away by Rob when he'd returned and found Eva so upset. Her husband had not spoken of it or anything else between them since then. He simply came to their chambers, enquired after her health and made certain that meals were brought and she was not disturbed. She knew he slept at her side each night. But, what he thought or what excuse or explanation he was giving the laird and lady and others, she knew not.

As she sent word to Arabella and asked for a moment to speak to her, Eva knew that what had happened had helped in some way to release all the pent-up grief and sadness she'd been carrying. Like a blister that finally broke and released its vitriol, her dammed-up grief was now free. Oh, she would bear the loss of her daughter's father and her inability to find the bairn and keep her forever. And she knew she must be strong if there was to be any hope of surviving such a loss as this.

When Nessa came to say the lady would receive her, Eva had still not decided what she would do when the inevitable questioning began. There was no doubt that Arabella knew the truth. She'd witnessed and heard Eva call the babe by a name. She'd seen Eva react to her advanced pregnancy, and she realised that Eva knew more than a maiden who'd never tended a birth knew. But, should Eva speak the truth or continue to lie as her father had made her swear to do?

Eva made her way to the lady's chamber and was surprised when Arabella opened the door herself and bade her enter. Eva prepared herself for the sound and sight and even smell of the new babe only to find they were completely alone.

'I thought we should have some privacy to speak, Eva. Would you like wine?'

'Nay,' she said. 'Sit. I should serve you.'

'All I have done is lie abed and be waited on these last two days. I need to move around a bit.' Arabella poured wine in two cups anyway and held one out to Eva.

'How do you feel? Is the babe…?' Eva looked around again, surprised at the babe's absence.

'She is well, thanks to your efforts.'

Arabella drank from her cup and then sat down. Eva sat on the nearest chair to the lady. After a few, heavy moments of silence, Arabella met her gaze. Eva tried to prepare herself for what the lady would say, but the words were a complete surprise.

'I would never have been so cruel as to have you attend me these last weeks if I had known, Eva. Pray forgive me for causing you such pain.'

Whatever she'd expected, these words, this apology, was not it. Tears came unbidden at words of such kindness. No one had truly ever cared about her comfort or peace until she'd come here to this place and these people. Eva wiped her eyes and shrugged.

'You did not know, Arabella. I knew you were not being unkind.' She could not pretend any more to this compassionate woman.

Arabella reached out and took her hand, entwining their fingers before asking the question that would lead to many others.

'Your daughter—did she die?' she whispered.

Eva shook her head and blinked at the tears. 'Nay. As far as I know, she still lives.'

'How old is she?'

'Nigh to three months,' she said. Had that much time passed already? Thinking on it, Eva realised it had—though much of it had been spent in a blur of loss and pain and confusion.

'When did you last see her?' Eva fought for control now.

'The day she was born.'

Silence met those words and then a harsh curse uttered by a woman who was known for her genteel ways.

'Does Rob know?' Arabella asked. Eva stood then and paced around the chamber.

'Nay. He thinks I mourn for a lost lover. I have not... I cannot tell him the truth.'

The lady grew silent then as though out of questions to ask, but Eva knew there would be more. There was so much yet unspoken over this matter, and the lady was a fierce defender of those she called friend.

'Telling him now 'twill do no good, Arabella,' she said. 'It will only cause more questions that I cannot answer. I should not even be telling you.' Her voice took on a sharper edge than she'd meant to do, causing Arabella to stare at her.

'Your father?' Arabella asked or guessed.

'He swore she would be safe and cared for if I did as he ordered. After he—' She stopped before the worst of it came pouring out. 'If I reveal the truth about her, he will not protect her.' Eva twisted her hands and met Arabella's stare now. 'I cannot tell.'

Arabella motioned for her to sit, so Eva did. Once again, the lady took her hand.

'In these situations, there is nothing you can do. Oh, believe me, Eva, you are not the first noblewoman to have a bairn in secret and have to let it be raised by oth-

ers. Unless you plan to challenge your father in this...'
Arabella paused and Eva shuddered her response '...you
must try to move on with your life. The life that your
father promised would protect her.'

Eva knew the truth of her words, but her heart could
not accept them. Not yet.

'I think you should tell Robbie the truth of it,' Arabella said softly. 'But I understand why you do not.
He's a good man, Eva. An honourable man who will
do his duty to his family and his clan. He would understand,' she urged.

But Arabella did not know the whole story. About
Eva running away and trying to escape the marriage.
About her suspicions of her father's part in manipulat-
ing Rob into it. It was Rob's honour that trapped him
in this marriage, even if he did not know it. And his
value to Brodie Mackintosh. So, in the face of all those
unspoken secrets, Eva remained silent now.

'Very well, I will accept your decision over this.
And, have no fear—this all remains between us. I have
not spoken of it even to my husband.'

Eva had some notion of how important that was, for
Arabella held nothing back from her husband. She'd
witnessed that many times since her arrival here. They
valued each other's company and opinions and kept
nothing from each other. She envied them that.

'My thanks, Arabella,' she said, rising to stand once
more. 'In some way, just speaking of it, of her, with
you has helped.'

'Mairead? You named her Mairead?' the lady asked.

'Aye.'

'And Mairead's father? His name?'

'I should not...' She shook her head. Speaking his

name hurt so much. Especially knowing his blood was on her hands.

'I will pray for them both, Eva. And for you, so that you have the strength you need to overcome the pain and grief that yet burdens you.' Arabella stood then and walked with her to the door of the chamber. 'Come to me if you have need to speak of such things. Do not let the sorrow of the past destroy any future happiness you might claim, or your father has won.'

Her words were like those of someone who had suffered at the hands of their father. Eva searched the lady's face for some clue of it.

'My father blamed me for my mother's death. We have only made our peace recently,' she explained.

'Ramsey MacKay will make peace with no one,' Eva said. 'I do not fool myself into believing that he would ever relent in this or forgive me for my…foolish and regrettable behaviour.'

'Then,' Arabella whispered as they reached the door, 'you must get revenge by living a life he would not want you to have. You must forgive yourself and move past this pain. Defy him, Eva. Defy him and live well.'

Eva smiled at the lady's determination and resolve. Without even knowing the MacKay, she understood. As Eva walked into the corridor, the other door in the chamber opened and Ailean entered, carrying the babe in her arms.

'You do not have to attend me every day, Eva. Take some time to learn our clan and the village,' she said, loud enough for the maid to hear. 'And your husband,' she whispered for only Eva's hearing.

Eva could only nod in reply. The lady's once-again unexpected kindness and consideration eased her pain.

She pulled the door closed behind her and stood there, feeling somehow lighter than she had in months. Mayhap the fact that someone else knew about Mairead made it different? Mayhap finally being able to speak to someone as though she existed, that she did exist, would bring her some measure of peace?

For now, Eva went back to her chambers. She'd been so mired in sadness that she had never truly settled in her rooms. The last weeks had been as a guest rather than one of the clan.

Was Arabella correct? Would claiming a life here be the best thing for her? Could she do such a thing?

As she walked around the chamber, rearranging some of the furniture, Eva considered the possibility of it and what it would mean. The first thing would be to give up on seeking her daughter.

The thought of it made her stumble, and she grabbed on to the bedpost for support.

She could never do that. Never. And Arabella had not suggested forgetting her daughter, she'd suggested moving on into the life she had now.

Taking a deep breath and letting it out, Eva took a fresh look at the chamber and decided to make it more her own...well, and her husband's. From the look of it, he was still living partly here and partly in his old chamber. Calling Nessa to her, Eva set out to make this room more comfortable.

A few hours later, she was quite pleased with their efforts and felt better for the exertion of the work involved.

After a short respite and a light meal, Eva decided to speak to Margaret. She took the empty bottle from the place where it yet sat on the table and brought it to return it to Rob's sister. With no clear decision made, Eva only knew she wanted Margaret's counsel, too.

Not about the babe but about...her husband.

It was becoming a common occurrence, it seemed. For him to be wandering through the keep and the village searching for his wife. But, if he was honest with himself, it pleased him that she was not lying abed with that lost expression in her eyes. When Nessa told him that Eva had left the keep after midday meal, he smiled and went back to his duties with Brodie.

Although he spent a good deal of his time at Brodie's side, serving as a counsellor, much of his time was spent in charge of training the Mackintosh warriors so they would always be ready to protect the clan and its interests.

One of their best fighters, honed in battle and practice, Rob was seen as the one to beat in any training session or challenge. And that afternoon saw many challenges made and answered before he called a halt to it.

The physical work kept his mind busy trying to outthink his opponents. He spoke to the commanders and recommended changes to the training routines, suggesting a few of their warriors to take on new or different roles. Content at what he'd accomplished, he returned to his, their, chamber, seeking Eva.

Even now, hours later, she'd still not returned. Without much thought on it, he soon rode to the village, first to Margaret's cottage, to find her.

Unlike previous times, he worried more about her endurance than her disappearance. Which brought him up short. His horse snorted and blew beneath him, not happy with the curt pull on the reins that brought them to a halt.

'Twas natural, of course, to worry over her condition considering these last days. Even when she'd awakened after the long, deep slumber brought about by the laudanum, Eva had not spoken unless he spoke first. She'd remained in their chamber, in bed, since. Now to find her gone from the keep did worry him.

Which worried him.

He touched his heels to the horse's sides and rode to the village. Following the paths through, he soon sat before Margaret's cottage. No voices or sounds came from within it, so he climbed down and opened the door.

No one was home. Not unusual, considering Margaret's tasks as healer. But what was unusual was the sight before him as he stood there wondering where Eva was.

She walked at his sister's side, carrying a basket on her arm, along the road that led west. Though not animated, they engaged in some conversation as they headed for Margaret's cottage. Eva managed to keep pace with his sister, who could walk faster than most, and only slowed when she looked up and saw him there.

'Good day, Robbie,' Margaret called out. 'I am glad you have come.' Margaret threw her arms around him and hugged him. 'Will you stay for the evening meal? 'Twill not be as grand as in Brodie's hall, but it will fill your belly.' At his hesitation, she nodded at Eva. 'Eva would like to, if you agreed.'

'Then we shall stay.'

He was transfixed by the hint of a smile that curved

the corners of her mouth ever so slightly. Her cheeks yet bore dark circles under her eyes, but she seemed recovered or, at least, recovering.

'Come, Magnus will return soon and you two can stay out of our way while I finish cooking,' Margaret said.

Rob opened the door and allowed the women to enter first. No matter when he came here, it felt warm and welcoming. Watching as Eva helped Margaret in sorting out the items in her basket before putting them away, ready for the next use, Rob thought her more at ease than when she was with him alone.

Magnus arrived, and he followed the man outside, where they chopped and carried in wood for the fire. Rob noticed that the man seemed very much accustomed to the task.

'Rob, I have a question for you,' Magnus said after they finished stocking the woodpile and seeing to the cows Margaret kept in the pen behind her house.

Rob suspected he knew what the question was, but he waited on his friend. He dipped his hands in the bucket nearby and washed the dirt from his hands as he waited.

'I want to marry your sister,' he said gruffly.

'What does Margaret say?' Rob asked back.

'The lass said aye.' Magnus met his gaze then and smiled. 'I did not think she would.'

'Because of Conall?'

'Aye. She loved him, I ken.'

'She did love him, Magnus, but I suspect she loves you, too.' Margaret and Conall's had been a love match, a surprise to their families.

'Aye, she does,' he said with a laugh. 'But marrying is a different matter, and I had my doubts. It would make her happy to have your blessing, Rob.'

'Though neither of you need it, you have it, Magnus. I wish you both much happiness.'

'Come inside, I want to tell her.'

Magnus led them into the cottage. Margaret and Eva were in the middle of placing bowls and cups on the table when the man ran to Margaret and lifted her from her feet.

'He said aye, Margaret!' he said before kissing her in what Rob could only describe as a scorching fashion. The love and heat between the two was so obvious that even he could see it.

'Mayhap this is not the best night for us to remain?' he asked, nodding at Eva.

Margaret pushed out of Magnus's arms and laughed as she smoothed her hair and her gown. 'Nay! You will stay and eat.'

He sat next to Eva and watched as the two never quite stopped touching each other. As Magnus helped carry the stew and bread to the table, as Margaret poured ale into the cups and all through the meal, their hands were never apart for long. His own wife noticed as well, as he discovered when their own gazes met as they both looked away from a more passionate caress.

Rob was glad for them. In spite of the condition of his own marriage, he was pleased that his sister had found love again. She had been integral to the success of their opposition to their cousin when he'd seized control of the clan through betrayal and subterfuge. And she'd paid the ultimate price for her involvement—the loss of her husband, killed because of her involvement…and his.

So, if giving her his blessing or approval mattered, she had it tenfold.

The meal was filling, and the conversation good as even Eva joined in. Much of it focused on him and Margaret and then on the struggle to regain their clan and lands. She asked questions, intelligent and explicit questions, and seemed truly interested in what had happened and the how of it. And when it ended with Margaret explaining how she and Magnus had grown closer through it, Rob knew it was time to go.

'Lady?' he said, standing and holding out his hand. 'If you are ready, we can return to the keep and leave these two to their own company.'

'My thanks, Margaret, for your company and counsel today. And for letting me accompany you on your visits,' Eva said. 'And Magnus, felicitations on your upcoming marriage. May you two have every happiness.' She followed him out the door.

'Did you walk here, lady?' he asked.

'Aye.' Rob glanced at her face and noticed the lines of exhaustion beginning around her eyes.

'If you speak to one of the lads in the stable, you can have a horse for your use. If you do not like the one who carried you to Glenlui, there are others you could ride.'

'I needed to walk. It felt good to move,' she said as she looked away.

Rob took the reins and swung up on to the horse. He held his hand out to her then.

''Tis your choice, lady. But not now. I can see the tiredness in your face.'

'Aye. I am tired,' she said, accepting his help.

Pulling her up, he seated her across his legs, trying to ignore the soft curves beneath his touch. Or the way she did not hold herself away from him this time.

'We will be at the keep, and you can seek your bed in a short while,' he said, guiding the horse to the road and beginning the journey up to the keep.

His words were the last until they reached their chambers, for she nearly fell asleep against him. He held her in his arms and carried up the stairs, and she did not resist him. She must be very tired not to refuse his touch.

He reached their chambers and placed her on her feet to open the door. She lifted the latch and pushed the door open.

Rob did not recognise the chamber before him.

'What happened here?' he asked, as his wife turned to face him.

Chapter Seventeen

'I thought to make it more comfortable for you,' Eva replied as Rob closed the door behind them.

Truly, she wanted to drop from exhaustion into the bed that now lay against one of the side walls rather than its original position. Placed there, it gave more room in the chamber for their trunks and even a small sitting area. Which she'd filled with two chairs claimed from a storage room below stairs after asking the steward. She would make cushions for both in the coming days.

'No wonder you are exhausted,' he said, though she thought she might have heard a bit of approval in his voice.

'I may have tried to do too much in one day, but I woke feeling the need to do something,' she admitted. 'Nessa helped, as did Fergus and one or two of the servants.' He stared at her then before speaking, examining her face closely. Pointing to the chest in the corner, he asked.

'Is that from my old chamber?'

''Tis,' she said, nodding and walking to it. 'We

moved your garments and cloaks from the two small trunks into this larger one.' Eva pointed out the other big change. 'By moving the bed to there, we could put the chairs on this side of the hearth, to capture the heat on cold days.'

Her stomach felt nervous now, waiting for his reaction. What had seemed so sensible this morn now might face his displeasure. She realised now that she should have asked him before she'd made the changes.

'I cannot believe you had enough strength to do all this, lady.' He turned around again, noticing more of the ways she'd moved or rearranged the items in the room. 'It makes it more comfortable and gives us a place to sit.'

'So, you do not object? I can move things back if you do not like it,' she offered.

'Nay. Leave it as you have set it.' He walked over and sat in one of the chairs, rubbing his hands along the wooden arms of it and nodding. 'Sit. Let me see you in your handiwork,' he said.

Eva walked to the other chair and sat down, the unexpected nervousness fluttering in her belly as she did. He seemed pleased over the changes. As she watched his face, he nodded again and smiled at her.

'This makes the question Arabella asked me more difficult.' He stood and walked to the hearth. 'After visiting Margaret this night, I thought I knew my own mind, but now, I am not so certain.'

'What did Arabella ask you?' Eva clasped her hands on her lap, awaiting his reply. He strode across the chamber and crouched before her, placing his large hand over hers.

'Why do you look as though disaster will befall you?'

'Mayhap because it does each time someone makes a decision on my behalf?'

The words were out before she could stop them. 'Twas the truth, but what man wanted to hear that for it was a clear question of his authority. Her father would have backhanded her by now. But Rob… Eva realised that she did not fear physical harm from this man who controlled her life in a way her father never had.

'Just so,' he said in a quiet voice before he stood and walked back to the hearth. 'Arabella asked if we would like a cottage in the village rather than living here in the keep. With everything that has happened, I had no chance to speak to you about it.' She remembered now Arabella mentioning something about this just before going into her precipitous labour.

'And what did you tell her?' she asked, awaiting his decision. He stared at her with wide eyes then, apparently surprised by her words. But why?

'I told her I would discuss it with you before making a decision.' His brow raised over his left eye in question. 'I thought you would like to have a say in this, since it affects both of us.'

A man willing to listen to a woman's, his wife's, mind on a matter under discussion was unfamiliar to her. These Mackintoshes were a strange breed. From their chief down through his men, they did things differently here than she had ever seen before. She nodded.

'What is your view on this?' she asked.

'At first,' he began, 'I thought you would be happier here in the keep, with the others and Arabella near. Then, today, this night, having a meal with Margaret and Magnus in their home, I thought you might like a place in the village.' He looked at her. 'It will be large enough to be appropriate for your status, and she will assign servants to see to your care.'

She would be happier? She might like a place? Appropriate to her status? What words were these? 'Twas almost as though he considered her more important than himself? How could that be? Her confusion must have shown on her face, for he approached once more and sat in the chair at her side.

'I have lived here all my life and know everyone here, so the place where we live matters not to me,' he explained. 'Here or in the village—either place would suit me.' He shifted to face her. 'What would be your preference?'

She forced her mouth to stay closed or it would have gaped like a fish caught on a line! Her opinions and preferences never mattered before. But his interest seemed genuine, so she gave it now.

'There is a part of me that yearns for a place of my, our, own, away from all the frenzy of the keep. But, I have only lived within one in my life and know not if I would be happy in a cottage away from it.'

'There is something else that might influence your opinion. Since our marriage and return here, I have not yet travelled on Brodie's behalf, but I will. Although you can accompany me on some of those assignments, many times you must remain here.'

'I may accompany you?' she asked.

Once more, her own experience was completely different from what he offered. Her mother rarely left their home, and when her father travelled for clan matters or pleasure, he left her behind—and usually brought along his leman instead. Now this man was offering a chance to do something she'd only dreamed of doing. Mackintoshes were so different than MacKays!

'You would do that? Take me along?'

'As I said, not always, but when it's possible and if you wish to join me…'

Eva tried not to be overwhelmed by his words and the promise in them. He'd asked her opinion and seemed sincere in his desire to know it. So…

'All of your duties centre on your chieftain, do they not?' she asked. At his nod, she continued, 'Then living here would be easier for you?' He nodded again, watching her in silence. 'It would seem that remaining here would work best, then.'

'So, you wish to live here in the keep?' he asked.

''Tis possible my opinion might change later, but for now, 'twould seem the right thing to do.'

''Twould be a waste of all your good efforts so soon after you'd done this. I will tell Arabella, or you can inform her on the morrow.'

He stood then and glanced around the chamber as though searching for something. Then he walked to the door and lifted the latch,

'I must speak to Fergus before he retires. I will return shortly.' And then he was gone.

Eva sat in silence in the chair for a few minutes, listening to the fire crackle and considering what had happened just then.

For one thing, she believed it was the first actual conversation between them that accomplished something other than raising suspicions or mistrust.

Another thing was that they'd made a decision together. About something of importance to both of them.

A decision and not an order from the man who ruled her life.

And now, just now, he'd left to give her privacy to undress and prepare for bed. Oh, he'd not said that was the reason he was leaving, but she knew it all the same. He gave her time each night to get into the bed before he entered the chamber. Some nights she pretended sleep and others she did truly sleep.

Nessa knocked and entered, seeing to removing her gown and brushing her hair, while the thoughts of the conversation just over consumed Eva. She did not remember her father ever asking her mother's counsel when making a decision. She could not remember her mother ever being bold enough to offer it.

Soon, she climbed under the bedcovers and Nessa left, extinguishing most of the candles that lit the chamber. The fire yet threw some shadows against the wall, but it would soon settle for the night, as well. Lying there, she noticed the first ache in her shoulders, back and legs. Aye, she'd done too much this day, although the results were most pleasing…

As was his reaction.

After so many confrontations and unpleasant words between them, this, this discussion and mutual agreement was a change and a welcome one at that. Is this what their future would be like? If she could finally accept it? Turning onto her side and wincing at the soreness, she thought it very well might be.

From all the things she'd heard about Rob Mackintosh from the women in his life, it might not be the marriage of fear that she'd expected after all. Though Margaret had shared some of his initial reactions to the news of the agreement reached between the Mackintosh and her own father, Eva could not blame him for them. With his habit and like of epithets and cursing, she was certain they must have been explicit. He had warned her, and Margaret had shared some of it so that Eva would not hear it elsewhere.

Now there was a chance for it to be different between them.

Her belly cramped then, reminding her of the other reason she ached so this night. Though not as bad as those she'd suffered before, these would keep her awake long into the night. Glancing across the room, she realised that Nessa had prepared a stone in the hearth but Eva had forgotten it. It would ease the pains, she knew. She'd slipped from the bed to get it when the door opened.

Rob had walked and waited for what he thought was a good amount of time before returning to the room where she would be waiting. Well, not waiting but there.

Abed.

He was not prepared for the scene before him when he pushed the door open.

She stood there between him and the fire, wearing nothing but her thin sleeping shift. The flickering light outlined the curves the gown could not hide to his sight. She bent over, reaching for something, and the enticing slope of her graceful back and arse made his hands itch to slide over the feminine form. When she stood, her braid, an unsuccessful attempt to control the riotous curls she had, swung down to just below her hip, almost an arrow pointing his attention once again to a place that he longed to caress.

The lady dropped whatever she was trying to retrieve in the hearth as she stood and met his gaze. He knew his lust showed in his eyes even while hers shone with nervousness. Not fear, though, this time.

Not fear.

That was a huge step and, even if she did not realise it, he did. Closing the door behind him, Rob stepped closer.

'Do you need help with something?'

She blushed then, the redness rushing up her neck and into her cheeks. Pointing at the bottom of the hearth, into the area beneath the grate, she stammered a reply.

'The large stone there,' she said, stepping back and taking her into the shadows and out of the revealing light. 'Nessa warmed it for me.' The lady held out a piece of plaid.

Ah, he understood what this was and what it was used for. Without another word, he used one of the tools next to the fire and scooped it up, placing it carefully in the fabric and wrapped it. Holding it out to her, he watched as she could not meet his gaze then.

In spite of the courage, foolhardy though it was, that she'd shown in running away alone, he needed to remember that she was actually quite reticent about dealing with men. Her every action seemed guided by fear of men, from her father even to him. Of course, she had good cause to fear her father—he was a cold-hearted brute who used his fists to enforce his will over his daughter.

Rob waited as she climbed back into the bed, pulling the covers up around her shoulders and turning on her side. He did not miss the moan she made as she shifted her body.

'Is it only your…?' He stumbled over the word to use. Rob did not ever remember speaking openly to a woman, other than Margaret, about a matter such as this before. It was no secret, but just not discussed.

'Nay.' She shifted again and rustled beneath the blankets. 'I did more this day than I have in a long time.' She shifted once more, her arse shimmying under the covers and grabbing his attention again.

Rob undressed and, after putting out the last of the candles, got into the bed. His wife did not move at all as he did. And she did not look back at him. He moved to his usual place and lay on his back, trying to ignore her nearness.

As he did each and every hour spent in a bed with her. So close and yet unavailable. Worse, unwilling. His body refused to accept the reality of their circumstances and prepared for what it wanted…and it wanted relentlessly. Relentlessly without pause since he'd first rescued her from the cave and knew she was his to claim.

Rob turned onto his side and stared at her back. Mayhap his body was remembering his decision not to claim her until she'd bled, showing she did not carry another's bastard? He'd not thought on it, for he feared she had. But now…

Now he knew she did not.

She moved once more, shifting and trying to stretch, but the moan caught his attention. Leaning up on his hand, he edged closer.

'If you are in pain, I know a remedy,' he offered. Fighting and training often led to pain or muscle cramps. And though in his experience, what he offered her now often led to other pleasures, it did not have to.

'Does it involve horse liniment?' she whispered back. He barked out a laugh at her question and then a few of his favourite words.

'Am I damned forever for that? It worked, did it not? Eased the pain in your ankle and foot?'

She half turned to him then and shook her head.

'I was not damning you for it. I was just enquiring.' There was a lightness in her tone, a bit of humour in her voice, and he smiled.

'Nay, lady. It does not involve my sister's ointment for horses.'

'Then what does it involve?' she asked.

'Turn away and I will show you,' he said. Pleased when she did so with little hesitation, he lifted his hands towards her. 'Where does it hurt the worst?'

'My shoulders ache, but my back is the worst,' she answered. He smiled, again pleased by this small show of trust.

'Let us see if this helps, then.'

Rob placed his hands over her shoulders, using his thumbs to press into the tight muscles there, easing and increasing the amount of pressure he used with each stroke. When her moan of pain became a sigh of ease, he knew he'd found the best touch for her. Unfortunately for him, the breathy sighs resembled the sounds of passion, and his body reacted, hardening as she sighed again and again.

He slid his hands along her spine, his thumbs leading the way, until he reached her back. A cry of pain when he touched one place alarmed him.

'Can you bear it for a moment or two? It will feel better quickly,' he urged.

'Aye,' she whispered, allowing him to massage the place.

He waited, repeating the kneading motion until she uttered those damned sighs. Then he began to slide his hands down, reaching her lower back and hips.

'Nay,' she said, pulling away.

'Hush now, do not move,' he urged. 'You will undo all of my efforts.' He kept his hands where he'd placed them, holding her still. 'Trust me, Eva,' he whispered.

The moment of waiting for her response seemed to go on for years. 'Twas such a small thing here and now, but the sign she could give him with her compliance was as huge as any step he'd ever taken in his life. He almost shouted in victory when she relaxed against his hands. Then the physical torture of touching her without doing more commenced as he pressed and massaged the tension and pain from her back and hips.

'It feels wonderful, Rob,' she whispered, her voice as she spoke his name sent waves of desire through him and into his manhood. 'How did you learn such things?' Oh, he knew so much more than this simple massage. For now though, he contented himself with touching her so.

'Training and fighting is not without pain and injury. 'Tis a commonplace thing, truly.' He lightened his touch, sliding his hands gently in wide movements across her hips and back and then up on to her shoulders. 'Margaret uses such a thing in her ministrations to the injured.'

'So you learned this from your sister?' Her voice was growing softer.

Not wanting to ruin the moment, Rob did not tell the whole truth. 'Some of this, aye. Some of it is just from trying it and seeing what works.' He finished, but left his hands on her shoulders. 'How does your back feel now?'

'So much better. You have my thanks for that.' He could feel her begin to shift, testing the now-relaxed muscles.

'Nay, do not move. Let them rest now that they are not painful,' he said.

'Truly, my body does not wish to move right now,' she said with a light laugh.

His body, however, did want to move and to do many other things to hers at this moment. Like touch her everywhere. Like tasting and kissing every tender and sensitive spot he could find. Like filling her with his flesh and marking her with his seed. He forced every one of those desires back under control then, knowing it was not time yet.

'Then do not. Rest here.' He slid a bit closer. He let his arm drape over her, his hand resting on the bed near, so near, to her breasts, but not touching her.

They remained so, for a short time. Then, the words just burst from him, without thought.

'How much longer will your courses last, Eva?'

Chapter Eighteen

Eva's face still flamed when she thought of him asking such a thing. Even two days later, when the bleeding ceased, she could not meet his gaze. Such an intimate thing to ask.

At home, she understood that even the servants knew the timing and length or even the absence of her courses. 'Twas how her mother and then her father had learned of her disobedience and her condition. Those who washed the laundry knew. Those who cleaned her chambers knew. From the time of her first one until the time she delivered her daughter, someone knew.

And now, the man she called husband knew. Eva pressed her cool hand to her heated cheek as she walked to Margaret's cottage in the village. He had not asked her again, but she understood the reason behind it. He'd suspected she had a lover and might be carrying. With the way she'd run away and everything else that had happened, it did not surprise her. He, and the Mackintosh as well, must have thought that was the reason for marrying her off so quickly.

He was not far off the truth of the matter and only in the timing of her disgrace by a few months.

Now though, she remembered every second of his touch as he soothed her aches and pains even while creating a wholly different kind of throbbing. Eva recalled being in the throes of passion with a man and, as much as she'd like to deny it even to herself, his strong hands and fingers made her want to turn to him and beg him to touch other parts of her.

Passion and desire had overwhelmed her before.

It would, she did not doubt, happen again.

Eva deciphered the desire filling his eyes and felt the changes in his body—his large, strong body—that spoke of his physical arousal and need. Each meeting, each encounter with him, brought with it a growing tension between them. The problem, the main problem, was she did not know how she felt about it.

To her, this was going to end in only one way—her husband would claim his marital rights on her body and she would have no way or right to stop him.

In being candid with herself again, which she felt she needed to be in order to prepare herself for the inevitable, Eva was not certain she wanted to stop him.

That brought her to an abrupt halt on the path to the village. Even when people passed her by, greeting her politely, she stood there shocked into silence by that realisation.

Accepting him in the marriage bed meant acknowledging that their marriage was true and permanent. Could she do that? Did that mean that she must give up on ever finding Mairead? And forget about the love she shared with Eirik? Was either of those things even possible now?

As Arabella had counselled, a noblewoman could not raise a bastard child and certainly not with her husband's clan. Men could acknowledge their natural children and often did, but that did not work the same way for women. The presence of a child born out of wedlock would simply never be accepted. How could she reconcile her past with the possible future, the probable future, life she had here with the Mackintoshes?

'Is there something wrong, lady?'

Eva turned and found Margaret there watching her. How long had Eva been standing in that mist of thought, and how long had Rob's sister been watching her? Before she could answer, Margaret laughed.

'And does the frown on your brow have anything to do with something my brother has done or said?'

Eva smiled then. Neither sibling missed an opportunity to tease the other. As the only child born to her parents, she'd never experienced that facet of childhood, either.

'Nay, nothing is wrong, Margaret. I was just thinking about the changes in my life over the last few months.'

'And Rob?'

'Well, aye, he is one of them.'

Margaret wrapped her arm around Eva's and began walking towards the cottages and crofts where she would visit to check on the sick and injured.

'He is a good man, Eva. He's been a bit full of himself and has had an easy time with women, but I think he will be a good husband to you.'

'Twas the first time the woman had ever pressed her brother's case before. Until now, she'd never said a word for or against him, other than telling her his reaction to the news of their impending marriage. What could she say in response?

'He has not been unkind to me, Margaret.' Didn't her lack of saying something more make him sound worse than she'd meant him to sound?

'Well, I do not wish to meddle...' she began and then laughed. 'That is not true. I want to meddle but know not how to get started with you.'

Eva laughed, too, at the woman's candour. The sentiment and the intent of it warmed her heart, for no one had ever cared enough about her to look too closely or become involved before. Though she wanted to accept their interest and caring natures, Eva had learned long ago that it would lead to nothing good.

The servant who'd noticed her missed cycles and went to her mother out of concern was thrown out of the keep and banished—her father wanted no witnesses to her shame. The man she'd loved and who'd promised to protect her and take her and their baby away was dead—pushed down a ravine when he tried to save Eva from her father.

So, revealing too much to these people could still result in harm to the only thing important to her now—her daughter. She knew what she had to say.

'I am certain everything will work out. We are married, and I must learn to accustom myself as his wife.' Now Margaret was the one who pulled them both to a stop.

'And Robbie? Mustn't he learn to accustom himself to you?'

Margaret muttered then, words Eva was glad she could not make out. Margaret was still talking to herself as they walked on towards their first stop. She did not speak or ask questions on the topic of her brother or his marriage for the rest of the morning. Eva did not fool herself into thinking that she would not have her say.

Just as Eva was leaving to return to the keep, Margaret took her hand once more and leaned in closer.

'You are safe here, Eva. I know not what has happened in your life before this, but you are under the Mackintosh's protection now. Be at ease and know that it can all work out for you.'

If only…

Eva smiled and nodded, accepting the words and the intent even if she did not and could not believe it. Oh, she believed herself somewhat safe and out of her father's control, but her daughter was not.

Walking back to the keep, she kept glancing out the corner of her eye, expecting Rob to show up. He'd turned up at the most unlikely times and places over the last days. Sometimes he seemed to be seeking her out and other times he simply was there, conversing with others or carrying out some task or duty. As she reached the place where the road forked and one path led to the keep, she found him waiting.

'Have you finished with Margaret, then?' he asked, swinging his leg over and jumping from his horse.

'I have,' she said, walking to him. 'I have learned so much from her in such a short time.'

'You do not have to do that,' he said, holding out his arm to her. 'A lady…'

'A lady learns her stitches. A lady learns to sing. A lady…' Eva said, mimicking the words of her own mother and one of her diatribes about the correct be-haviour and pastimes for a lady.

'Sits on her arse and looks pretty while doing so,' he finished for her. Eva laughed at that. He watched her and then a smile broke on his face.

Good Lord, when he smiled she could get lost just watching it! She'd found herself staring at him when they were with Margaret or Arabella, when his smiles were easy and frequent. He was a handsome man, nay, a gorgeous man when he smiled like this.

'Apologies, lady,' he said with a nod. 'My language is, as my sister and Arabella tell me, deplorable and not fit for polite company.'

'I have noticed,' she said. 'I confess though, I am not offended by it.'

And she wasn't. Once the surprise of it wore through, she accepted it was simply something he did. From his thorough examination of her face, it was clear he did not believe her. He shook his head at her ad-mission.

'I do not want you to exhaust yourself, Eva,' he said. 'You came here barely recovered from a fever. You do not rest well. You drive yourself relentlessly, never tak-ing time for yourself.'

'To sit on my arse and look pretty?' she asked. She gasped and covered her mouth with her hand. Eva did not know why she'd said such a thing, but his words, tinged with concern, were too close and too personal. It unnerved her. And yet, she found herself longing to see him smile again.

'If you have a longing to say such things, I could teach you,' he offered, his expression that of a young boy urging someone to join in his wickedness. His wink was devastating to her control. 'The truly bad words.'

'I fear you could,' she admitted, enjoying the light-hearted moment far more than she would have anticipated. 'I will consider your kind offer.'

He laughed aloud once more and patted her hand where it lay on his arm.

They walked side by side up the road, his horse being led instead of ridden. It was a companionable silence for a time until he slowed their pace just before entering the gates.

'Brodie asked me to do something, asked us, and I wanted to tell you before he approaches you.

Rob watched as that expectation of doom entered her blue eyes once more. He hated the fear that dwelled within her. He hated the way she began to gather herself for an expected blow. But, he'd watched her these past weeks and her avoidance of the bairn was conspicuous.

Though neither Brodie nor Arabella mentioned it or seemed concerned by it, he had watched as a carefully arranged process was set in place. Eva's visits to Arabella always happened when the babe was napping or otherwise being cared for by her nursemaid. No matter that he had held the wee bairn several times already, as far as Rob could tell, his wife had not seen the babe since that day when she helped bring her into the world.

And that was damned odd, even to him.

The fact that he noticed was another peculiarity.

At some time in the past days, Rob had accepted that she did matter to him. And she mattered more than simply the woman he was forced to marry.

When they'd first met, and even until this last week,

he would have thought her fear was of him. However, he now understood, knew somehow, that she had let go of any fear of him. This reaction now was of another matter completely. He knew it.

'What does he wish us to do?' she asked. He heard the slight tremble in her voice that she tried to control.

'He wishes us to stand as godparents to the babe.'

Her gaze narrowed slightly at his words. Other than that, there was no visible reaction. Well, others might not notice anything but he did. She began to clasp her hands, rubbing one over the other in slow motions while the rest of her body moved not at all. It was the one gesture that seemed to escape her control in times when she was frightened or upset.

'An honour,' she whispered. 'To be asked is an honour.' Her words and tone seemed to seek to reassure herself as much as an answer to him.

''Tis an honour. And I would like to accept but wanted to know your mind on the matter.' She blinked then, several times, before speaking.

'As you wish,' she said, nodding.

Unfortunately, he'd expected exactly this. She never refused him anything outright, no matter that he could see the cost to her. None of that explained her lack of interest in Brodie and Bella's daughter.

'Eva, I do not know what makes you uncomfortable about this babe, but I can see it that you have avoided her. If you do not wish to do this, you can decline Brodie's request. Your help in bringing Arabella safely through delivery means Brodie will refuse you nothing.'

In the space of a single moment, her expression

emptied and a vacant gaze met his. It was not the re-action he'd expected.

'Forgive me, sir,' she said after a short silence. 'I left…something with Margaret that I must retrieve.'

His wife turned and walked away from him, back towards the village without another word and without waiting on his reaction.

She was running away.

Again.

He did not know and could not fathom why the subject of the babe should cause her to do so, but, as he watched her almost trip over her hasty steps to get away, Rob knew it linked one to the other.

Mayhap she feared childbirth or having children? They'd never discussed having children because it was expected. Had she lost someone close in childbirth? Was that the name she often called out when she was dreaming? *Mairead.*

So, as he watched her disappear down one of the pathways to the village, Rob wondered whether or not to follow her.

He did.

Tying the horse there, he followed her on foot. She had not gone towards Margaret's cottage but in the other direction. Not knowing he pursued her, she continued on until she reached the edge of the village and stopped near the stream there. Eva was so caught up in her thoughts, she clearly did not hear his approach.

Rob waited as she fought some battle within herself. Gazing at the water as it flowed past, she did not move and barely breathed. After some minutes, he decided it was time to take action in a different manner.

He'd been kind. He'd been patient. He'd ignored

her behaviour and allowed her refusal to accept him as husband to remain between them. And none of that worked. She was, with little change, as distant from him as almost the day they met.

It could not go on like this between them.

Rob walked to where she stood and said her name. 'Eva.'

She startled and turned to face him. Although he'd planned a different strategy, something in him released and the words he said surprised him, revealing his long-festering wound of his own.

'I grow weary of being judged by what others have done in the past. I tire of the constant fear and doubt in your eyes when you look upon me. And most of all, I will not wait on your acceptance of me as your husband in spite of the way it all came about.' Her hands began that twisting motion—at least until he reached out and took her hands in his own.

'Have I harmed you in any way?' She shook her head. 'Have I threatened you or beaten you as your own father has?' Another shake. 'Then when will you judge me by my own merits?'

And that was the true problem in this—she did not see him for himself. So many looked on him as Brodie's closest friend, as Brodie's counsellor, as a path to the chieftain's ear or notice. Rob Mackintosh the man, who offered his blood and sweat, heart and soul for kith and kin, disappeared once Brodie ascended to the chair of their clan. And he discovered there and then that he wanted her to see him for the man he was, not what others saw him to be—a means to an end. When she opened her mouth to speak, he placed his finger over her lips to forestall any false promises or apologies.

'Nay,' he said. 'I want not empty words to ease my temper in this matter. I want a wife. I want the wife I pledged myself to and the one who gave her vow to me. And I want her now.' He released her and stepped back. 'I am unwilling to wait any longer, Eva.'

Rob had thought to walk away from her but did not want to give her time to give in to her misgivings and fears. So, he held out his hand to her and waited for her to accept or reject him, once and for all.

Chapter Nineteen

Rob waited at table as long as he could before returning to their chamber. If Arabella, returned to the table for the first time since the bairn's birth, noticed his anxious behaviour, she'd said nothing. But Rob had noticed the glances exchanged by Brodie and his wife when Eva excused herself.

Well, Arabella's notice or not, Rob could not stop himself from touching his wife during the meal. Oh, not in the way he wanted to, planned to, but simple touches—his hand on hers, his mouth whispering in her ear, his leg pressing against hers—that she allowed him with no resistance. It was as though they'd broken through a dam when she reached out and took his hand earlier in the day.

And he would not be stepping back from her.

'Oh, Robbie,' Arabella whispered from her place on the other side of her husband. 'Go. Just go.'

He tried, truly and well, not to rush up the stairs to the room they shared, but from the laughter that followed his leave-taking from the hall, Rob knew he'd failed to make a decorous departure. He took the steps two at a time and found himself standing in the corridor outside the room, his hand frozen in the space between him and the latch.

Chiding himself for his own nervous behaviour, he lifted the latch and found Nessa brushing Eva's hair. He left the door open a bit, took the brush from the maid and knelt behind Eva. With a nod, Nessa was dismissed. Rob began to ease the brush through the long, riotous curls of his wife's hair, trying to calm his own breathing with each stroke.

He continued until all the tangles were smoothed out and then placed the brush on the table before her. He slid his hands under the length of it and gathered her hair in his hands, lifting it up to expose her graceful neck. Rob leaned in and kissed the curve of her neck and down on to her shoulder. Although she hesitated, she did not pull away. A good sign, that.

When he kissed along the side of her neck and along her jaw, she turned to him. Releasing her hair, Rob placed his hands on her shoulders and eased her to face him. Cupping her face, he drew her mouth to him, kissing her the way he'd wanted to...forever, it seemed. When she opened to him, he plundered her for the taste that was only hers.

His tongue played with hers, teasing it forward until he could suckle on it. Leaning closer, he felt her nipples harden as his chest grazed hers. The thin gown and robe she wore was no impediment at all to feeling them. He canted his head and took her tongue into his mouth, urging her to taste him.

And she did!

Soon, Eva followed his lead, matching everything he did, kiss for kiss, taste for taste. Rob slid his hands down over her arms and then around her waist, lifting her from the stool as he stood. Her slight weight was nothing to him as he held her to him, one hand now on her bottom, urging her to wrap her legs around him.

'Twas then he realised that her own arms now wrapped around his shoulders, holding on to him as he moved across the chamber. Her legs straddled his hips, his erection nestled against her, as Rob carried her to the bed.

Breathless from their kisses, he placed her on the edge of the bed and stepped back from her. Never breaking gazes with her, he loosened his belt and let his plaid drop to the floor. Smiling, he untied the laces of his tunic and pulled it over his head, tossing it aside as he waited for her to look at him. Oh, he knew she'd stolen furtive glances at him when he climbed out of bed in the morn, but he was daring her to look her fill now.

And she did. Her eyes dropped and his body reacted as though she touched his flesh, his shaft lengthening and growing thicker. The best part was that there was no fear in her eyes when she drew her gaze off his rampant flesh and back to his face. He smiled at her then, but knew his own lust must be in his gaze.

Rob reached out and loosened her belt, drawing the robe aside. Then he gathered the gown in his hand, easing it up inch by inch along her legs. With his other hand, he caressed her, following the path of the fabric until he reached the junction of her thighs. Pausing to give her one last chance to object, he slid his hand between her legs, finding her flesh heated and wet.

She reached out and steadied herself by holding on to him then. Her hands clenched and released, over and over, as he caressed those sensitive folds of flesh. But the best part, truly the best, was the wonderful little gasps with which she answered each and every stroke. And the way she began to arch against his touch. His shaft wanted to be buried deep there, but he waited. He would pleasure her first and discover all the secret places on her body that triggered those gasps and sighs.

He kissed her again, not ceasing the caresses between her legs, pleased more than he could say by the growing wetness there. Rob trailed his mouth down her throat, down the slope of her breasts and did not stop until he reached the taut tips that begged to be tasted. The gasps turned to moans as he pulled one and then the other into his mouth, teasing them with his teeth and tongue. She grabbed him then, sliding her hands into his hair and holding him there.

'Easy,' he whispered against her, the fabric growing wetter against his own mouth.

He leaned back, pulling against her hold and then used both hands to tear the gown and rid it from his path. Finally naked before him, he gazed at her breasts and down her belly to where he wanted to be next. Giving her no warning, he slid his hands beneath her legs and pulled her down and spreading her wider for his gaze.

Though he'd worried that she would be reticent or hold back, Rob was stunned by her sensual reaction to everything he did. Her body asked for more at each pause, arching and warming to his touch. The muscles in her belly rippled as he kissed and licked a path down and down until he reached the springy curls that covered her mons.

She'd fallen back onto the bed, writhing under his mouth, but now pushed up on her elbows and watched him with a passion-filled gaze. He caressed the inside of her thighs, first with his hands and then his mouth. Her own mouth opened and she licked her lips, making his prick throb at the sight of it.

Rob waited no longer to taste the very core of her, spreading her legs and placing his mouth there. She did not moan or gasp then. Nay, she fell back to the bed in silence, though her body spoke for her. He licked along the folds and searched for the small bud that would send her over the edge to pleasure. Finding it, he caressed it with his thumb before using his tongue.

Her body bucked, her hips left the bed and she arched against his mouth, her hands in his hair now, holding him, nay pulling him closer. So he went deeper, thrusting into the place where his prick ached to be, causing her to scream out as her release came upon her. Rob did not stop, he used fingers and tongue to urge her on, pleasuring her flesh as he'd wanted to for so long. When her body began to quiet, he stood and eased her back onto the bed, kneeling between her legs.

When he slid his fingers into her, her flesh tightened around them, yet trembling from arousal and orgasm. She was ready. He placed his flesh there, dipping the head of it into her opening, ready to claim her.

'Eva,' he whispered as he climbed over her and meeting her eyes then. 'Am I the first?' he asked.

Rob had doubted it from the first, even used his own blood to cover the possibility or probability of her condition, and so the slight shake of her head gave him no surprise. Indeed, it gave him the freedom to take her as he wanted to, for a maiden would need more time than... So, he took her—fully, madly, deeply.

'Then I will be the last,' he said before thrusting into her, filling her as he wanted to.

Eva heard his declaration as he entered her, nay, claimed her body. His flesh, hard and thick, slid deep inside her and her body took him in, every inch of him. He let out a sigh and closed his eyes above her for a moment.

His suspicion did not surprise her, but his asking did. But, she knew the reason for it, and it was not for blame or condemnation. It was out of consideration for her.

Now, she simply felt. Her body was like a thing unknown to her—the recent pleasure had not even dissipated before he stoked it again. This time, instead of hands and mouth, he used his own flesh to plunge deep into her and bring her body alive again. Her breasts pressed against his chest and swelled as he moved. Her skin ached for his touch. And, the woman's flesh tightened around him with every thrust. Tighter as he pulled out and thrust again and again. His mouth found hers and he searched for her tongue. She gave it, suckling on his, tasting her own essence there.

Then, Eva let go and did nothing but feel—his flesh, his strength, his body and hers. He drove her relentlessly towards that place she'd just come down from and she allowed it.

Right or wrong, it mattered not, for she'd decided in that moment earlier that she must walk away from her past and take the chance it would, it could, be better with him.

Her body tensed, something deep inside wound tighter and tighter and then snapped, releasing wave after wave of pleasure. Her blood carried it through every part of her. She felt him swell there and then, with a shout, he spilled his seed within her. It did not stop him from thrusting inside her, he did several more times before slowing and then halting. He remained deep within her, his flesh still hard there, and he kissed her over and over again.

Then, they lay there joined by flesh as their hearts and breathing calmed, his face tucked against her shoulder and neck, his breath still a warm caress on her skin. Soon, she thought him asleep, for he did not move or speak at all.

Eva tried not to look too closely at what had happened between them. Well, other than the quenching of his lust. And her enjoyment of the act. 'Twas nothing more than had happened in countless other marriages made out of political necessity or out of convenience. That he was considerate of her, seeing to her pleasure before his, was not unexpected after all.

Now, she understood why those women smiled like a well-fed cat when they looked on him. It was not only his looks or strength—it was his manner of bed play. She glanced at his relaxed body and felt his flesh yet within her. Aye, no wonder they wanted him to return to their beds.

'What are you thinking, wife?' he asked. 'I can practically hear thoughts ruminating inside that head of yours.' He lifted his head and looked at her. He narrowed his gaze and examined her closely. 'Do you regret it?'

'Nay. No regrets,' she said truthfully.

'Then what plagues you now?' He eased his upper body from hers and stared, his gaze demanding the truth. 'I want your candour in this, Eva.'

She did not want to share her thoughts about the other women he'd had before her, but decided that having truth between them from this day on was important. Even knowing his probable reaction, she revealed her thoughts to him.

'I understand now why Fiona and the others want you in their beds.'

Silence greeted her revelation, not at all what she expected. Then he laughed, sliding free of her and lying back next to her. Eva rolled to her side and watched him. After a few moments, he met her gaze.

'I did not expect those to be your thoughts, Eva. Though, I admit, it does please me to know you enjoyed this.'

'Will you be insufferable now?' she asked.

'Nay, wife, not insufferable at all,' he said, rolling to his side and facing her.

He slid the torn gown and robe off her shoulder, leaving her completely naked and open to his sight. Reaching out, he slid the back of his hand down over her breasts and then her belly, leaving it resting on the curls between her thighs. She fought the urge, the need, to open her legs and invite him there once more. She noticed that his flesh moved and began to lengthen.

'I take it as a challenge,' he said, easing only a finger deep into her cleft and finding her eager flesh. 'What has happened so far is only a taste.' He leaned over and kissed her then, open-mouthed and possessively. 'But I plan to show you why you should keep me in yours.'

And he did.

By the time the sun's light shone into their chamber, there was not a place on her body he had not touched or kissed or tasted. There was no response he had not drawn from her, from laughing to crying to screaming out her pleasure or whimpering her need of him.

He would not tolerate her compliance in his demands, he urged her to participate in their pleasure and passion. She touched and caressed his body, enjoying the chance to run her hands over the masculine, sculpted muscles of his chest and back and thighs she'd only been able to see before. And Eva learned a few things about pleasing him, as well.

Though she expected to go about their daily routines, Nessa discovered a very naked and rampant Rob Mackintosh when she opened the chamber door to bring in water that morning. A squeal and a slam and they were alone once more.

When the sun reached high in the sky, he made no attempt to leave. Indeed, after several more inventive joinings she'd not thought possible in her inexperience, they slept, limbs entwined. A second knock at their door went unanswered until Nessa said Arabella's name.

Instead of a summons back to duty and daily tasks, they found a bucket of steaming water and a tray filled with food. Nessa had long run off, probably fearing what she would witness should Rob open the door as he had the last time she attempted entry.

The rest of that day and night were a blur to her—his hunger spurred on her own and they would join, then rest, eat when food appeared outside their door, and then begin again.

And again.

And again.

* * *

Only Brodie's loud knock and call back to duties drew Rob from her but not before paying her attention he claimed was so she would not forget him in his absence.

As though it would be possible.

Once he left their chamber, a bath appeared as did her maidservant. Nessa fell into her pattern of chattering about the goings-on at Drumlui Keep in her absence these last two nights and a day. Only when she approached the hall, with its curious people and servants, did she hesitate.

How did a lady keep her dignity when everyone around knew what she'd been doing since her hasty departure after supper two nights ago?

Arabella saved her. The lady met her in the corridor outside her chamber and walked with her the rest of the way. Many were already about their business, but those in the hall stopped and watched her enter and sit at the table. Arabella smiled knowingly and nodded her encouragement.

Then, everyone lost interest and Eva moved into the day's tasks as she had this last week or so—visiting the sick and injured with Margaret in the morning and attending Arabella later in the day.

But if she'd thought that two nights and a full day of pleasures of the fleshly sort had satisfied her husband, she quickly discovered how wrong she was in that. He'd sneak up to her and drag her into an alcove, or an empty stable or into the shadows of a thick copse, kissing her senseless and breathless.

By the time she thought to whisper a warning or beg off from such a scandalous place or time, she found herself thoroughly tupped. Sometimes, if a private place, he would strip off her clothing and his and it would take some time. Other times, hidden from view only briefly, he would toss up her gowns and his plaid and take her quickly. No matter how or when, Eva found herself completely satisfied and yet still hungering for another touch, another caress or kiss, another…tupping!

When once he lured her onto his horse and she found herself straddling him in a most shocking manner, she thought she should object. By the time they reached the small clearing next to the stream some distance away from the village, she'd lost all coherent thought…and her garments.

But a few days later, during a bout of bed play that lasted hours and was filled with soft, slow, gentle caresses and kisses and sighs, she realised the true danger of her situation.

As Eva MacKay watched her husband claim her once again, she knew that she wanted to claim him. Worse, if she did not take care, she could find herself falling in love with the man she'd once run away from.

Chapter Twenty

One month later...

'They will begin arriving within days. I expect everyone to be present within the next seven to eight days.'

Brodie was explaining the plans for visits by the four neighbouring and allied clans—some part of the Chattan Confederation and one, the MacKays, allied by their treaty. Though only a small group from each clan would participate, it would fill the keep to overflowing and tax even the efforts of Fergus, the steward, and the cook.

Rob knew no one would complain, but he knew things would be tense here, balancing between hospitality and the challenges of hosting a large number of visitors. He also knew of Brodie's aspirations for this gathering and the benefits it could bring to them.

'I will make the arrangements for those not staying here,' Rob offered. 'And organise some training exercises to keep them busy,' he said.

The talk continued for a while, until Brodie was satisfied with all the preparations and plans. This would be the first time he hosted such a gathering since becoming chief and laird here. Rob understood the importance of it all.

He heard her laugh before he saw her.

Eva entered the hall, arm in arm with Arabella, and looking happy. He let out the breath he did not know he held then.

'So being married is not as bad as you thought, then?' Brodie asked under his breath. 'Time has helped?'

'Aye. 'Twould seem so,' Rob admitted.

The last weeks since she'd accepted his hand and his offer had revealed a woman to him he'd thought might be hidden away under sadness and longing. She had taken her place at his side since then, becoming a helpmate to Arabella and to Margaret, who both sang her praises loudly and often. To Eva's utter embarrassment.

And, her playful side had been exposed. He fulfilled his offer to teach her some wicked words, and she learned and used them well, even if only between the two of them and only in bed. She especially liked to use them as exclamations when he pleasured her, and the memories of her calling out in that breathy, shallow and aroused voice made him hard even now.

The women did not approach them but went off to see to something else, giving Rob a chance to regain his control. Sliding his hand through his hair, he wondered if he would ever be able to stop wanting her.

'Her father will arrive first, within days,' Brodie said. 'Tell me more about him.' Holding out a cup, Brodie filled it and his own before nodding at Rob. 'I have never met the man.'

'He is a cold-hearted, brutal son of a bitch.' Rob

drank deeply of the cup and then continued, 'He beat Eva…he beat her with his own belt the morning of our wedding.'

Brodie's cup crashed on the table and fell over. His friend could be a son of a bitch when he needed to be, but his strength did not lay in brutality, especially not towards women.

'Why did you not tell me of his true nature?' Brodie asked, righting the cup and pouring more ale into it. 'And he yet lives?' Whether in jest or not, Rob appreciated the sentiment.

'I thought it might interfere with your agreement if I killed him,' Rob said, drily. Not that he had not thought of it many, many times since then. 'I stopped him.'

'So, their reunion will not be a happy one when next they meet? Will Eva be…?' Clearly, Brodie could not think of how to ask the question that bothered him so much. Brodie faced Rob and met his stare. 'Will there be problems?'

'Oh, my friend, there are always problems at gatherings such as these, but I will make certain she is seen safely through any encounters with him.'

'And if you are busy with your duties to me?'

'I will ask Margaret and Magnus if need be to attend her.'

Rob stood then, anxious to see her and warn her about her father's arrival. Or mayhap he just wanted to see her? Or just wanted…her? No matter the reason, he nodded to Brodie and left him there with his steward sorting out details of supplies.

She would be in Arabella's chamber, the room where her women gathered. He stood outside the slightly open door and peered inside. There she stood at Arabella's side as usual. But when she turned, he realised she held wee Joanna in her arms. She did not see him watching her.

The first thing he noticed was the glint of pain in her eyes. It lasted only a moment before disappearing, so quickly that he thought he might have not seen it at all. But he had.

Then, she smiled and cooed to the babe, rubbing the wispy hair on her head. And in that moment, the need to see her body swelling with his child nearly forced him to his knees. The need to glide his hands over her belly and feel the life they made within her became so strong he must have made a sound, for she turned to him then.

'Robbie, I did not see you there,' she said, walking to him. 'I was…'

'I could see—paying attention to the babe,' he finished for her. 'Arabella,' he said, nodding at the lady.

'She is getting big so quickly,' his friend said. 'If she follows her father's bearing, she will tower over me.'

'Bella, nearly everyone towers over you,' he said, leaning over to run his finger down the babe's cheek. 'Can I borrow my wife?' Rob asked, glancing first at Eva and then the lady.

'Rob, you must give her some rest,' Bella argued.

'Bella!' both he and Eva called out at the same time.

A lovely blush rose in Eva's cheeks. It somehow satisfied him to see her reaction when she thought about his physical demands of her.

Oh, and he was demanding! Everything about her pleased him, but mostly the trust she placed in him. She allowed him any use of her, urged him on and begged for more. Kiss for kiss, swiving for swiving, she matched him in both wanting and doing more together.

When he'd asked her just the other night if he'd made her glad she took him to her bed, she'd laughed and just nodded. He took that as another challenge to show her how much she was gladdened by him there. Neither of them got much sleep that night.

'I do have a matter to discuss with you, wife,' he said.

Eva glanced at Arabella and then handed the baby to her.

'I want her returned to me, Rob. We have tasks to see to before Margaret and the others arrive.'

He took Eva's hand and led her out of the chamber, up the stairs instead of down, until they reached the door leading out to the battlements of the keep. Other than the guards always on duty, they would have some measure of privacy. If he took her to their chambers, Bella would not get her back anytime soon and not in any condition to see to whatever tasks needed to be done. Rob walked to one corner and nodded to the guard there. The man walked some paces away, far enough that he would not hear them, and took up a place there.

'Is something wrong?' she asked, as he let go of her hand.

He hated the fearful expression in her eyes. He'd not seen it for some weeks and knew now exactly how much he hated it. But now he knew it was not about him or her feelings for him, which he was sure she had.

In that moment, Rob understood what had happened— he'd fallen in love with Eva MacKay. He stumbled and she grabbed hold of him.

'Are you unwell?' she asked, touching the back of

her hand to his forehead. 'I feel no fever but I should summon Margaret.'

He grabbed her hand before she could go.

'Nay, I am well.' He glanced down and kicked some stones there on the walkway. 'I only tripped.' Disbelief shone in her eyes, but she did not leave.

He loved her. When it had happened or how, he knew not. He only knew it had.

He loved her courage and her spirit and her willingness to take his hand that day and not look back. He loved the way she sighed when he entered her. He loved the way she moved into his embrace every night when he climbed into bed.

He loved the way he could be only a man to her and with her and not a conduit to anyone or anything else.

He loved her. And he would do whatever was necessary to protect her. Even from her own father.

'Kiss me, Eva,' he said. Without a moment's hesitation or question, she moved closer and stood on her toes to reach his mouth. He did the rest, holding and lifting her, and possessing her mouth. When he eased her back to her feet, she looked on him with a suspicious glint in her eyes.

'What is this about?'

'Brodie just told me that your father arrives in a day or two. I thought you would want to know.'

As he observed her reaction, he recognised the old Eva pushing forward. Her physical demeanour and posture changed as she became more defensive and her face lost its colour. He would not allow it. Taking her by the shoulders, he shook her gently.

'Do not do that,' he urged. 'Do not lose what you have become.' She searched his face then. 'You told me you trust me? Then you must trust that I will protect you from him.'

The haunted expression left her, and she shuddered then. He pulled her into his arms and rubbed his hands over her back. She clutched his shirt and held on to him. 'All will be well,' he assured her. By the time she left his embrace, she was not shaking.

'If you would like, you could stay with Margaret and Magnus in the village while he is here.' He would hate not having her at his side, but if she would be at ease there, she could.

'I am your wife, Rob. To not be here to greet my father would be an insult to you and to Brodie.' Spoken like the lady she'd been raised to be. 'And with you at my side, I promise not to cower before that piece of shite now.'

He laughed and wrapped his arm around her, holding her close. It was not the coarsest curse or worst words she could say, but her attempt warmed his heart.

'I love you, Eva MacKay,' he said, kissing her once more. He could not keep those words in now that he knew the truth.

She searched his gaze then, touching his cheek. Then she cupped his face and brought his mouth to hers, kissing him gently. He felt the caring there. He felt her response to his words. Rob suspected fear kept her from speaking of her own feelings. She never had, as though saying the words would make everything good go away. When she lifted her mouth from his, tears tracked down her cheeks.

'Come. Bella will be cross if I made you cry,' he said, wiping her tears away. 'Or if I keep you too long,' he said. Reaching up, he pulled some tendrils of her hair free from the elaborate concoction of knots and twists that Nessa used to control her curls. 'Let her think the worst.'

Saying nothing, she smiled and shook her head at his antics. He did it just to keep touching her. Now that he recognised the feelings coursing through him, he did not wish to relinquish her yet. But, they both had their duties to carry out, so he escorted her back to Arabella, who crossed her arms over her chest and looked exasperated.

'I will not be at the evening meal,' he whispered to her. 'Wait for me,' he urged. He walked away quickly and without looking back at her, for if he did, he would forsake his duties and take her to bed.

And that night, their joining and passion had an edge of desperation to it, in spite of whatever words he spoke. No matter the number of times he assured her of his love. Then when spent, she clung to him, never letting go of him completely. Neither one slept.

He knew it was tied to her father's arrival, but he knew not what it meant. Unfortunately, she had never spoken of the matters between her and the MacKay, nor the true reason for her attempt to run from their marriage. Without the truth, he was going into a battle without weapons.

And Rob Mackintosh did not go into battle unprepared.

Brodie thought he was in an armed camp instead of his hall welcoming honoured guests. Rob stood on his right, his arms crossed over his chest, ready for a fight. His wife on his right stood stone-faced as her fa-

ther entered the hall and walked towards them. She'd
flinched several times just standing there when someone turned suddenly or approached without warning.

But the most puzzling was his Bella.

Standing on his left, she bristled with anger and fury.
Dressed in the finery expected of Lady Mackintosh,
she resembled a fairy princess of legend—beautiful,
ethereal, breathtaking. And yet, all she needed was a
sword in her hand and she could be a Valkyrie of old
Norse tales.

Something or someone had raised her hackles, and
she stood stiff and ready for a fight. A good thing that
weapons were not permitted here. He turned to her as
the MacKay came closer.

'Bella, what is it?'

She shushed him and nodded towards the powerful
clan chief of the north, who now stood at the bottom
of the dais from where they did, waiting for Brodie's
acknowledgement. The look of hatred in her eyes and
aimed at the man told him that his wife was privy to
much more than even Rob had let on. Another glance
told him that she knew more than Rob did, which somehow made him feel better. And yet it did not.

He smiled grimly then and nodded to the man.

'Laird MacKay,' he said, reaching out his arm in
greeting. 'Welcome to Drumlui Keep and the lands of
the Mackintosh Clan.'

'Mackintosh,' he said, accepting Brodie's arm and
clasping it with a nod.

'May I present my wife, Lady Arabella Cameron?'

Arabella smiled, but it was the one he'd always
hated. The MacKay did not notice or know it for the
imitation it was, for he bowed to her. When she did not

hold out her hand in greeting, Brodie frowned at her and motioned with his head. His wife ignored him and only offered her words.

'Welcome to Drumlui Keep, Laird MacKay.' She nodded to Fergus, who stepped forward. 'Our steward Fergus will see to your comfort while you are here. Places have been arranged for your men, and a chamber is ready for you and Lady MacKay.'

Brodie glanced at the group assembled there and saw no other woman of an age or description to match that of Eva's mother. The only woman in the group was younger, almost the same age as Eva. She stood, eyes cast down, until the MacKay spoke her name. Then she walked...nay, that did not describe the way she moved to the laird's side. Every step made her hips sway, and every man watching her noticed it.

'My cousin Sigrid has accompanied me on this journey,' Eva's father explained, though not a single person in that hall mistook the woman for anything but what she was—his leman. 'Lady MacKay was unwell.'

He heard the indrawn breath and thought that the MacKay did, as well. Brodie felt as though control of this situation would quickly begin to falter. He would like to have avoided what he must do next, but there was no way to do so.

'And, of course, my kinsman is known to you.' Brodie gestured to Rob.

'Laird MacKay,' Rob said gruffly as he bowed to his father by marriage. Brodie noticed that Eva moved closer to her husband and slipped her hand into his. A telling gesture, that.

'Eva, have you no greeting for your father?' the MacKay asked before Rob could say more.

'Father,' she said, curtsying to him from her place at Rob's side. 'Welcome.'

The MacKay looked ready to say something, but he just narrowed his gaze and studied his daughter. With a wave of his hand, two of his men came forward carrying a small chest, which was placed before Rob.

'The rest of my daughter's dowry, Mackintosh,' he said to Rob.

'I thank you, Lord MacKay, for seeing to it,' Rob said, with the first hint of genuine appreciation he'd heard since this scene began to unfold. Brodie's hopes for a good ending diminished when the MacKay replied—the man's gaze lay on his daughter and not Rob or even him.

'An agreement is an agreement, is it not?' he asked. Eva stared at her father, and it appeared that some message was exchanged between them in that moment, though Rob answered.

'Aye, Laird MacKay. It is.' Rob nodded to Fergus, who saw to moving the chest to the strongbox for attention later.

'I keep my agreements,' the laird said, not taking his eyes from his daughter.

'There will be food and drink to refresh you from your journey,' Bella interrupted...finally. 'Let Fergus show you to your chambers, where you can rest first.'

The MacKay nodded at her and then turned to follow the steward to the far tower. He stopped right in front of Rob and smiled, one to rival Bella's coldest.

'From the looks of it, you took my advice then, lad?'

The older man laughed and did not wait for a response from Rob. He was gone from the hall and did not see Rob try several times to draw the sword that would normally be hanging in its scabbard from his belt. But Brodie wanted to know what he was up against with this man, so he called him closer, even as Bella moved to Eva's side.

'What was his advice?' Brodie asked in a low voice.

'To beat her well and often, or she would not learn who was in control.'

His wife gasped then, and Brodie knew she'd heard the words in spite of Rob's attempt to keep them between himself and Brodie.

Well, at least it confirmed what Brodie had heard about the man, even years before from his uncle. Ruthless. Brutal. Powerful.

And now his ally.

Brodie nodded to Rob then. 'Bella, would you take Eva to your chamber until the evening meal?'

For once, his wife did not argue with him or question his reasons. With her arm at Eva's waist, she guided the woman from the dais and out of the hall.

'What is his purpose, Rob? Why is he here?'

'You invited him, Brodie. How the hell should I know?' Rob snapped back.

'Nay, I mean why connect himself and his clan to ours?' Brodie watched as his friend never took his gaze off the retreating figure of his wife. 'Why sell his daughter to me? To us?' Rob turned his attention to Brodie, finally, and shrugged.

'He is sworn to the earl of Orkney. He owes fealty to him,' Rob said. 'But you are high in the King of Scotland's favour. He might simply wish a foot in each camp?'

'It could be as simple as that, in addition to the trade

we have promised and the ability to meet with our allies. Expand his possibilities through us.'

Brodie thought on that and was satisfied. It was the way of diplomacy and trade. But he would be watchful of the MacKay in the coming talks.

He just did not trust a man who needed to rely on his fists to control those weaker than himself. Especially not a wife or a daughter.

And Brodie did not like a man who shamed those he should protect. Having a leman was an acceptable practice, and most noblemen kept a mistress for comfort. But to bring her and present her to Brodie's lady wife was an insult to both wives…and to his daughter who stood witness to it all.

'See to his men, Rob. We will speak again later.'

Though he knew Rob wanted to see to his distraught wife, his cousin followed his orders and left the keep. Brodie thought Bella was the better remedy for Eva's distress right now.

He hoped he was correct.

Chapter Twenty-One

Eva smiled.

She did not have to speak a word, for Arabella expressed all the outrage she'd felt in the hall as her father had arrived.

About his behaviour. About his leman. About everything.

And she used words that Eva would not have imagined were in the lady's vocabulary. And with as much style as Rob did. Mayhap the habit was contagious?

Bella only sought to calm herself when the nurse-maid brought the babe in to be fed. Still nursing her daughter herself, the lady sat down and sipped some ale. If she remained this angry and tense, she explained, her milk would not release and the babe would not feed.

In the last weeks, Eva had grown more at ease with being in the chamber when Arabella tended to her child. She still startled in those first few seconds, but then grew less tense in her presence. And though she knew that it would never replace the emptiness in her heart over being forced to give up her daughter, Eva found herself more and more thinking about having a child with Rob.

His words of love had made her heart soar and think it was be possible for them to have a happy life. She'd wanted to say them back, to share the feelings that filled her heart for him, but to do so would obligate him in ways she could not.

She knew the cost of loving someone, and she would not tie him to her in that way.

No matter that she did love him. In spite of knowing the danger of it, she did. Now her father's arrival reminded her of his power over her. His words just now had confirmed to her that he was not done using his daughter as a pawn.

Marriage to Rob was not the whole of his plan. But what was?

Eva tried to remain busy during the hours before the evening meal. Rob would be there at her side, as would Brodie, who was now her laird. So she tried to remember that she had allies who would support her if needed.

None of that mattered or helped at all, because her father held the one thing that would force her to capitulate to whatever he wanted or demanded. Unless she revealed the truth to the husband she loved, and mayhap even if she did, he could not do a thing on her behalf or her daughter's.

Finally, she sat at Rob's side at the table, and her father was far enough away from them that she did not hear his every word. She tried to enjoy the meal and listen to the musicians that played as the rest ate, but knowing he was there and knowing there would be a demand placed on her soon made her tense and made the wonderfully prepared food taste like dirt in her mouth.

The meal was done when it happened.

'I would like to speak to my daughter, Laird Mackintosh,' she heard her father say. 'With your permission, of course.'

The deference was all for show and meant nothing. Her father stood and Brodie did as well, so now she could see them—as could everyone else. By asking Brodie, he removed any chance that Rob could object.

'If you would send her to my chambers?' Her father nodded and began to leave the hall.

'Only if she consents, Laird MacKay.' Brodie's words startled no one who knew him but shocked her father, who turned and shook his head in disbelief.

'She has no choice in the matter, Laird Mackintosh,' he said, sputtering in anger at the challenge. 'Surely, her laird makes those decisions for her, if not her husband?'

This was going to escalate into something terrible; Eva could feel it. She knew her father—standing up to him, questioning his authority, was the worst thing to do. She stood quickly, nearly knocking over her chair.

'Laird Mackintosh, I will attend to my father's summons,' she said, surprised her voice did not tremble or hitch. 'I would welcome a chance to become reacquainted after so much time apart and so many changes in our lives.'

She felt Rob's gaze burning into her, and she knew he wanted to object. Eva knew Brodie wanted to as well, but it would go better in all aspects if she made it appear as though she willingly answered his call. Rob took her hand and tugged her closer as the two lairds considered this battle of wills between them.

'I will come with you,' he said, entwining their fingers.

'Nay,' she whispered. ''Twill all be well, Rob.'

Brodie finally nodded his consent, and Eva walked out after her father, following him to the chamber in the far tower that had been assigned him. Though it should have surprised her, finding Sigrid there and already in the bed waiting for her father did not.

'Get out,' her father ordered.

Without hesitation and without a stitch of clothing on, Sigrid slid quickly from the bed and walked past Eva without a glance. She would be seen naked if Ramsey MacKay ordered it so. Well, Eva did not wish to embarrass any of the servants who might find the woman, so, before she could shut the door, Eva grabbed a blanket and tossed it at the woman, who had no shame.

Closing the door, Eva turned as her father filled a cup with the costly wine provided to him by Brodie and then took a seat on the only chair in the chamber. He offered her neither courtesy as he drank the wine. He held out the half-empty cup, expecting her to serve him.

And so she did, waiting for the true reason for this call to become clear.

'So, you have certainly thrived here with these people.'

'I am well, Father.'

'Better than well, I would say from what I have heard. You managed to ingratiate yourself with the laird and his wife. You must be spreading your legs for your husband, for he practically swives you with his eyes every time he looks at you.' He drank more of the wine. 'At least you have used your natural talents as a whore to smooth your way here.' She gasped at his crude language.

'I am no wh—' She'd barely begun to deny his words when he lunged from his chair and made a fist. He stopped just before hitting her.

'You forget, I have the proof of that. Tucked away, safe and sound as long as you do as I tell you.'

'I did as you ordered. I married the Mackintosh's man,' she whispered. 'I left your lands and your keep.' She twisted her hands, trying to keep control, when she wanted to fall to the floor and weep, even beg, for his word that Mairead would be kept safe.

'Ah, but now there is a new task for you.' Now he approached and held out his hand to her, guiding her to sit in the chair. 'The provisions of your marriage contract were favourable, but this new treaty does not give me enough consideration.'

'I have nothing to do with Laird Mackintosh's negotiations, Father. You must know that.' All the weeks of comfort and security faded into the dark around her. The fear that had been her constant companion, that had kept her from accepting Rob sooner, flooded back in now.

'I have been told of the Mackintosh's words after you helped his wife deliver their child. He pledged himself in your debt, as did she. Now, all I'm asking is that you use that debt in my favour.'

'I cannot.'

She uttered the words softly, but it was the first time she'd ever refused an order or request from her father.

He turned and walked across the chamber, staring at her from there.

'You do not wish to protect your daughter any longer? She's still such a wee thing, 'twould take almost nothing to do away with her.' Eva tried not to react to his threat, searching her heart and soul for the strength to stand against him.

'I think you may have done that already, Father,' she said calmly. Though the thought of it turned her stomach, it had occurred to her more than once since her daughter's birth and disappearance. But, her doubt would leave him without a weapon to use against her.

'Do you love him, Eva?'

The soft words, asked quietly, were like a nightmare returned to haunt her. Months and months ago, her father had asked her the same question of her, but the man involved was Eirik. Foolishly, she had admitted her love and claimed they would never be parted. In spite of Eirik's kinship to the Earl of Orkney, her father had tossed him down a ravine, claiming an accident when questions were raised.

She'd learned that lesson. It was why she'd not told Rob. Eva shook her head.

'Nay, Father. He is just the man you forced me to marry.'

Her father studied her face, even walking closer to see her more clearly. She tried to keep her gaze empty. She tried.

'You, as your mother before you, have a tendency to fall in bed with whatever man shares your bed and brings you pleasure. Young Eirik did that. Now the Mackintosh's man does. Does he declare his love for you, as Eirik did? Will he defend your honour to me?'

She failed then, for he read the truth in her eyes and laughed in her face at the revelation.

'It will be interesting to see what he thinks when he discovers your part in the scheme to force him to marry you.'

'I played no part!' she denied his words. 'I ran away to avoid marrying him. If you…'

'Come now, Eva,' he urged. 'Let us examine the facts that I will remind your husband of. First, he discovered you missing and found out the direction in which you'd run.'

She shook her head as he began to explain it all— every word of it would damn her to Rob.

'That was not difficult to arrange at all. My man fed him the information in enough time for him to track you by the signs you left in your flight of escape I arranged.'

Eva gasped then, realising she'd been a pawn in her father's plan all along.

'He made no secret of finding you, but the miller sent word to me as soon as he had, so I could arrive and *discover* you together. I knew you were ill, and that helped give me time to set up the rest of it.'

He paused and then smiled. Her stomach spasmed, and she nearly fell to her knees.

'And why would he believe me? I know you are asking yourself that question now.' He lifted her chin with his finger, forcing her to meet his gaze. 'He did not find a virgin in his bed when he finally took you, did he? And he knows it.'

Walking away, he filled the cup once again and drank it down before speaking. She knew he would finish the matter between them with a threat and a promise—'twas his way.

'All I want is to better terms from the Mackintosh. And the right of first refusal before he offers anything to the clans who arrive next. Not so much to ask.' The terms were offered.

Eva stared at the man who'd raised her and wondered how it had ever come to this. Like a spider weaving his web, he was terrifying and fascinating at the same time.

'If you do not use your influence on my behalf, I will kill her and I will tell him of your part in the plan that deceived him and his chief and forced him to marry you.' He laughed then, and she trembled at the sight of it. 'Did he spill his own blood on the sheets because he already suspected your part in all of this, or did you, I wonder?'

The threat. Clearly, word had spread faster than she had seen to the sheets that morn. She tried to breathe as she waited for the last part. It followed quickly.

'If you do as I ask, the babe is safe and your husband will never learn of your perfidy. You can live your happy little life and no one will know the shame of your past.' The promise.

He walked past her and lifted the latch on the door, not waiting for a response from her, for he knew he would get the answer he wanted—her capitulation to his will. Again. Always.

'You may go now,' he said, nodding to her to leave. 'There are only a few days before the others arrive, so do not delay. There will be consequences for that.'

Eva pushed to her feet and struggled out of the room, passing Sigrid in the corridor. When the door closed, she stumbled down a few yards and then leaned against the cold stone wall to pull together the tattered bits of control that she had.

She could not face Rob in this condition. She could not return to their chamber and defile it with more lies and deceit. She could not go to Arabella or Brodie, not yet.

Where could she go? Where could she find peace for at least time enough to consider her choices?

Eva made her way back to the hall and then avoided everyone by going through the kitchen and storage area. Climbing the steps that led to Brodie and Arabella's chambers, she walked quietly past their door and down to the next one. Lifting the latch and using her fingers to muffle the sound, she eased the door open and nodded at Joanna's nursemaid. An offer to keep watch over the little one sent the girl away for a short respite.

She sat staring at the babe for a long time, her mind empty of all the matters and choices before her. But when the sweet one began to fuss, Eva lifted her up and placed the babe against her shoulder. Rubbing her back in the circles she'd seen Bella use to soothe her, she sat and whispered softly, singing a lullaby she'd learned while expecting her own bairn.

It turned out that the little girl liked to be walked rather than remaining still, so Eva did that, walking to the window and back countless times while her problems spun inside her thoughts.

She could simply do what he'd asked of her—speak on his behalf to Brodie. Though she could not guarantee Brodie's agreement with what her father wanted, it might be enough to satisfy him…for now.

And that was the rub here, giving in to his demand now would only assure his continued demands later. Each time she did it, he would use it against her for something more.

The little one fussed and squirmed a bit, a sign of growing hunger that meant her time here was limited. But holding the babe soothed her somehow, and she was reluctant to give her up so soon.

Her other choice was to go to Rob and confess it all before her father accused her. She would see the love in his gaze wither and die right before her eyes as the truth of her past was laid bare to him. She'd lied to him countless times—lies of both fact and omission. Lies that kept from him the truth that he was indeed only needed as a conduit to Brodie Mackintosh.

And that was the one thing that would destroy his heart and soul—to think she had finally accepted him only because of his connections. The truth of it, that she loved him for all the good things he was, would never be heard once he felt the sting of her betrayal. Everything that he'd given her—his strength, his support, his trust, his love—would die in that instant.

Her heart hurt at the thought of it, but she'd run out of choices in this. Do her father's bidding and be woven into his web of deceit forever. Confess her sins and lose the man she loved even while she suffered the possibility of her daughter's death.

By the time the nursemaid returned, Eva knew what she must do. She handed Joanna to her and walked out of the chamber before Arabella would be summoned to feed her. She'd nearly made it to the stairs when the lady whispered her name.

'Eva? Are you well?'

'I am, Arabella. Just tired. I seek my chambers now,' she said, easing away a step at a time.

'Eva? What did your father say?' This was the only person to know her truth, but she knew only part of it.

'May we speak of this in the morn?' There was a long pause before an answer came, and she was saved from further scrutiny only by the cry of the bairn.

'Aye. In the morning, then.'

Eva would leave. She would disappear. This time, without her father to leave clues to be followed. No one would find her. No one would care.

Without her to do his bidding, her father would have to make his own agreement with the Mackintoshes. Even if he exposed her past, she would be gone before Rob knew the truth. She would not have to see his face when he learned it. And the sick feeling in the pit of her gut told her that Mairead was gone forever.

But first, she wanted one more night with him. One night to remember for the rest of her days. One night that no one could take from her in the empty months and years that stretched out before her.

One more night of love before the hatred began and her life descended into hell.

One more night.

Chapter Twenty-Two

Rob sat in the dark and waited for her. The keep had quieted for the night some time ago, so he listened to the stillness and waited.

She would want to run, he knew that. The impulse to escape was something within her that nothing and no one could change. Facing down her father was not something she could do well—a lifetime of punishment for just such behaviour would have beaten it out of her.

So, he waited here, knowing that she would have to pack some of her things before leaving. To help her pick up the pieces. To help her see her own worth. To love her.

To beg her to stay.

He heard her footsteps coming down the corridor and listened as she paused there outside the door. He'd seen her do what she was doing there now—gathering herself back inside. The latch lifted and the door eased open. Eva stood there, her body outlined by the torch behind her in the wall.

Once, she'd stood before the fire here, not knowing that her shape was revealed to him. Now, he needed no light to know that body. He had touched and tasted every curve and crevice, every inch of the skin, every bit of her.

More than that though, he now knew her heart and her soul.

And he knew that she held his heart and soul.

Eva turned then and noticed him. He would wait on her, for he recognised that fragile expression in her gaze as it fell upon him. She walked across the chamber to him and knelt before him. Without a word, she undressed him, easing his belt and plaid out of her way and pulling the shirt over his head.

Then, she loved him the way he had her—with her mouth and hands and every part of her body, even her hair. He never took his eyes from her as she went about the task of giving him pleasure and bringing him to release.

She was relentless in her attentions, and his good intentions of allowing her to have her way without saying a word failed when she slid her mouth over his flesh and suckled it. He shouted her name, and it echoed off the walls as she cupped his bollocks and sucked him until he spilled his seed.

When he finished and would have pulled her into his arms and shown her the same consideration, she shook her head and laid it on his chest, as though listening to his heart. They remained there, in silence, touching and yet not, for some time. When his flesh responded once more to her nearness, she began to stroke it.

'Nay,' he said, moving her hand away. He held her shoulders and helped her to stand before him, between his legs.

And he undressed her, kissing every inch as he un-

covered her to his gaze. She was panting by the time
he finished, and he guided her forward, to kneel over
his hips. Entering her a scant inch at a time, he slowly
filled her until she could take no more. But then she
seated herself the rest of the way on his shaft. Her head
fell back, her now-loosened hair swung around her hips
and the sigh she released heated his blood.

Rob reached out and stroked her body, sliding his
hands over her breasts and teasing the tips with his
thumbs. She arched against him, rocking her hips and
gasping with each movement. He traced a path down
over her belly and into the curls, seeking the spot that
drove her to madness. Filled by this flesh, she could
not move much, but her body reacted when he slipped
one finger and then two into the folds and found the
bud there.

'Come for me, Eva. Let me watch you as you do,'
he urged.

His fingers moved faster and harder on that en-
gorged flesh, and she rocked more and more on his
shaft and against his fingers, seeking the release she
knew she could find. When he felt the first tremors of
it, he pushed them free of the chair and walked them
to the bed. Without leaving her body, he laid her down
and thrust deeply inside her to touch her core.

Her body rippled inside that place and he felt as
though fingers tightened around his manhood. He was
not ready yet, so he plunged into her and pulled out,
over and over as she screamed out her pleasure. And
when his body readied to pour his seed into her, he
said the words he needed her to hear and to believe.

'I love you, Eva MacKay,' he said, thrusting in and
hearing her gasp. 'You are mine.'

He was close, damn it, so he moved harder and harder into her, whispering those words over and over and hoping she heard them and accepted them. His bollocks tightened then, his flesh swelled and one more thrust brought on his release.

They lay on the bed in silence, the air heavy between them. Rob knew she needed this, and he would give her whatever she needed. The night moved slowly, and they loved several more times before she was spent. As she nestled closer to him, pulling his arm across her waist and holding it near her heart, Rob could feel her body finally seeking rest.

'Do not run away from this,' he said quietly. Her body startled. 'Stay here. Stay with me, Eva.' He waited for her to say something, any words at all, but none came. 'I beg you, do not run this time.'

He had ruined her plans completely.

Her body and soul sated with this night of pleasure and love, she'd planned to leave in the morning when the gates opened and the keep and village were caught up in the activities of welcoming so many guests. Once Brodie called Rob to his side, her path and opportunity would be open and she would leave Glenlui and the Mackintoshes...and Rob...forever.

He did not understand yet that it was his best protection. He thought he knew and could stand against her father. He thought right would win out in this situation.

But she knew better. Eva had lived her life trying to stand against Ramsey MacKay and learned the lesson after paying the most terrible and steep price for her resistance. Leaving would protect him best.

But now, how could she? How could she walk away

when Rob knew what she planned to do and asked, nay begged, her not to? Damn her own weakness in this!

One more day, she decided. She would stay one more day and see if she could find a solution to this dilemma. One more day to lull his suspicions, too. 'Twould make her escape easier if she did not rush it.

His breathing slowed against her ear. He slept, never loosening his hold on her, as though he feared she would slip away in the night.

One more day.

Rob and Magnus were training in the yard when the knock came on his door. Brodie had expected her sooner, but she waited until they would not be interrupted by her husband's attentions. He opened the door and bade her enter.

He'd seen many sides of Ramsey MacKay's daughter, but this was a new one for him. The ill woman, the insecure and fearful one, the one who fell in love with his best friend, the friend to his own wife. There were many facets to this woman, but now she was confident and purposeful as she entered the chamber and faced him.

'You are here to collect your debt then, Eva?'

'Aye.'

A simple answer, and yet one that could and would cause many consequences. His offer of a favour was not something simply uttered in an uncontrolled emotional outburst to be denied later when cooler heads prevailed. He stood by it and would honour her request, no matter the cost of it. Brodie poured some wine in his cup and offered her some. She declined with a curt shake of her head. Business, then.

'What will you have?' he asked.

'My father wishes to have better terms in the coming negotiations. He asks for the right to accept or reject what you offer first, before you offer them to the others who are coming.'

It all fit what he was beginning to recognise as the man and the pattern of behaviour of the head of the Clan MacKay. But Eva speaking on his behalf did surprise him.

'And this is what you ask from me as payment of what I owe you?' he asked.

He watched her carefully as she considered his words. Her blue eyes flashed with anger, and she shook her head.

'Nay,' she said, meeting his eyes. 'I would not plead his case to you. I but thought you should know what he wants and what he will press for.'

She took the cup he'd offered before and drank it down in a long swallow. Brodie thought he saw her resolve softening, but the look of determination in her gaze told him otherwise when she placed the empty cup down and faced him directly.

'Your debt to me will be paid if you find Rob a way out of this marriage.'

Of everything the woman could ask him for, this had never entered his mind. Brodie thought himself well versed in strategy and negotiations, but this, this was a surprise.

'I thought that both of you were finding the marriage to be satisfactory,' he said. Though neither realised it, they both were walking around in a constant state of bliss for the last month. Satisfactory? Hell, they were happy in their marriage, which Brodie knew was a huge step since their unhappy beginnings. When she did not answer his implied question, he asked it aloud. 'Why would Rob want a way out?'

'The truth will out soon,' she said in a toneless voice. 'When he knows, he will not wish to be married to me.'

Good Christ! What the hell had happened between them that could make Rob forsake the woman he so clearly loved? 'And you? Do you wish a way out? Do you not want some consideration if your marriage ends?'

'There is no way out for me, Laird,' she said plainly. She stared off into the corner of the chamber for a few seconds before clearing her throat. 'So, will you do this service for me or not?'

'Mayhap you should speak to…'

'Will you do this for me or not, Brodie?'

She let out a breath then and walked to the door, not waiting for his answer. It was an inevitable one, for his honour demanded he accede to her request. Much as he'd like to argue and convince her otherwise, it was what she asked in return for his promise.

'Aye, Eva. I will find a way to dissolve your marriage. For Rob.' She nodded and left without another word or glance at him.

Brodie gave her a few seconds and then followed her as she left him and sought out Arabella. Was Eva MacKay collecting all the debts owed to her? Later, from his wife's unhappy face and refusal to speak of it, Brodie knew she was tying up all the loose strands of some thread.

But not for a minute did he think she had some nefarious plot planned against them. Nay, her methods seemed more like a woman trying to protect those she loved. Using his favour for Rob rather than to appease her father was another sign of it.

Hours later as they gathered in the hall for supper, Brodie knew he must honour his promise. He just prayed he could find the right way to do it.

Rob made his way through the crowded hall towards the dais. The day of training proved a good diversion for him from the fear she would leave without a word. She'd been at Arabella's side most of the day, or so Margaret had reported to him. Still, until he could discover the reason behind it, he would keep a close watch on her.

He was passing some of the MacKay warriors when he first heard the whispers. Drunken ramblings they might be and too furtive to be heard, so he tried to ignore them. But, like good gossip, the words grew louder and clearer.

'Her father said she would spread her legs for any man.'

'She brought shame to his name.'

'She whelped one bastard before returning to seek her father's favour.'

'And she found it, did she not? Her father needed the Mackintosh's man, and so she did what she does best.' Rob tried to ignore the gesture that followed those words.

'The MacKay gets what and who he wants!' The one saying that raised his cup in a mock salute to his laird.

'The Mackintosh's man fell for her act.' A laugh and then, 'He went sniffing after her like she was a bitch in heat!'

The last one broke Rob's control, and he stopped behind the man who'd spoken the words. Grabbing him by the collar of his shirt, Rob pulled the man off the bench to face him.

'What say you?' he demanded of the man. Even the stench of too much ale did not ease his anger. 'Of whom do you speak?'

His words caused much amusement, for the whole group of men from Tongue burst out laughing. They nudged each other with elbows and nodded at him. A sick feeling spread from his gut to his head. Not waiting for an explanation, he punched the man and threw him to the floor.

It took little time before the whole of the hall noticed the beginnings of a brawl. Mackintoshes gathered behind him, ready to fight, when Brodie's voice rang out.

'The training yard is outside. If any man feels he needs more time there, he can leave now.' Rob stood and faced his laird. 'Cousin, your counsel is needed here. Join me...now.'

It was not an invitation no matter how the words were phrased. Rob shook out his fist and made his way to the front of the hall. Anyone in his path moved aside, trying to both get a better look at him and trying not to appear so eager. Well, he was not the only one to hear the words spoken, the claims made, so he had little doubt that it would be known throughout the keep and the village by nightfall.

He reached the dais and climbed up the steps, bowing in front of Brodie and Arabella before seeking his seat. Eva sat there stone-faced and silent as he took his place next to her. Brodie did not speak to him through the rest of the meal.

He could not look at her. If only half of what he'd heard was true, her deceit and lies were of the worst kind. Her lack of reaction spoke louder than any admissions or objections could.

She had not been running away—she'd been leading him along a merry chase. Though she had not feigned the fever, the rest of it was set up to make certain he could not refuse the marriage.

Every word she'd spoken to him now flooded through his mind, and he heard the other meanings in them. He heard her deception. At that moment, her father leaned forward and winked at her, confirming his worst doubts.

But the reason eluded him. He thought on it through the meal, barely touching his food or his cup. Only at the end, when Brodie rose and spoke did it make sense.

'Laird MacKay and I have come to terms on an agreement that will enhance both of our clans. Raise your cups now! *Loch Moigh!*' He called out the Mackintosh battle cry, which everyone in the hall repeated. *'Loch Moigh!'*

Then the MacKay rose and called out theirs. *'Bratach Bhan Chlann Aoidh!'*

He forced himself to his feet and did what was expected of the Mackintosh's man. After a few minutes, the hall quieted, and Eva's father took his leave. Walking behind them along the dais, he placed his hands on Eva's shoulders and whispered to her. The words were loud enough so he could hear, and they simply confirmed the gossip told below.

'I am proud of your efforts, Daughter. For speaking to the Mackintosh on my behalf.' More words were spoken, but the only two Rob could discern were *our agreement*.

Rob glanced at Brodie, but his cousin did not look his way. Or would not. He waited, his world crashing around him, until he could no longer. 'Brodie.'

This time Brodie did meet his gaze, and the truth was there—Eva had been at the heart of her father's plans. When the nod of permission came, Rob stood and left, not waiting on Eva. He walked blindly but ended up in the one place he did not wish to be—their chambers.

He stood there, as memories poured over him, now knowing that every word she'd spoken was a lie. Part of a plan to use him and his nearness to Brodie to get what the MacKay wanted.

When the door opened, he knew it could be only one person and it was the one he did not wish to see at this moment.

Chapter Twenty-Three

Eva followed him when he'd left the dais. He'd heard most of her story but needed him to know some parts others did not. Now though, watching him pace like a lethal animal, she thought she should not have returned here. She'd not feared him in a long time, but now, his anger was palpable and dangerous. She leaned against the door, waiting in silence for him to say something.

'How many were there?'

'What?' She did not understand the question. It was not what she expected he would ask. He strode over and stood right in front of her, his height and girth blocking everything else from her view.

'Goddamn it, Eva! How many men have you lain with? They said you spread your legs for any man, and I want to know. How many have had you?'

She'd slapped him before she even knew she'd lifted her hand. Lies or not, 'twas an insult.

'And now you play the lady?' He touched his cheek and smiled grimly at her. 'Just so,' he said, stepping back. 'What did you tell Brodie on your father's behalf?'

His fury made him seem larger than he truly was. He kept making tight fists with his huge hands and releasing them.

'I only told Brodie of my father's plans. I asked him for nothing on his behalf.' The words did nothing to abate his anger. Instead, it seemed to make it worse.

'You expect me to believe that? After the rest of it?' he shouted. 'What other part did you play in his plans? From the start of it?'

'I did not know, Rob,' she began, but he was there, so close she could feel his breath on her face. She turned away rather than see the hatred and disgust in his eyes. But he came back to his first question, yelling it at her again.

'How many before me, Eva? How many times did you play whore for your father's aims?' He leaned his head back and rubbed his face. 'And you watched me spill blood to mark the sheets that morning. What a laugh you and your father must have had over that!' Then his voice dropped, and it was filled with a plaintive tone, making the demand sound more like he was pleading for her to answer.

'There was one man before you, Rob. Only one,' she said. '

It seemed to knock some of the rage from him. He stepped back, thinking on her words. But he was not done, and her hell began with his next words.

'You have a child?'

The words were softer than she could have expected, but the pain of hearing them from his lips cut her in two. She could only nod, for it hurt to breathe or think or even live in that moment.

'Mairead.' He said her name before Eva could or did.

'The name you call out in your sleep. Your daughter.' She nodded again. He staggered back away and fell into one of the chairs, staring wildly at her. 'You gave up a child to gain your father's favour?'

Her control snapped at that accusation. Before she knew it, words spewed out of her mouth, calling him every foul name and word he'd taught her and others she'd only heard. She ran over to him to...do something to make him stop. He grabbed her hands in one of his hand and backed her up against the wall. Trapping her legs between his, he stopped her from kicking and flailing.

'You stupid miscreant!' she yelled. 'I did not give her up. He took... He took my...' She stopped then, losing all desire to explain or to fight him. Her body collapsed, and he released her. She slid down the wall and sat on the floor. He walked away then and took a place on the other side of the chamber.

'Mayhap it was for the best that he took her,' he said. 'Where is she now?'

Her head snapped back against the wall as though he had backhanded her. Could she tell him all of it? What if her father did still have her somewhere? Dare she confide in him now? One glance at his face, distorted by anger and disgust, gave her the answer.

'She is gone. The price I paid for defying his wishes.' She could say no more about Mairead.

After a few minutes of silence, she managed to climb to her feet. Stumbling, she crossed the chamber and sat on a chair. He watched her but said nothing. When he finally headed for the door, she knew she must say the words now, for it would be the last time she would see him.

'I may have married you because of my father's plans, but I did not fall in love with *the Mackintosh's man.*' He stopped but did not face her.

'I fell in love with Robbie Mackintosh, a man loyal to his cousin. A good man who did not strike back when it was his right. A kind man who took care of a woman he should have left behind. A faithful man who did not stray from his vows even when he was refused by his bride.'

Tears flowed freely now, making it difficult to speak. She brushed her hand across her eyes.

'An honourable man who would not give up because he had given his word.' He turned and looked at her then. 'I love Robbie Mackintosh, the man. Not the bloody Mackintosh's man.'

Without acknowledging her words by action or sound, he left, closing the door behind him.

Strange, once he left, she could not cry. Enveloped in complete sadness and utter devastation, the tears would not come.

Eva remained there, not speaking to anyone for the next two days. Servants came and removed Rob's trunks and belongings from the chamber. Nessa tried to see to her, but she waved the girl away. Calls to meals were ignored. Summons to Arabella's chambers went unanswered. She sat, unable to do anything at all.

Rob never returned. She had no idea of what he was doing or what he would do, so she contented herself knowing that Brodie would find a way to dissolve their marriage. What that meant for him or for her, she knew not.

Nessa was the only one who returned, unbidden, to

clean around her. And to force her to drink something from time to time.

She learned her father was leaving from the girl on that second day. And learned of Rob's hasty departure two days later.

It hurt too much to wonder over where he went. It hurt too much to even breathe. Eva had not thought that anything could hurt more than the loss of her daughter. But this loss did.

She took to her bed on the fourth day and lost track of the passing of night and day after that. When the door slammed against the wall, she barely heard it. But, the foul words did make her smile as Margaret cursed her way across the chamber.

'I am away for three days, and everything and everyone has gone to hell in my absence?' she shouted. 'What in bloody hell is happening?'

Eva did not have the strength to answer her. Nor the desire to speak of it. Nor to defend her acts against the woman's brother. Luckily, Margaret did not need anyone to carry on a conversation. She forced Eva from the bed, washed and changed her and had her sitting in one of the chairs without ever pausing to allow for an answer if Eva wanted to give one.

'Drink this,' she ordered, placing a cup of something warm in Eva's hands. When she would have put it down untouched, Margaret lifted it to her mouth and poured it in. Eva had no choice but to swallow.

Margaret called Nessa, and the two cleaned the chamber thoroughly. Some hours later, when satisfied of her condition and the chamber's, Margaret sat in the other chair. Eva understood what that meant but did not wish to speak about Rob.

'Arabella wants to see you. She sent me first to tend to you. I will get her.'

'Nay,' she whispered. 'No one.' Margaret must have heard the desperation in her tone, so she nodded.

'For now.' She stood and walked to the door. 'Do not get back in that bed except to sleep. When you tire of sitting, walk. When you tire of these four walls, leave it. You are not a prisoner here.'

She appreciated the woman's common-sense approach to everything, even if she knew she was more prisoner than she'd ever been anywhere before.

'I will return on the morrow. I want to see you dressed when I arrive at midday.'

But on the morrow, it was not Margaret who invaded her privacy first. Arabella accepted the word 'nay' no more easily or happily than Margaret. She knocked twice, loudly, and then entered, not waiting to be asked in. Standing before her, the lady tapped her foot impatiently and then grumbled.

'You must give me leave from my promise, Eva,' she said, kneeling before her. Grabbing both of her hands, she shook her head. 'They do not understand. Let me explain your reasons.'

'You do not know all of it, Bella,' she said. 'And you gave your word.'

The lady began cursing then, using some words she recognised as Rob's favourites and others favoured by Margaret. She wanted to smile, but just could not.

'I would ask the favour of you that you promised me,' she said softly.

Eva could not stay here in the keep and be reminded of the fleeting joy they'd found. This place belonged to

Rob and when he returned from whatever called him away, he should be able to live here in peace. Once Brodie carried out his promise, she would disappear from their lives forever.

'What do you need? What can I do for you?' Arabella asked her.

'You once offered the use of a cottage in the village. I would like to move there until Brodie arranges an end to things.'

'End to things? What do you mean?' The lady stood and studied her for a long moment before shaking her head violently. 'What does he arrange?'

'He will see to the dissolution of our marriage.'

'Nay!' she cried out. 'Nay!' Bella began pacing, long strides across the chamber and back. 'You are married. You love him. He loves you. There can be no ending of it.' Her voice rose in volume until she was shouting.

''Twas a marriage based on deceit and lies, Arabella. Not a valid one in the eyes of the Church or law.'

'But you were forced to it. To protect your child. Surely, Rob understands your reasons?' It took but a moment for the lady to realise that Eva had not made things clear with him. 'You did not tell him the truth? He does not know,' she whispered. 'Why? Why would you let this happen?'

'Because I love him, Arabella.' She smiled then, thinking of the man. 'You know you would walk through hell for Brodie. Well, this is, I suspect, my walk through hell. But he will be safe and free of involvement with me and my father. He can find happiness elsewhere.'

Arabella looked up and muttered what sounded like

a prayer before looking at her. 'Let me help you. I pray you, give me leave to speak to Brodie on this.'

'The only thing you should speak to him about is if he will permit me the use of a small cottage while he handles the situation. It could be months or more, and I do not wish to live it here in the keep.'

The lady gave a brisk nod and then left and the quiet descended once more into the chamber. Word came later that Brodie had given permission for her to move to the village. A few days later, she moved there and began the process of living alone and on her own.

Brodie had been a damn idiot over the whole thing. Instead of telling Rob what he wanted to know, the man insisted on being his usual, close-mouthed self. But Rob would not answer his questions except to say that he had not raised a hand to her.

The same could not be said of her.

He'd been so angry when he left their chambers that Brodie sent him to the village on some made-up matter, anything to get him away from Ramsay MacKay and his daughter. Then he was sent to help repair the mill, which took another whole day. By the time he'd returned, the MacKay had left and Eva restricted herself to their chambers.

He'd sent the servants to remove his belongings and clothing, and he now slept in his old chamber. Well, he stayed there but sleep eluded him.

Sleeping meant dreaming, and his dreams were filled with...*her.*

Finally, a few days later, Brodie sent him off to escort their last guests from the coast to Glenlui. They both knew the assignment was a farce, but it removed him from the place he did not want to be. He'd ridden off alone, just like the last time. And as with the last time, he spent the first days of the journey cursing... cursing a lot.

The first day, he did not think about her or the expression on her face when he'd raged.

The second day, he did not think about her answers to his questions or the way she'd raged at his words.

The third day, he did not think about her declaration.

But on the fourth day, all he could remember were her words about the child she'd had. And the pain that tore her apart when faced with delivering Arabella's bairn. It had not been the pain of her courses that had driven her, sobbing and curled up, to the floor. Rob understood that now.

It had been the loss of her child that had driven her actions from even before they'd met.

When he'd suspected another man, a lover whom she'd lost or was separated from, she had been mourning the loss of her daughter. When he thought she'd run from him, she'd been running to find the child. The melancholy that afflicted her with every mile they travelled south was fear and hopelessness, because it meant she would never see the child again.

That realisation drove him to his own knees and to prayers that he would be forgiven for his part in the travesty played upon her.

He walked most of the fifth day, memories and thoughts of her, of them, plaguing his every step. And, when he reached the coast without ever encountering the guests Brodie had sent him in search of, he knew the real reason Brodie told him to leave.

He also knew what he had to do.

And no one would stand in his way.

Three weeks later, after discovering that brutes could not bear up under the kind of punishments they so freely gave to others, Rob was back on the road south.

To Glenlui and to his wife.

Chapter Twenty-Four

Her life took on a regular pattern now. In spite of her efforts to hide away from the strange, questioning glances or the whispers about what she'd done to their Robbie, Margaret would not allow it.

As she'd told Eva that first morning and any morning when Eva objected to joining her on her visits, every woman should have some skill to live by. And, if Eva planned to follow through on the annulment Brodie promised to arrange, she would, more than most, need a way to make a living.

So each morning and some afternoons as well, Eva carried Margaret's supplies and listened and watched and learned. She could dress a wound now, could stitch the deeper cuts and she could treat a fever. Eva had also helped Margaret when she'd set several broken bones, though she'd lost the small amount of food she'd eaten while watching the procedure.

Four weeks had passed since Rob left Glenlui, and she existed in limbo. Brodie said his legal advisors were searching for a solution and they'd consulted with the bishop. He never mentioned Rob other than his reports on his progress, or lack of it, and she never asked.

It was the worst part of all of this.

To feign disinterest when she wanted to ask many, many questions and know that he was well. She hoped that, in time, he would not hate her for the lies and deceit.

This day had dawned bright and clear and, since it was close to midsummer, it would be a long one. An overturned cart in the fields had caused a number of injuries, forcing Eva to help Margaret for many hours. When they finally arrived back in the village, Magnus told her of Brodie's invitation to sup in the hall.

When she tried to beg off, Magnus told her it was actually an order and, since he must obey it, he would carry her over his shoulder if she would not walk at his side. Though certain he could not be serious, she thought the better of it when Margaret did not tell her otherwise.

Walking between them up the path to the gates, she realised it would be the first time she'd returned to the hall since the night when her betrayal had been exposed to Rob. Nervous about being in the middle of his kith and kin, Eva tried to come up with a way to avoid it. By the time she knew there was no way, they stood at the steps leading into the keep.

'Eva,' Margaret said. 'Fear not, Magnus and I will stand at your side. If Brodie has called you here, no one would dare insult or harass you or they face his wrath.'

'Come, lass,' Magnus said softly. 'Give me your arm.'

So, with the two people who should be most angry at her side, the three made their way through the door and into the hall. Though some whispers swirled around her, no one said anything aloud. Eva was halfway through the large chamber when she saw him.

She could not do this. Not now. Not yet. He had returned and waited there with Brodie and Arabella… and a young woman stood at his side. Eva stopped suddenly, forcing Magnus and Margaret to do so.

'I cannot,' she began, shaking her head and trying to back away from them and him. 'I pray you, do not force me to do this.'

She pulled free then and turned, prepared to run if she had to in order to get away from him. Eva had only taken three steps when his voice called out to her.

'Running away again, Eva?'

Eva stopped at his words, but she could not face him, not when he'd clearly found another and had brought the woman here to his home.

'You were the one who left,' she whispered to herself, reminding her of his actions after the terrible disclosures of her sins against him. She clenched her fists and felt the sting of her nails pressing into her palms.

'Look at me, Eva,' Rob said.

She could not look at him. She must not look at him. She would not survive it.

She would not…

Her heart pounded and her lungs would not take in a breath at his words, his order. If she looked at him and saw the same disgust and hatred in his gaze, it would destroy what little of herself that still remained.

'You said you loved me. You said you trusted me. Then turn around and face me, wife.'

A gasp escaped before she could stop it. Surprised that he would speak of love and trust at this moment,

she shook her head and tried to make her feet move…
away from him. Tears poured down her cheeks and
the sobs trying to force free nearly overpowered her.

'I pray you, Eva, turn around.' His voice was softer
then, almost pleading with her to face him.

She wanted to resist these soft words. She wanted
to leave here, leave him, and never feel this kind of
pain again. But she was the sinner in this, and he was
the victim of her wrongdoings. Margaret hovered in
the fringes of her sight ready, she knew, to intervene
in some way. Eva had no wish to cause more problems
between Rob and his sister, so, she turned slowly to
face him. Swallowing deeply and blinking against the
tears, she stared at the man she loved.

Oh, God, he looked even more handsome than before! It took nothing more than a quick glance to prove
how weak she was about him. Most likely, seeing him
after such an absence and knowing he would never
be hers again had made her want him even more. He
stood there in silence and waited until she raised her
gaze to his before he spoke.

In that moment, everything and everyone else in the
hall disappeared and it seemed to be only the two of
them. Eva waited for him to say whatever drove him
to have her summoned here, though she suspected it
would drive her to her knees. Taking in a breath and
trying to let it out, she nodded at him.

'What do you wish to say?' she asked. His gaze
narrowed as he seemed to examine her face. 'Brodie
said…'

'This is between you and me, Eva.'

She closed her eyes for a moment. This was worse
than she could have imagined. Margaret's promise

about Brodie's protection clearly did not and would not extend to her estranged husband. Losing him was not enough of a punishment? Now he sought her humiliation before everyone she had called friend?

'We left Durness and Tongue rather hastily those months ago,' he said, stepping closer. 'And I discovered that you had left something behind. Something very important.'

She did not understand what he meant and could not remember anything left behind. Then Eva watched as Rob slipped his free hand inside his cloak and lifted it aside. He held a small bundle in the crook of his arm. Eva shook her head, staring at it and trying to ascertain what it was and why it meant anything to her. For a moment, she thought it looked like a... She looked at him and shook her head.

'So I went back and retrieved it, her, for you, Eva.'
Her?

Her?

Her heart filled with dread and fear at his words. Her whole body trembled as her gaze dropped once more to stare at the bundle he carried.

A bundle? Dear God, was it a baby?

It could not be...

'She is bigger than the last time you saw her,' he said as he held out the bundle towards her, and Eva realised he did hold a bairn, wrapped snugly and asleep. She?

It was not possible. Do not hope. Do not think it. The words repeated inside her thoughts, but it was her heart that began to hope for the impossible in that moment. Her hands itched to reach out, but she could not. She could not breathe, and she could not dare to hope against hope that this was… It was his next words though that shattered her world.

'Mairead,' he whispered to the babe sleeping there, ''tis time to wake and meet your mother. She has waited too long to see you again.'

Eva shook her head even as she stepped closer to him, staring in disbelief at what, or rather whom, he carried.

'It cannot be…it cannot be…my Mairead.' The words came out on gasps as she tried to consider what he was saying.

She'd last seen her daughter on the day of her birth, and this infant was nothing like her. This bairn was so much bigger with a thick thatch of pale straw-coloured hair. Her Mairead had been nearly bald, with eyes that were neither blue nor brown. He held the babe out to her, and Eva could not help but notice the similarity of the shape of her eyes to…Eirik's!

This *was* Mairead!

She reached out to touch the babe when her body began shaking violently. Any thought of taking the bairn in her own arms ended as the world around her first flashed in brightness then sank into darkness.

'Mairead.'

Eva whispered the name and reached out to touch the babe. In the next moment, her eyes rolled up into her head and she crumpled. Rob barely caught her with his free hand and kept her from hitting the floor. He called out for help.

'Magnus! Help me with her,' he said. As Magnus lifted Eva in his arms, Margaret moved to take the babe but he shook his head. 'No one holds her until Eva does.'

Pride, he thought, shone in his sister's gaze then, and she stepped back and let him follow Magnus forward. Brodie pulled the large chair he used from the table and Magnus placed her there.

There was so much to say and so many things done and not done, for which he needed to beg forgiveness. He was not certain she would forgive him, considering the terrible things he'd said to her the last time they'd spoken. Worse, he had, in fact, broken faith with her. He'd demanded that she have trust in him when he had not the same in her. But, he hoped and prayed during his journey that she would forgive him for that lapse.

Only a minute or so passed before her eyes began to flutter open. Rob crouched before her, holding the very well-behaved child there.

'Eva? Are you well?' he asked. Margaret handed her a cup of wine, which he thought she would refuse. She drank it down before reaching out to touch the baby.

'Is it truly her?' He nodded. 'Can it be?' Her voice quivered in fear but with a hint of hope. 'How did you find her?'

'I had a…talk with your father and discovered where he'd sent her,' he explained briefly. Eva still had not touched her daughter. Shifting the bairn in his arm, he leaned over and placed Mairead in her mother's arms. He would give her a full explanation later. For now, she needed her bairn.

Eva sat motionless, staring at the child but not saying anything, her hand suspended in the air over the baby's face, as though afraid to even touch her. The expression of shock over the bairn's return was there on her face for all to see. Even Arabella cried softly, and Brodie took her in his arms to comfort her. Margaret just rested her hand on Rob's shoulder, patting it in approval. Then, Mairead, who'd been easier to travel with than most women, decided to wake up. Peering at all the unfamiliar faces, she scrunched up her face and screamed out her displeasure and discomfort.

If he thought Eva would be ill at ease handling her, she proved him wrong in seconds. She brought the babe up and kissed her cheeks, whispering something to her, as she soothed her daughter for the first time since the day of her birth. Rubbing the bairn's head, she rocked to and fro as she spoke little nothings to the babe.

In that moment, Rob regretted leaving Ramsay MacKay alive, but his death truly would have caused more problems. Although he was not unscathed by Rob's fury, he'd learned quickly that brutality was not as pleasurable when one was on the receiving end of it.

When Eva began to sob as she rocked the babe back and forth, Rob knelt closer to her and motioned for the others to back away. There would be time for speaking about all this later. Except for one introduction that must be made now, if he read the signs correctly.

'Eva, this,' he said, waving the young woman forward, 'is Gunna, Mairead's nurse. She agreed to move here and see to the bairn's needs.' He motioned Gunna closer. 'Gunna, this is my wife, Mairead's mother, Eva MacKay.'

Now, Rob moved away to give the woman a few minutes to speak about the bairn. Brodie moved to his side.

'How long did it take you?' Brodie asked.

'How long did what take?'

'To realise you were wrong about everything.' Rob

laughed then, not willing to admit it even to his friend. 'And the MacKay?'

'He will be pissing blood and drinking his meals for some time,' Rob swore.

'Not dead?' Though his first impulse was to kill the man, the calm part of him that guided him during battle had prevailed.

'I thought it might interfere with your agreements if the man was dead.' His words echoed his previous explanation, but Rob knew that the man had hovered near death for several days after Rob had beaten the truth from him. And that pleased him greatly.

The bairn's renewed crying interrupted any other conversations, and Arabella ordered the women to her chamber to see to Mairead's care. When Eva would have stood, he instead lifted her into his arms and carried her up the steps. They would have time enough later to speak more fully on matters between them. For now, it was more important that she become re-acquainted with the child torn from her so viciously.

He placed her in one of the chairs there and turned to leave as the women gathered around Eva and the babe, but her voice stopped him.

'Rob,' she said. He met her gaze and saw the love there. 'I cannot thank you enough for this, for her.' She stroked his face and smiled.

'There will be time enough later,' he said. He lifted her hand and kissed her palm before leaving the chamber.

As he walked down to the hall to speak with Brodie, Rob knew it was true—there would be time enough for them now that he accepted that Eva was his and would be his forever.

He might not have been the first man she loved, but he would make certain that he would be the last.

Epilogue

Five months later...

He held out his hand and she took it without hesitation. They'd not danced or celebrated really at their own wedding, so they would at his sister's wedding to Magnus.

Mairead was safely in Gunna's care and the young woman had turned out to be a godsend in more ways than the one. For while Arabella glowed and seemed enhanced by carrying a child, Eva suffered through most moments each day.

So, when she looked well, he took advantage of the short time…as he did now.

'Just do not spin me too much,' she said with a laugh as they took their places with the others. 'You will not like the results.' He nodded and held on to her hand as they began the pattern in step with the music.

He watched her face and loved the expression of joy that sat there now. No longer in fear of her father. No longer hopeless without her daughter. Her life was now filled with love and laughter and joy and family as she'd not known before he'd been forced to marry her.

Deciding there was a better use of any time when she did not feel ill, he wrapped his arm around her waist and guided her out of the area they were using for the dance and into a nearby alcove. Pulling her into his arms, he held her close and kissed her until she melted against him and was breathless.

'I hope this sickness passes soon,' he said as he turned her around and slid his hands over her growing belly. 'I love feeling the way your body is changing.' When she arched back against him, Rob knew she wanted it, too.

'I love to feel your hands on me,' she whispered back. 'But 'tis been so long that I do not remember why I should be glad to have you in my bed.'

'You will pay for that challenge, wife,' he threatened.

Her laughter and her acceptance of his touches and his kisses told him she did not fear such a challenge. And he was glad of it. He took her mouth then and tasted her. She leaned back and smiled.

'Margaret said to fear not, the sickness should pass long before we should stop...your attentions.'

'She would know,' he said. One more kiss and he led her out of the alcove and back to the table.

Margaret had been so busy caring for everyone else that she'd missed the fact of her own condition until the day she passed out at Magnus's feet. A miracle, she and the midwife claimed, for Margaret had never become pregnant in her first marriage. Magnus walked about quite 'insufferably proud,' as Eva called him. Rob was simply happy for them both—for they'd found joy when and where neither of them expected to.

Glancing over at Eva and considering the events of the last year, he realised that was their story, too. When she wrapped his hand around hers and then entwined their fingers, Rob knew he should be insufferable, too.

But first he would prove to Eva once again why she was happy she'd accepted him into her bed…and into her heart. Knowing it might take some time, he stole his wife away and they were not seen again that night, or the next day, either.

* * * * *

REQUEST YOUR FREE BOOKS!

⬙ HARLEQUIN®

ℋISTORICAL

Where love is timeless

2 FREE NOVELS PLUS 2 **FREE GIFTS!**

YES! Please send me 2 FREE Harlequin® Historical novels and my 2 FREE gifts (gifts are worth about $10). After receiving them, if I don't wish to receive any more books, I can return the shipping statement marked "cancel." If I don't cancel, I will receive 6 brand-new novels every month and be billed just $5.69 per book in the U.S. or $5.99 per book in Canada. That's a savings of at least 12% off the cover price! It's quite a bargain! Shipping and handling is just 50¢ per book in the U.S. and 75¢ per book in Canada.* I understand that accepting the 2 free books and gifts places me under no obligation to buy anything. I can always return a shipment and cancel at any time. Even if I never buy another book, the two free books and gifts are mine to keep forever.

246/349 HDN GH2Z

Name _____ (PLEASE PRINT) _____

Address _____ Apt. # _____

City _____ State/Prov. _____ Zip/Postal Code _____

Signature (if under 18, a parent or guardian must sign) _____

Mail to the **Reader Service:**
IN U.S.A.: P.O. Box 1867, Buffalo, NY 14240-1867
IN CANADA: P.O. Box 609, Fort Erie, Ontario L2A 5X3

Want to try two free books from another line?
Call 1-800-873-8635 or visit www.ReaderService.com.

"You do care, no matter how much you deny it."

Azhar stepped out onto the terrace, indicating that she should follow. "It is incumbent upon me, Julia, to behave honorably, that is all."

"As a prince of royal blood, you mean?"

"Yes, but also as a man."

"That, I would never doubt. You could easily have left me at the oasis, but your conscience would not let you, and for that I will always be eternally grateful. To the man, not the prince."

It was dusk, and though they were in the middle of a palace, in the middle of a city, it was that time of the evening when a stillness, a silence, fell over everything like a cloak. Azhar slid his arms around her, pulling her toward him. There were only a few layers of cotton and silk between them. His hand slid down to rest on the small of her back. "Julia?"

Her stomach knotted. She ran her fingers through the short, soft silk of his hair. "Azhar?"

"We are not on a camel now."

"No, we are most certainly not on a camel…"

"So I wondered if it might be possible that the moment might be…?"

"Propitious?"

"Precisely," Azhar said, dipping his head toward her. "Very, very propitious. And very well chosen, in my humble opinion."

Her eyes drifted shut as his lips caressed hers, sending shivers of delight over her skin. He kissed her slowly, flattening his hand on her back to mold her to him, as his lips shaped themselves to hers. He kissed her as if he was tasting her, as if he was savoring her. The combination of the twilight, the pent-up heat of the desert sun glowing on her skin, the alluring desert man holding her tightly against him, the seductive shimmer of her desert clothes, the persistent flicker of desire that had lingered all day, waiting to be ignited, made her stomach flutter, and it made the blood sparkle in her veins. She ran her fingers up his back, relishing the sensation of fine silk rippling against the knot of his spine, and their kiss deepened. His tongue touched hers, and Julia let out an odd little sigh of delight. And then, as slowly as it had begun, the kiss ended, fluttering to a stop.

Don't miss
THE WIDOW AND THE SHEIKH
by Marguerite Kaye,
available April 2016 wherever
Harlequin® Historical books and ebooks are sold.

www.Harlequin.com

Turn your love of reading into rewards you'll love with
Harlequin My Rewards

Love the Harlequin book you just read?

Your opinion matters.

Review this book on your favorite book site, review site, blog or your own social media properties and share your opinion with other readers!

Be sure to connect with us at:
Harlequin.com/Newsletters
Facebook.com/HarlequinBooks
Twitter.com/HarlequinBooks

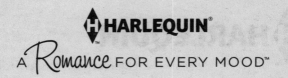

HARLEQUIN®

A *Romance* FOR EVERY MOOD™

JUST CAN'T GET ENOUGH?

Join our social communities
and talk to us online.

You will have access to the latest
news on upcoming titles and special
promotions, but most importantly,
you can talk to other fans about your
favorite Harlequin reads.

Harlequin.com/Community

Facebook.com/HarlequinBooks

Twitter.com/HarlequinBooks

Pinterest.com/HarlequinBooks